CARRYING THE GENTLEMAN'S SECRET

Helen Dickson

MILLS & BOON

Published in Great Britain 2017
by Mills & Boon, an imprint of HarperCollins*Publishers*
1 London Bridge Street, London, SE1 9GF

© 2017 Helen Dickson

ISBN: 978-0-263-93261-4

Printed and bound in Spain
by CPI, Barcelona

Helen Dickson was born and still lives in South Yorkshire, with her retired farm manager husband. Having moved out of the busy farmhouse where she raised their two sons, she now has more time to indulge in her favourite pastimes. She enjoys being outdoors, travelling, reading and music. An incurable romantic, she writes for pleasure. It was a love of history that drove her to writing historical fiction.

Books by Helen Dickson

Mills & Boon Historical Romance

Destitute on His Doorstep
Miss Cameron's Fall from Grace
When Marrying a Duke…
The Devil Claims a Wife
The Master of Stonegrave Hall
Mishap Marriage
A Traitor's Touch
Caught in Scandal's Storm
Lucy Lane and the Lieutenant
Lord Lansbury's Christmas Wedding
Royalist on the Run
The Foundling Bride
Carrying the Gentleman's Secret

M&B *Castonbury Park* Regency miniseries

The Housemaid's Scandalous Secret

Mills & Boon Historical *Undone!* eBook

One Reckless Night

Visit the Author Profile page
at millsandboon.co.uk for more titles.

Chapter One

1852

Beset with nerves, self-doubt and just a little terror at the speed with which events had taken her over, Lydia stood beside Henry Sturgis, the man who in a few minutes from now would become her husband. The realisation of the fact struck her anew and, as it did, she asked herself again if she was doing the right thing.

When Henry had told her he wanted to marry her, at first she had not been sure of herself, not really. The little time they had spent together had been exciting, but she had resolved to make no resolutions. With the death of her mother one year ago and after a lifetime of fending for themselves, to unite in such intimacy with another human being was a hard step for her to take.

Why? she asked herself. Why was it so difficult? Why was she so sensitive to committing herself to the challenging emotions of love, honesty and trust? Other people didn't have a problem with it. Why should she?

Fear! Fear of what? Of moving forward, she supposed, of letting another person into her life and pledging herself to them. Pledging yourself meant holding another's heart in your hand, of offering a secure place where anything was possible and everything between the two involved was understood. Pledging yourself meant facing what life had to offer together in the name of love. The problem was, she didn't know if she wanted to. It was a risk, like leaping into a void, with no idea what she would find there.

Would it work? That was the question. Unable to make up her mind whether or not to marry Henry, she had decided she would carry on with her work as normal and see how things turned out. But Henry was in a hurry and after further persuasion from him and the resurrection of an unwelcome ghost from her past—a ghost in the shape of her father, who had cruelly abandoned her as a child and now wanted to reinsert himself into her life, which she wanted to avoid at

Quite inexplicably Lydia's heart gave a leap of desire, and when her gaze settled on his mouth she was lulled into a curious sense of well-being by his closeness as a rush of warmth completely pervaded her and her lovely eyes became blurred.

'Just a kiss then,' she whispered.

'Just a kiss, Miss Brook,' Alex murmured in a husky whisper.

Very slowly he lifted his hands and placed them on either side of her face. His eyes darkened as he leaned forward, and at his touch Lydia trembled slightly—with fear or with excitement? She didn't know which, but she did not draw away as he lowered his head the final few inches and placed his mouth on her soft, quivering lips, cherishing them with his own, slowly and so very tenderly.

His gentleness kindled a response and a warm glow spread over her—but also fear began to possess her…a fear not of him but of h̶e̶r̶s̶e̶l̶f̶ ̶a̶n̶d̶ ̶o̶f̶ ̶t̶h̶e̶ ̶d̶a̶r̶k̶ ̶h̶i̶d̶d̶e̶n̶ ̶f̶e̶e̶l̶i̶n̶g̶s̶ he ar̶

Author Note

I have really enjoyed writing this story. It is about Lydia, a working woman in early Victorian London, who takes control of her own life before the emancipation of women—although calls for change were gathering pace in the last decade of the nineteenth century.

Lydia is an experienced seamstress and designer of ladies' clothes. Intent on opening her own establishment, she is disheartened but not defeated when the bank refuses her a loan on the grounds of her being a woman. Along comes Alex Golding, a wealthy and influential businessman who deals with business ventures and legalities on a daily basis. He admires her intelligence and knows he is looking at a fighter. When she tells him she is looking for a loan to open her shop he offers her the money, confident that she will succeed…

all cost—she had relented, trying to convince herself that Henry was the living promise of all she desired and her escape from fear. But she wouldn't think of that now. Not here. Not now, not ever.

The minute she had said she would marry him, Henry had set the wheels in motion with what she silently considered indecent haste. She'd had no say in the necessary arrangements. Two days hence they were to travel to Liverpool to take passage for America. Henry lived in America and his father was very ill. Should anything happen to him, he didn't want to be on the wrong side of the Atlantic. It was for this reason they had come to this Scottish village called Gretna Green, the first changing post over the border, which was also a fashionable and romantic place for couples to marry immediately and without parental consent.

Now they faced the self-appointed priest who, for a substantial fee, had agreed to oversee the ceremony. The house where they had chosen to be married might not be as sanctified as a church, which Lydia would have preferred, but in the hushed quiet of the room and with the requisite two witnesses hovering behind them, it had all the solemnity she could wish for.

Lydia wore a costume of vibrant raspberry,

simply styled and unadorned, with a well-fitted bodice. Her bonnet with its wide semi-circular brim, decorated with a small bunch of pink and white rosebuds, matched the dress. A profusion of black curls escaped the confines of the bonnet and caressed her face.

The priest leaned forward. 'Are you ready to begin?'

Lydia nodded dumbly.

'Yes,' Henry was quick to reply, unable to hide his impatience to get the proceedings over with as quickly as possible. 'Get on with it.'

Lydia looked at the priest when he asked them if they were of marriageable age. Yes, they replied. There was a disturbance at the back of the room as the door was flung open and someone entered.

'Halt the proceedings.'

Lydia thought she must be mistaken. She thought she had heard someone say the ceremony must be halted. Startled, she turned at the same moment as Henry. It was simply unreal—the people, the priest, the sunshine streaming through the window. Two men had entered the room. The taller one who had spoken strode towards them. She looked him over openly. His tall, broad-shouldered physique radiated stamina and command, seeming to dwarf the other inhabitants of the room.

'Can this not wait?' the priest said crossly. 'You are interrupting the ceremony.'

'With justification.'

A sudden silence fell over the room. Lydia felt the cold at the back of her neck. It insinuated itself and slithered like tentacles down her spine. She stared at the man who had made the announcement.

'What justification can there possibly be that allows you to burst in here and interrupt a wedding ceremony?' Lydia retorted sharply with a fine cultured accent like cut glass, her gaze passing over the intruder with cold disdain.

The man's gaze flicked from Henry to her, regarding her with an arrogance that was clearly part of his masculine nature. His eyes narrowed dangerously and his lips curled fractionally, but what passed for a smile was merely a polite obligation and a cool, dismissive one at that.

'I apologise for any inconvenience caused, but I have justification enough—as you will, I am sure, soon agree. This man is not who he says he is. Had I not come in time he would have committed a criminal act.'

Astonished, Lydia stared at him. 'Are you a policeman?'

'No, I am not.'

From the tone of his voice and the set of his head and shoulders, Lydia knew that he was going to tell her the truth of the matter that was the reason for his intervention and her instinct told her that it was going to be worse than her worst imaginings. She stood rigid beside Henry, scarcely daring to breathe, waiting for him to continue.

'It is my duty to inform you that this man you were about to marry already has a wife.'

Uncomprehending, Lydia felt her eyes widen and she stood immobile as a marble statuette as time drifted by in this sunlit room. In the time it had taken him to utter the words, all the devastation and bitterness of her expression could not be concealed.

There was a ringing silence. Nobody in the room said a word. Henry's face had faded to the colour of dough. He was the first to recover. His mouth formed a grim line and his expression was guarded and wary—not unlike a small boy's who has committed a wrongdoing and suddenly realises he has been caught out.

'What is this?' he demanded, his gaze fixed on the intruder. 'And what the hell are you doing here?'

'Surely I don't have to spell it out?' the tall

stranger said, his voice dangerously quiet. 'Of all the stupid, irrational— Have you lost your mind?'

In the face of such intimidation, Henry was visibly shaken, but it only lasted a moment. 'Damn you,' he uttered, his mouth forming the words which were barely audible.

Lydia tore her eyes from the stranger and looked at the man she had been about to wed, telling herself that whatever was happening had to be a mistake, that it was some kind of nightmare. It could be nothing else, but the stranger wore an expression of such steely control that she knew he was telling the truth even though she couldn't comprehend it just then.

'Do you know this man, Henry? And how does he know you? Answer me.'

Henry was emanating enough antipathy to suggest he not only knew this man, but that he was likely to commit violence. Anger had replaced his initial shock. Ignoring the woman he had been about to marry, he took a step towards the man, his back rigid and his fist clenched by his sides.

'You followed me. Damn you, Golding!' he snarled. 'Damn you and your interference to hell.'

'And you'd like that, wouldn't you? I didn't

think it was asking too much when I insisted you remain faithful to Miranda—after all I have done for you. If it were not for me, your noble pile would have fallen into ruin and you would be living on the family farm, eking out a meagre living off the land. Instead of that you are living the life of the lord you were born to be and still chasing women.'

'How did you know where to find me?'

The man didn't so much as flinch. 'It wasn't difficult. You left my sister. She became bored and followed you to London. When she failed to locate you she came to me. I decided to pay a visit to your club where your friends were most accommodating with the truth. What lame excuse did you intend giving your *wife* for your absence?' He spoke with an edge of aggression in his voice, which suggested that he was a man used to being answered at once.

'I would have thought of something.'

'I don't doubt it. You've become rather good at lying to her. Damn you, Henry, you were about to become a bigamist.'

'Until you stepped in. You could not have orchestrated your arrival with greater skill or better timing.'

'I will not ask for an explanation—the situation speaks for itself. But how the hell do you think it would stand up in a court of law? Now I am here and though I am tempted to kill you, the love I bear my sister forbids it. Any wife faced with one sexual scandal after another would have her faith eroded in the man she married. She has just grounds to divorce you for this, but I doubt she will. She has a will of iron and your unacceptable, disgraceful behaviour since your marriage has only hardened her further. She is Lady Seymour of Maple Manor, a member of the peerage and no matter what you do to her she means to keep her place in society. Damn it, man, you have hurt her deeply. I hope you're proud of yourself.'

He switched his attention to Lydia, bearing down on her like a tidal wave, his thick, dark brown hair, with just a hint of silver at the temples, gleaming in the light of the sun slanting through the windows. Tall, lean of waist with strong muscled shoulders, attired in a dark frock coat and cravat and light trousers, his gaze with a touch of insolence passed over her. His mouth tightened and his eyes, cold and unfriendly, flashed dangerously as he glared at her.

He studied her as Lydia studied him. She felt herself chafing under it.

'What in God's name did you think you were doing,' he exclaimed irately, 'careering round

London with a notorious rake before embark-
ing on this mad escapade?'

Lydia felt a swelling of righteous anger, a
powerful surge of emotion to which she had no
alternative but to give full rein. After all, she
was as much a victim of Henry's cunning as his
sister. Her eyes flashed as a blaze of fury possessed her and added a steely edge to her voice.
'None of this is my fault,' she flared, suddenly
furious at having some of the blame shoved on
to her. 'I had no idea Henry had a wife—or that
he was a notorious rake since I do not inhabit
his world.Polite society is outside my normal
sphere, sir. Nor did I know his real surname is
Seymour. I only know him as Henry Sturgis.'

The man stood with his hands on his hips,
his light blue eyes like ice set in a deeply tanned
lean face with a strong determined jaw and his
voice like steel. 'I wasn't accusing you, Miss...?'

'Brook. Lydia Brook,' she provided, getting
her voice under control and her features into
a semblance of their normal expression. 'And
you, sir?'

'Alexander Golding.'

Lydia faced him, resolute and defiant, her
small chin thrust forward. She favoured him
with a gaze of biting contempt before dismissing him and looking again at Henry. The words

the stranger had spoken lapped round her like a wave threatening to engulf her at any minute. Her head felt suddenly weightless and she had to stiffen her spine to remain upright.

She studied Henry's face and read what he couldn't hide. In the space of a moment his expression had changed from the amiable, loving man who had been impatient to make her his wife, to that of a self-seeking, cunning being who was clearly thinking quickly what he could do to turn this situation he had not anticipated to his advantage. With the arrival of his brother-in-law, no longer at ease and in control, beads of perspiration began to dot his brow. She could almost hear the workings of his mind.

She squeezed her eyes shut and forced the tightness in her throat to go away. The sun that had shone so brightly had gone out of the day. How gullible she had been to let herself believe after Henry's passionate kisses and soft persuasive words that he really did want her, for she now realised that his words had been hollow, his passion no different from the passion he might feel towards any woman he was attracted to. The fact that she hadn't succumbed to his attempts of seduction—indeed, she had adamantly refused to do so without a wedding ring on her finger—had only served to make him want her more and try harder. When she thought she could speak in a normal voice, she opened her eyes and looked at him, trying to stand on her dignity before these strangers.

'Tell me why you have done this.' He cast a look at her. She wanted to see it as a look that asked her to understand, but she saw instead the calculation behind it.

'If only you knew,' he said, his voice so low that she hardly caught the words. 'I did want you—'

'But not as your wife,' Lydia bit back scornfully, noting that he didn't look her in the eye.

'No. I care for you—'

'You do not ruin someone you care for.'

'From the first time I saw you, I wanted you. I couldn't help myself. I have waited so long for this. I thought my chance to possess you would never come. My desire for you subverted whatever sense of right and wrong—of breeding—I have. It's not something I am proud of.'

'No. You should be ashamed. We were to have been married. You deceived me and brought me here to make me your wife. You were to take me to your home in America—your father was ill, you said, which was the reason you didn't want to wait the requisite three weeks for the banns to be read out in church. None of it was true.

What a gullible idiot, what a stupid blind fool I have been. How you must have laughed. What you have done is underhand—despicable. Oh, how dare you? You have treated me abominably.'

'Lydia—if only you knew—'

'Knew? Knew what?' she flared, anger flowing through her veins like liquid fire. 'That you already had a wife? What did you plan to do with me? Abandon me in Scotland following one night of connubial bliss and return to London flush with your success?' Seeing this was exactly what he had intended, she gave him a look of profound contempt. 'You disgust me, Henry. How dare you make me an object of pity and ridicule?'

'What will you do?'

'What I have always done—get on with my life. Let's be honest, Henry. You didn't love me any more than I love you.'

'You mean to say you didn't develop a *tendre* for me?' he quipped sarcastically.

'Your intention was to seduce me and when that failed it only served to make you more determined. Instead of doing the decent thing and walking away you went one step further, playing on my ignorance and vulnerability, and offered me marriage—even though you had no right to do so. You are a liar and a cheat. The worst of it is that I fell for your lies. I didn't know what you were trying to do to me. Your aim was to diminish me, but I will not be diminished—not by you. Not in any way.'

Knowing he had played with her as a cat plays with a mouse was almost more than Lydia could bear. She looked at him, at his curly fair hair and his lean athletic body. His face was sensuous with heavy-lidded eyes and a full-lipped mouth, which, no doubt, women found appealing. He looked just the same, this man who had shown her kindness and consideration and been attentive to her needs. But now, looking behind his handsome facade, she saw that man did not exist any more, if indeed he ever had. Now she saw a man emotionally devoid of those things. She saw boredom and greed, self-interest and contempt for her as his inferior. He looked at her as he would at some low creature—arrogantly and insolently.

She hated him then. She felt a mixture of rage and humiliation that was so profound she almost believed she would die of it.

'How could you be?' Henry retorted, her words having roused his anger. On the attack and uncaring how wounding his words could be, he went on to regale her and those present with her many shortcomings, much to his brother-in-law's irritation.

'You, my dear Lydia, would make an amusing bed warmer were you not as cold as the proverbial Ice Maiden and set with wilful thorns. Some might think your virtue admirable—personally, I consider it a damn waste of both time and a beautiful woman. It's unfortunate since beneath the ice you have spirit and should have proved highly entertaining in a chase—which I was about to experience for myself until my brother-in-law blundered in. Any man who shows an interest in you, you hold at arm's length until there is the promise of a ring on your finger.'

'Including you, Henry,' his brother-in-law said sharply in an attempt to silence him on seeing the young woman's shocked expression and how she had paled beneath the force of his attack.

Henry lifted his arrogant brows, drawling, 'Including me. I wanted her—rather badly, as it happens—and was prepared to go to any lengths to possess her.'

'Even to commit bigamy. You have failed, Henry, which is why you are so ready to point out Miss Brook's faults to anyone who will listen.'

'Indeed, I confess to having been afflicted

by a strong desire to possess her, but perish the thought that I would actually marry a woman of such low character and without a penny to her name.'

'Your failure to seduce her will do nothing for your self-esteem when you are back in town and you have to face your acquaintances and admit your failure to win the wager and have to part with the five hundred guineas.'

Lydia stood like a pillar of stone, her mind numb. Her senses and emotions would return when she realised the nightmare she was experiencing now was no nightmare at all, but an extension of reality that would affect the whole of her life. But at the moment she was too traumatised to feel or see beyond it. Henry's insulting words and the stranger's revelation hung in the air like a rotten smell. No one had insulted her as much as this and it was more than her pride could bear. She saw it all now.

Dazed and unable to form any coherent thought, she backed away as the implication of what she'd heard rammed home. Her heart began to beat hard with humiliation and wrath. She was appalled and outraged—there was no possible way to deny the awful truth.

Henry had made a wager with his friends to seduce her and, should he win, he would be richer by the sum of five hundred guineas. It was more than her lacerated pride could withstand. Her face glazed with fury. Oh, the humiliation of it. Any tender feelings that might have remained for him were demolished. The discovery of his treachery had destroyed all her illusions.

'How dare you?' she said, her voice low and shaking with anger. 'How dare you do that to me? I do not deserve being made sport of.'

'Miss Brook,' the stranger said. 'Please believe me when I say I regret mentioning—'

Her eyes flew to his. 'What? The wager? Is that what you were about to say? Why should you regret it? Why—when you were telling the truth? I have a right to know the extent Henry went to in order to get me into his bed.' She looked at Henry. 'What you have done is despicable. From the very beginning you set out to degrade me in the most shameful way of all. I am not too proud to admit that in the beginning I was foolish enough to fall for your charms. You're no doubt accustomed to that sort of feminine reaction wherever you go,' she said scathingly, 'even though you have a *wife*. It would give me great satisfaction to know that handing over five hundred guineas for your failed wager would ruin you, but I doubt it will.'

Faced with such ferocity, Henry took a step

towards her. 'For heaven's sake, Lydia, it was just a wager—a moment of madness. I never intended to hurt you,' he said in an attempt to justify his actions, but Lydia was having none of it.

'A moment of madness!' she flared, her eyes blazing with turbulent animosity. 'Is that what you call it? There is no excuse for what you have done. What is true of most scoundrels is doubly so of you. You would have ruined me, defiled me without any regard to my feelings and then cast me off as you would a common trull, you— you loathsome, despicable lech.'

'Lydia, listen—'

'I am not interested in anything further you have to say. But you listen to me, Henry Sturgis—Seymour—whoever you are,' she said, her chilled contempt meeting his spluttering apologies head on. 'I will never forgive you for this. From now on you will keep your distance from me.' She turned from him and walked away. She couldn't bear to look at him. The man and woman who had been brought in to witness their wedding stood side by side, rigid, their faces blank and expressionless as she brushed past them.

What he had done to her and what it would mean for her in the future spooled before her like a long ribbon of anger and grief. She wanted to lash out at him, to claw his face and pound him with her fists. Hate, disgust, disappointment and a deep sense of humiliation and hurt throbbed inside her skull and tightened her chest until she thought she would choke.

He had brought her all this way for a pretend wedding on the strength of a wager with his friends. She felt as if he'd taken a knife to her and sliced her into little pieces. Gripped by a terrible miasma of pain and deprivation—feelings she recognised, having grown up with them—she turned and ran unseeing out of the room which she had so recently walked into with a happiness she could not conceive. Now she saw nothing, heard nothing but the heavy pounding of her heart as she left the house and out into the street, hurrying to goodness knew where—anywhere, as long as she didn't have to go back into that room and face them all, to confront the truth of what Henry was and what he had done to her.

Rage, white-hot and fierce, coursed through her, bringing a suffering so excruciating as to be unsupportable. She felt cruelly betrayed, lost and abandoned, the immensity of it causing her intense pain.

She knew she'd feel better if she could only get away. If she could escape from him. She didn't want to stop because then she wouldn't have to think about anything else. But eventually she would have to stop and when she did she would have to feel, which she didn't want to face. She didn't want to see Henry. She didn't want to look in his eyes. She hadn't loved him. She didn't know what it meant to love anyone, but it did nothing to lessen her humiliation and the pain of such a public betrayal.

She kept on heading out of the village. What she was planning to do when she stopped running she couldn't say. The most important thing was to get away. She heard her name being called. She kept on going. Her heart was racing in her chest and she felt a sharp pain in her side.

'Wait,' someone called.

She heard herself gasp and saw the road ahead of her blur. She kept hurrying on. She heard footsteps behind her and then another call of her name. Not until a hand grasped her arm did she halt, breathing hard. She turned, her mind and her senses disjointed, the people and carriages passing by in a maze of confused colours and muffled sounds. Her confusion was exacerbated by the colour of light blue eyes surrounded by thick black lashes, the sound of a deep, mellifluous voice and the pleasant aroma of a sharp cologne. Still holding her arm, Alexander Golding led her to the side of the road, out of harm's way of passing carriages.

The eyes that looked into hers were as transparent and as brilliant as sunlight on water. His sharp, sceptical gaze seemed to bore into her brain.

'Are you all right? You are upset.' He spoke evenly, without sympathy, seemingly uncaring of her plight or the cause. Her chest was rising and falling in rapid succession.

'Of course I am upset,' she replied irately, trying to pull herself together. 'What Henry has done to me is unforgivable. What was I? Some tender titbit he decided to play with, a simpleton to fill his needs for a night or two. What amusement he must have had playing his sordid little game with me. And how disappointed he must now be feeling, knowing he has lost his wager.'

Nothing moved in his face, but his eyes darkened. Quietly, he said, 'I am sorry you had to find out like that.'

'Yes—so am I, but thank goodness I found out before it was too late. Now would you please let go of my arm?' He obliged at once.

Her anger somewhat diminished, Lydia stared at the darkly handsome stranger. He possessed a haughty reserve that was not inviting. There was also an aggressive confidence and strength of purpose in his features, and he had the air of a man who succeeded in all he set out to achieve. From the arrogant lift of his dark head and casual stance, he was a man with many shades to his nature, a man with a sense of his own infallibility. With her mind on what Henry would have done to her had this stranger not intervened, she was unnaturally calm, as calm as the Ice Maiden Henry had accused her of being.

'I—I…' Words seemed to stick in her throat, almost choking her. She felt exposed and vulnerable, knowing this man was seeing her like this. Normally poised and in complete control of herself, she felt so undignified. It was all so humiliating. When she had first looked at him she had seen by his face that he was a hard man not easily softened, so she was surprised he had even come after her. 'Please excuse me. This is all so sudden—so confusing.'

For the first time, Alexander looked at her and she at him. Something passed between them. Each felt that this moment was one of great importance, that they stood on the edge of something tangible, but they did not understand what it could be. Lydia swallowed hard. She could not seem to look away. She thought she should scream or try to run away. She did neither. Noise and bustle went on around them, but the sounds and people were lost to them as they looked at each other. It was a look that stretched for only seconds, but seemed far longer before Lydia averted her eyes as her heart swelled with such a bewildering array of emotions that she was overwhelmed.

Caught off guard by the effect this young woman was having on him, Alex immediately recollected himself. He could see she was still in the process of reeling from the truth of what Henry had done. She was dressed with tasteful simplicity in a gown the colour of raspberries. Her features were striking, her hair beneath her bonnet a rich, shining black. Her large dark green eyes tilting slightly upwards were moist, droplets of tears caught in her thick fringe of lashes glittering like diamonds. Her mouth was as red and ripe as a berry, her lower lip full. The sun was warm and the light glinted softly against her. It made her skin luminous. Quite tall and slender, she was wholly arresting and he could not seem to drag his eyes away.

When he had burst into the room to halt the wedding, he had been unable to focus on anything else but his brother-in-law. When he had learned Henry had come to Scotland and his reason for doing so, he had taken the young woman to be one of the high-spirited good-time girls who thought of little else but the frivolous pursuit of pleasure, whose life was one constant round of uninhibited fun and who thought it necessary to be a rebel, to outrageously defy the order of society—hence her easy compliance to adhere to this mad escapade.

The anger provoked by Henry's reprehensible behaviour began to subside a little, and Alex felt a faint stirring of admiration for the self-assured way in which the young woman faced him. Anger burned like a flame in her eyes and he was touched, despite himself, by her youth. When he looked at her, there was no hint of the softening in his mood. His eyes, harsh and impenetrable, met hers, and, if she had but known it, they were adept in keeping a legion of employees in their place.

'I imagine it is,' he said at length. Beginning to see how devastating it must be for her to realise she had fallen prey to a seducer, he suddenly showed a hint of human feeling. 'This cannot be easy for you. You did not know Henry had a wife.'

Wishing herself anywhere but where she was, facing the lonely place that rejection and anger had taken her, Lydia blinked hard to make the tears of hurt, anger and frustration disappear, hating herself for a weakness which ordinarily she would never show. 'Had I known that, I would not be here. I cannot believe he has done this to me. How could he?'

There was a desperate, almost wild look about her. She seemed ready to bolt like a wild horse at any moment. The cords in her neck were strained and the glimmer of tears slipped like melting dreams from her eyes. Alex felt a curious need to treat her with gentleness, to say something to comfort her. But he didn't know her or understand the nature of her grief, or her true relationship with his sister's husband.

'It's all right. I am not about to judge you.'

She didn't look convinced. Distrust clouded her eyes. Fiercely, she wiped away her tears with the back of her hand. 'But I think you will.' She tried to sound scornful. She only sounded afraid. The stranger would know, hear her inner weakness, and she despised him for knowing. Her natural resilience began to reassert itself. She looked at him, eyes flashing, defiant chin lifted. 'I thank you for arriving when you did.'

'There's no need.'

Alex noticed her posture—arms stiff, hands clenched by her sides. Her face was white like alabaster and her eyes glittered. He could not take his eyes off her—in fact, she looked quite magnificent. She reminded him of a rapier blade made of steel. Drawn up to her full height, she was standing on her dignity. He could see that the fear had left her and she was in the grip of an ice-cold, venomous rage. He waited for her to conclude whatever inner battle she was engaged in and he tried to keep his face as noncommittal as possible.

'I imagine you were looking forward to going to America.'

'Yes. I can't pretend otherwise—a new start—I'd hoped.'

'You must be disappointed.'

'One has to learn to live with disappointments.'

'Really? You seem rather young to be stacking up the bitter lessons of life.'

'No one knows at what age life will deny us.'

Alex looked at her. He tried to read her face, to see what emotion and meaning were behind her words, but he couldn't. He suspected that this young woman had a great deal of pride and courage, and both those things would force her to brave out the situation no matter how devastated she was.

Lydia stood and stared about her. What was she to do? Until now there had been Henry, experienced and decisive, to give her guidance and to take ultimate responsibility of the journey north in the hired coach and of their wedding. Now, she realised, she was on her own. Her hopes and dreams for a future which she had built were fractured suddenly. But, God willing, it was not irreparable.

'I will not go back into that room,' she said. 'I do not want to see Henry again. Not ever.'

Alex noted the even tone of her voice and the directness of her contact with his eyes. 'No one expects you to. Return to the hotel. I will make sure Henry does not trouble you. I want to say it was remiss of me not to enquire as to how what has happened has affected you. I do apologise most sincerely. I am not usually so unmannerly and I realise I spoke to you most unfairly earlier. I do beg your pardon.'

'Since he is married to your sister your anger was justifiable. Believe me, sir, when he proposed marriage to me I took time to weigh my options, considering every possible outcome of permanently tying my life to his.' She smiled bitterly. 'When it comes to making decisions I am the least impetuous person you could meet. I should have thought about it some more.'

'You weren't to know he was already married. How could you? Come. Let me walk with you back to your hotel.'

'Thank you.' She fell into step beside him,

slanting him a look. 'You have gone to a lot of trouble.'

He shrugged. 'I was left with no choice. Believe me, Miss Brook, I would not have halted your wedding without good reason. Consider yourself lucky that I discovered what he was up to before it was too late. I am sorry if this has inconvenienced you, but you must see that I have done you a favour.'

'Yes—yes, I realise that.' She stepped away from him. 'I will return to the hotel. I shall be boarding the coach going south in the morning.'

Having reached where she was staying, they stopped outside and Alex looked down at her, noting a tiny cleft in her chin that was almost invisible. She had style and bearing, and there was a tone to her voice and an imperious lift to her head that spoke of breeding, of being superior to the ordinary woman. He suspected she was very much her own person—a woman of her time. In the sun's bright light her colouring was vivid now. She dazzled him, drawing him to her with a power that enthralled him, and he stared at her with a hunger that went beyond anything physical.

He was quite bewildered by what he felt for her. It was an emotion he had no words for. All he knew was that it was different to anything he had felt in a long time, something that had sprung up suddenly, taking him by surprise, and he knew he couldn't and didn't want to walk away from her.

'I, too, will be staying at the hotel. It would give me great pleasure if you would dine with me tonight, Miss Brook?'

Lydia took a moment to consider his request, thinking that she really should refuse in the light of everything that had happened. But feeling restless and dissatisfied and having no wish to be alone on what should have been her wedding night, she accepted.

'Why— I— Yes, thank you. I would like that.'

Returning to the wedding venue, Alex immediately sought out Harris, his manservant—the man he relied on implicitly in both his business and personal life.

'Where is my brother-in-law, Harris?'

'Still inside—doing his best to placate the minister who was to conduct the ceremony. His attitude is of a man who is not at fault.'

'Which comes as no surprise to me, Harris.'

'He wanted to go after the young lady, but I told him to wait here.'

'You did quite right. He's the last person she wants to see right now. I've taken her back to the hotel. It grieves me to say so, but my sister's husband is a wastrel with a warped sense of humour and his reasoning, to put it mildly, is perverse. He is capable of gross infidelity and would have boasted of the conquest to his worthless friends had he brought it off and to hell with his reputation and the hurt it would have caused both his wife and Miss Brook.'

'Well, you did try to warn your sister against marrying him.'

'Since when did Miranda listen to anything I have to say?' Alex retorted crossly. 'I sometimes wonder about the family she married into—that the very fabric of the Seymour line is flawed in some way. As you know, I have no particular liking for my sister's choice of husband, but I did not imagine he was capable of this. His father had a dubious carry on—a gambler and a womaniser who left a pile of debts. There's a dark thread running through that family, Harris, and who knows where the devil it will appear? I pray to God not in my as-yet-unborn nephew or niece.'

'I very much doubt it,' Harris said.

'Let's hope not. I would protect Miranda from this—but when she gets a bee in her bonnet she won't give up until she is in full possession of the facts. She knows he's been seeing another woman—but not the extent of it. For her sake I would like to keep this whole thing quiet. Should the story get out the dirt will stick and the unsavoury backlash will cause her unbearable hurt.'

Alex strode into the house, meeting Henry coming out. Alex was a serious individual and known as a hard, unyielding taskmaster by those subordinate to him. He was also a ruthless businessman who had made a large fortune in shipping and mining in the north of England and an even larger one in clever investments in the railways and abroad. He had settled a more-than-generous dowry on Miranda, knowing of Henry's debts and his run-down estate which would benefit. Alex looked at him with contempt.

His normally arrogant brother-in-law was now subdued, demoralised by the events that had overtaken him, existing in a numbing vacuum of his own uncertainty. 'Well?' Alex demanded. 'Things have ended this way because of a miscalculation on your part—Miranda's failure to remain in Surrey and your friends' willingness to talk. It was a stupid mistake, the sort of error that could cost you your marriage. What have you to say for yourself?

'What can I say? You appear to know everything.'

'Quite. You care for nothing but your own self-indulgence. How dare you treat my sister in this despicable manner! You disgust me.'

'You must listen—let me explain...'

Alex shot him a look that would have stopped a racehorse in its tracks. 'Hold your tongue! I don't have the stomach for it now. I would like to spare Miranda the details of what you have done, but I do not see how it can be avoided. She will be deeply wounded by your betrayal, but no doubt she will forgive you eventually—foolish girl. You are undeserving of her devotion. I believe you hired a coach to come here?'

Scowling and tight-lipped, Henry nodded.

'I want you to leave here without delay, even if it means travelling through the night. You will go straight home to your wife, where you will confess what you have done and beg for her forgiveness. Is that understood, Henry?' Henry flinched before his cold anger. 'Damn it all, Henry, I will not rake over the sordid events that have brought you here. My anger will probably get the better of me and I won't be responsible for my actions. I have to remain in the north for a few days. When you reach Surrey you will remain at home—close to your wife— and keep a clear head. Where your friends are concerned you will maintain a discreet silence.

I expect your full cooperation in this. You and I have important matters to discuss.'

'Lydia—Miss Brook, she…'

'Has no wish to see you. You will not try to approach her. Is that understood?'

Henry nodded and swallowed audibly. 'Yes.'

Alex turned and walked away.

Alone in her room at the hotel and hidden from prying eyes, Lydia felt her whole body tightening as something tried to escape her, yet as fierce as she tried to suppress it, it was to no avail. Tears started to her eyes and began to flow, in sheer frustration and desperation. She wept for the present, in which her dreams and every wish seemed to be shattered, and she wept for the future, which now looked empty and bleak.

Henry's appearance into her life and his proposal of marriage had meant a liberation from a life that had held her chained to Alistair's workshop. Alistair, who had been her mother's lover and her employer, worked her hard, the constant pressure he put on her making her long to be free, to own her own establishment and create her own designs. Her dream had been her mother's dream, too. Before she had died she'd said it didn't matter that she hadn't realised her dream because she, Lydia, would carry forward her dream. Through her she would live on.

Henry had been a means of escape.

As his wife Lydia would have had a freedom from responsibility she had always dreamed of. Marriage to him promised great changes in her life. If she did actually marry him, her circumstances would alter dramatically. In short, she thought bitterly, he was a means to an end. But it had not been like that and now, with hindsight, she saw how he had skilfully manipulated her during the time she had known him. Determined to possess her, he had used patience, cunning and ruthlessness to gain her trust and devotion to get her into his bed.

Chapter Two

From his vantage point inside the dining room of the hotel, Alex watched Lydia enter. She stood in the doorway, her gaze doing a slow sweep of the room. Seeing him rise from the table, she walked towards him. Instead of the pale, humiliated woman he'd feared to see, she had lost none of the quiet, regal poise that had struck him earlier. She was the personification of calm, giving no indication of what had transpired earlier—or the tears that unbeknown to him she had shed in her room. Alex felt his admiration for her grow. He reacted to her. It was automatic after too long a period of celibacy.

Her body moved serenely as she crossed the room. Her ivory skin was flawless. In contrast to this, her hair, parted in the centre with a profusion of heavy corkscrew curls on either side, with the rest of her thick hair braided and pinned at the back, glistened like polished jet. Her eyes, surrounded by a heavy fringe of dark lashes, were large and luminous green. She was darkness and light, shadows and moonlight. Completely enchanted, he stepped round the table and held out her chair. As she took her seat and thanked him he breathed in the heady scent that came from her. She really was quite stunning. Little wonder Henry had been unable to resist her. How could any man with blood in his veins withstand her?

'My compliments,' he remarked softly, his eyes appraising her as he took his seat across from her. 'You look lovely. How are you holding up?'

Lydia's flesh grew hot and a tremor passed through her now she was face to face with him once more. A smile of frank admiration gleamed in his eyes when he looked at her, his sternly handsome face stamped with nobility and pride, his powerful, muscular body emanating raw power and sensuality. She smiled at him, the smile lighting her eyes with intelligence.

'I am very well—considering what has happened,' she replied, frustrated by the slight quaver in her voice. 'Where is Henry?'

'You will be relieved to know he has left Gretna.'

'Yes, I am—extremely relieved. I trust he has gone back to his wife?'

'Yes.'

'And the gentleman you were with earlier. I do so hope I have not deprived him of your company at dinner.'

'You mean Harris. He's my valet—secretary—whatever he wishes to call himself on the day and he's been with me for longer than I care to remember. What I will say is that he's indispensable. I am a busy man, Miss Brook. Harris takes care of my needs. At present he's making the most of some time to himself.'

The hotel dining room was filled with elegant, fashionable people. But it was these two that caught the eye and drew the most attention. They were a striking couple, Lydia still attired in the dress she had designed and made herself for her wedding. She knew light-coloured gowns were popular for brides, but Lydia had had to make do with the fabrics available to her. With its sloping shoulders, full sleeves and close-cut bodice tapering to a small point at the waist, the full skirt pleated into the waistband, it drew many an admiring glance. Alex, over six feet tall when standing, created a strong presence in the room in a way other men failed to do.

The waiter poured the wine. Alex sat looking at it, but he didn't drink it at once. His countenance was brooding and something vibrated off him, some sort of curious life force akin to restless energy.

'Did you not consider accompanying Henry to London?' Lydia asked.

He shook his head. 'At present I have no wish to spend time in his company if it can be avoided. Besides, I have business in the north to take care of. I expect to be here for at least a week.'

'I see.' Taking a sip of her wine, Lydia glanced at him over the rim of the glass. 'Does your sister know about me—about what Henry intended?'

'She is aware that he left London with a woman—not her identity,' he replied, fascinated by her, noticing how her face captured and absorbed the soft glow of the candles on tables and in wall sconces around the room. 'As far as I am concerned that is how it will remain. I have no doubt she will deal harshly with him, but she will not leave him. Her marriage means everything to her. She made vows. She said until death.'

'I'm sorry—truly. If I have caused her further

grief, it was not intentionally done. I was quite taken in by him. He appeared genuine. I had no reason to doubt him. But the truth is that once you begin to trust someone, to allow them into your life, to allow yourself to be touched by what you believe to be someone's inherent goodness, then not only have the walls been breached but also the armour has been pierced. He has made a fool out of me and I have no one but myself to blame for trusting him.'

'You are too harsh on yourself, Miss Brook.'

'I don't think so.' She managed to smile thinly. 'At this moment I am feeling more than a little bewildered, ill used and extremely angry.'

'I can understand that. What is your profession, Miss Brook?'

She hesitated. 'I am a seamstress. My employer, Alistair, also employed my mother— until her death a year ago.'

'I am sorry. Were you close?'

'Yes, very close. I miss her greatly.'

'And are you good at what you do?'

'Yes, I believe I am. I also like my work— which I will have to return to even if I have to grovel to Alistair to take me back.'

'Henry has much to answer for.'

'I cannot argue with that.'

'He has a chequered past—you weren't to

know. Life is one huge lark to him. He has a weakness for a pretty face. I have come to know him well since he married my sister and I have become familiar with his appetites. Like those he associates with—a pack of wild, swaggering, privileged young lordlings—he is known for his excesses and is one of the very worst examples of the ruling class and his upbringing.'

'Are his parents still living?'

Alex shook his head. 'As an only son, an only child, he was the pride of his parents with his future laid out. While those less privileged had to fight their way through life, Henry had it all handed to him. But he didn't realise that. He did not have the perspective that allowed him to recognise how lucky he was. He thought that whatever he wanted he could have.'

'Are his parents alive? He never spoke of them?'

'No. On the death of his mother his father drank and gambled the estate into the ground, leaving a heap of debts which forced Henry to make an advantageous marriage.

'Hence his marriage to my sister, who presented him with a generous dowry and who doted on him. He was raised in the belief that he is entitled to do anything his privileged birth tells him is his due. Not only is he charm personified, he is also expert in the art of persuasion. He has a habit of dazzling young ladies.'

'Especially a humble seamstress who doesn't know any better,' Lydia said, beginning to suspect that her companion's family must be very rich to have settled such a large dowry on their daughter.

Alex gave a lift of one eyebrow and he smiled suddenly, a startlingly glamorous white smile that unbeknown to him made his companion's heart skip a beat. 'Humble? Miss Brook, I suspect you are many things, but humble is not one of them.'

She returned his smile, a soft flush staining her cheeks. 'Perhaps not as humble as I ought to be—but stupidity cannot be ruled out. I thought it odd at first that he paid me so much attention. Me! A seamstress—and the daughter of a seamstress! He gave me flowers, presents—he flattered me. It had never happened to me before. I let him lead me on. My behaviour was a reaction to a weakness in myself that caused me to fall victim to his plethora of charms.'

'You were flattered by his attentions. You cannot be blamed for that.'

'No, perhaps not,' she said with a sigh. 'Why does Henry's wife put up with his philandering?'

'At first, in her blissful state of a new wife,

Miranda, secure in her marriage, didn't react to the attention Henry was getting from other women. His infidelities were subtle initially. Happier than she had ever been, even when she heard the whispers, she was unwilling to believe them. And then the knowledge grew from a practical examination of the facts at hand—his absences from home, from the marital bed, returning reeking of another woman's perfume. During one particular amorous encounter, when the lady Henry was pursuing refused his advances, she made it known to Miranda. Naturally, she was devastated and had cause to wonder where Henry's infatuation for other women was going to lead them—not to mention what potential for unhappiness lay in his seeming inability to control it.'

'I cannot understand why she doesn't leave him?'

He shook his head. 'She's become resigned to it—not that she likes it, not one bit, but she knows she will never change him so she gets on with her life regardless. She insists on discretion. He always leaves them in the end. Yes, Miranda loved him as soon as she set eyes on him. But apart from the emotional side of their relationship marriage was mutually beneficial to both of them. She hankered after a title and, financially, Henry needed the money from her dowry to restore his crumbling estate.'

'I see. Then I wish her joy of him. Knowing what I do now, I cannot envy her. I can only fear for her. He is a baron, you say? I did not know that he was titled, but I knew he was different from me. But what of you? Are you titled, too?'

'No.' As a self-made businessman, Alex chafed beneath the privilege of meaningless titles, family history, and velvet capes and ermine.

'Then what do you do?'

'I am a businessman, among other things.'

'I see.' She didn't really, but considering it rude to appear too inquisitive, she let it go at that and began eating the food the waiter had placed before her. 'And do you have a wife, Mr Golding?'

'My wife died.'

'Oh—I'm sorry.'

'There is no need. Blanche, my wife, was killed when the carriage she was travelling in overturned.'

'How tragic. You…you must miss her.'

His face became guarded. 'Yes.'

'I…I hope you don't mind me asking. My mother always did say I talk too much.'

He looked at her and met her eyes, staring at her for a moment, then he shrugged and smiled, the moment of melancholy having passed. 'I don't mind. It happened three years ago. I have no need to hide anything. It is better to speak of such things than keep them hidden,' he said, but Lydia saw his eyes held more seriousness than his voice, which told her it still affected him more than he would have her know.

'I agree. It is always best. You…have not thought of remarrying?'

'I am not looking for a wife,' he told her, his words and his eyes conveying a message. 'I am quite content to remain as I am, to go my own way and to enjoy female company from those who desire my company.'

'And always careful to elude capture,' Lydia said softly.

'Always.' He smiled. 'I have not known you twenty-four hours, Miss Brook, and already you are beginning to know me a little too well.' He looked down at his plate. 'We should eat before the food gets cold.'

Picking up his fork, after toying with his food, Alex gazed across the table at her lovely face. My God, he thought, she really was a beauty. Her long lashes drifted down as she looked at her plate, her soft red lips slightly parted. Her hair and gown were both unadorned, yet the effect was almost like nakedness, and Alex was

both embarrassed and ashamed of the animal
thoughts that flew through his mind as he looked
at her.

Looking up, Lydia met his gaze and raised
her brows in silent enquiry.

He smiled. 'What?'

'Why are you looking at me like that?'

'Why shouldn't I look at a beautiful woman?
You, Miss Brook, would make a saint forget his
calling.'

Lydia swallowed, feeling her cheeks redden.
The very fact of this weakness was an irritant
to her, making her vulnerable to her own body.
'I've heard many flowery compliments in my
time, but that, Mr Golding, is the most flowery
of them all.' Later she would realise her mistake.
The delicious food and the quiet, warm atmosphere of the room had lulled her into regarding
her companion as an equal, a person whom she
could relax with.

'You are a strange young woman, Miss
Brook. I find your company both pleasurable
and enlightening.'

'I'll take that as a compliment.'

'You are more intelligent than most women
of my acquaintance and, if you are not careful,
you will have me falling in love with a woman's mind—but her physical attributes cannot

be ignored,' he murmured, his gaze languidly sweeping over her, his eyes settling on the gentle swell of her breasts straining beneath the raspberry dress, measuring, lingering, a slow smile curling his lips.

The soft sincerity of his voice, the tone of it, rippled over Lydia's flesh and took her breath away—behind the words she detected an intractable force, coercing, seducing, and she was drawn to it, but then she remembered her purpose for being there. She tried to think of something to say, something that would restore the camaraderie and repartee of a moment before, but she was unable to say anything for the moment.

'What else did Henry tell you about himself, Miss Brook?' Alex asked, aware of the awkwardness of the moment and trying to steer clear of the direction in which his mind was wandering, but unable to take his eyes off her.

'That—that his home was in America. When he proposed marriage I told him we should wait, to give it time until we knew each other better. But he said time was something he didn't have. His father was dying across the Atlantic Ocean and he had to go home as soon as possible. I had no reason to doubt him. I cannot match him in education or experience—what knowledge I have was taught me by my mother. She was the daughter of a clergyman in Yorkshire. I have to work to make my living. Our backgrounds are dissimilar in every way.'

'And yet you were prepared to marry him.'

'Yes. He promised me so much.'

Alex smiled, noting that her every movement as she sat was graceful and ladylike. There was a serenity of expression and stillness that hung about her like an aura and just being with her was an experience he had not sufficiently prepared himself for. She really was quite beautiful, far more beautiful than any woman present, and she intrigued him, troubled him. His instinct told him that hidden desires were at play beneath her layer of respectability. He noted a certain unease in her eyes and what lay behind the unease was a sense that something was not quite right. Yet exactly what it was, not knowing anything about her, Alex couldn't have said.

'You saw Henry as a purveyor of dreams.'

'Perhaps it is best not to dream at all,' she said softly.

'How long have you known him?'

'Three months.'

'Where did you go? Where did he take you?'

'Why do you ask?'

'He is well known and popular among members of his club, his reputation that of a man about town who likes a good time.'

'My time off from work was limited. We saw each other on Sundays and sometimes I could manage an afternoon during the week. We were alone mostly.'

'That stands to reason. He wouldn't want to advertise the fact he had taken a lover.'

'We were not lovers,' Lydia was quick to inform him, her cheeks flushing pink with indignation that he thought they were. 'Never that.'

'No? Then I have no doubt this is the reason why he insisted on a sham marriage. His desire to possess you must have been overwhelming— even though he never had any intention of leaving his wife.'

'On occasion he did introduce me to a selection of his friends. Surely they would have said something—unless they didn't know he was married either.'

'Believe me, Miss Brook, they knew,' he said drily.

'You mean they were in on the deception? So I really was just some kind of amusement to liven up their bored lives?'

'I'm afraid so. I told you it is not the first time he has done something like this, although he has never gone as far as being prepared to enter into a sham marriage to get what he wants. You must have something the others lacked.'

She bristled. 'No, I'm just another one in a line of women.'

'Were you impressed by him?'

She looked at him steadily. What woman would not be, she thought, having been raised as she was. 'It was all so new to me. A different world.'

'And now? Will you go back to what you were doing?'

'I already told you that I have to. I have to work to live, Mr Golding. Throughout my life I have lived with the belief that happiness, security and future success would be available to me through the mainstay in my life—my mother— with her calm and gentle but firm ways. When she died all that changed—until I met Henry.'

Alex nodded with understanding. 'I am sorry. And your father?'

Immediately Lydia's eyes darkened and her face tensed. She looked away. 'He…he is not in my life.'

'I see.' There it was, Alex thought, that was the something which was not quite right. He was intrigued. Why the reluctance to talk about her father? Sensing that his enquiry was sensitive to her, he did not press further. It was not his concern. 'And your employer? Do you get on with him?'

'I have always tried to, for my mother's sake— they were lovers, you see.'

'Then if that was the case, will he not help you?'

'Alistair is a hard master. Working for him, I will never be more than an overworked, under-paid employee. I want to have a chance to make my own way, to be the dressmaker I know I can be—that my mother wanted me to be. I want to be a woman in my own right.' She sighed. 'I don't expect you to understand. How could you possibly?'

Alex did understand—more than she would ever realise. As the deprived son of an impov-erished and more often than not inebriated es-tate worker, on the death of his parents when he was just a boy, his maternal grandfather had paid for his education at Marlborough and then Cambridge. Alex would be eternally grateful to his grandfather for making this possible, even though he'd spent almost every penny he had doing so.

When Alex was eighteen, with his entire for-tune of one hundred guineas given to him by his grandfather, he had worked his passage to America. Life had taught him that he had to grasp the opportunities when they arose. Nothing was going to be given to him. Gambling his money on a series of investments had paid off. Thirteen years later he had made his fortune and never looked back.

He continued to excel in business like Midas. The only other venture he had engaged in was the pleasurable pursuit and conquest of the opposite sex.

Though thoroughly put out by this whole sordid affair with Henry which had disrupted the smooth order of his business life, he was impressed by this young woman's astuteness and he was amazed she hadn't seen through Henry's deception. She exuded tension and a certain authority and despite everything his curiosity was aroused as they ate their meal. She had an easiness of manner and a self-assurance and poise that was entirely at odds with her background. He was warmed by her sunny smile, the frank gaze and artless conversation, and he found himself sparing the time to listen to her.

There was an air of determination about her that manifested itself in the proud way she held her head and the square set of her chin and a bright and positive burning in her eyes when she outlined her plans for the establishment she hoped to open one day.

She told him how she was apprenticed at thirteen and how she had gained a thorough knowledge of fabrics and the business of supplying dressmakers. She had made a study of ladies' fashions and, inspired by what she had learned and her own ideas, she had high hopes for the future. She told him she had a small nest egg put by and when she had saved enough she would realise her ambition and her mother's before her. Alex found himself being carried along by the wave of her high expectations.

Finally falling silent, she looked at him and sighed. 'I'm sorry. I didn't mean to talk so much. You must wonder how I can speak so enthusiastically about my work after what Henry has done. He told me all my hopes and dreams would be fulfilled once we got to America. Well, that won't happen now—but I refuse to let what he has done to me ruin my hopes for the future. I cannot believe how I let myself be duped like that.'

'No? They say love is blind.'

'Love?' She laughed at the absurdity of it. It was as humorous as it was bitter. 'Oh, no, it wasn't love. I was flattered that a man of such glamour and charm—with a merry smile and a certain devil-may-care approach to life—should pay me attention.'

'So you didn't love him?' Alex felt curiously relieved on being told this, but once again he felt there was an edge to her manner—subtle, yes, but there—which led him to think there might be another reason why she had been so ready to accept Henry's proposal of marriage, that she might be running away from something and she had seized on the opportunity to escape. After all, she had admitted she didn't love Henry. So what other reason could there be?

Lydia smiled, a faint frown puckering her brow, and when she spoke it was as if the question was directed against herself. 'How does one analyse love? It has always been one of life's great mysteries to me. How can anyone adequately explain it? It's like trying to explain why the sun shines, why the earth spins and why the moon controls the tides.'

He laughed. 'The things you mention are rational to me. They are divined by nature.'

'That's another thing. How to explain nature.'

'You sound very cynical, Miss Brook. Love does not need an explanation, surely? Love, so I'm told, is something that grows out of nothing and swells as it goes along. No one can tell another why if happens—only how it is.'

Lydia smiled at his teasing tone. 'Now who is the cynic?'

'Touché, Miss Brook. Tell me. Why would you want to go back to working for Alistair if you were not happy?'

She looked at him. 'Happy?' She pondered the question a moment. 'I don't think the world has much to offer in the way of happiness,' she said, more to herself. 'There's too much grief—too much pain.'

'And you have known both, I suspect.' He looked across the table at her, his eyes curiously intense. 'You have just told me that you do not love Henry, which I find curious since you agreed to marry him. Why, I ask myself, would a woman who is both beautiful and clever do that, unless you are running away?'

She looked at him sharply. 'What makes you think that?'

'It's merely a suspicion I have. I am right, though, aren't I?'

She looked down at her plate, tension in the angle of her jaw. 'Yes—at least—something like that.'

'Running away is not always the sensible thing to do.'

She looked at him from beneath her long lashes. 'You may be right, but sometimes one is left with no choice.'

'That's true, but generally I think it is better to face the problem head on and deal with it.'

'That's easy for you to say.'

'Why are you running away? That is if you want to talk about it.'

She eyed him with wary indecision, wondering what he would say if she were to divulge the more sinister truth behind her acceptance of Henry's proposal of marriage, a marriage that would take her away from London—from England—far away from the awful truth that the man she had come to realise was her father, a man she had believed was dead, was very much alive. Having no wish to discuss this highly personal matter with a complete stranger, she shook her head. 'No, thank you, I really do not want to talk about it.'

'I understand, but I suspect it is connected to the grief and pain you mentioned.'

'Yes, I have known both, borne out of attachment to the person or people who cause it, and knowledge.'

From bitter experience her mother had told her that knowledge was life's blood in this world, that once gained it should not be thrown away, but used sensibly, ruthlessly, if necessary, that with knowledge a person could rule the world. And so she had applied herself diligently to her learning and then set about doing what her mother had told her to do. But when she had met Henry it hadn't worked out that way.

She was a woman who had encountered hardships for most of her life. Even working for Alistair where her performance was valued and he paid her slightly more than the other girls, she'd learned to take care of herself, never allowing others to venture too close—her mother excepted when she had been alive—never completely letting down her guard lest the price of that familiarity would mean an equality of mind. She had allowed Henry into her life, but she had only given of herself as much as she had wanted to give.

'My dream was that one day my luck would change and I truly thought it had when Henry came into my life. Suddenly I had a wonderful future before me, but it was not to be.' She smiled, a smile that was quite enchanting and unbeknown to her did strange things to her companion's heart. 'Please do not mind me, sir. Considering who I am you are being most kind and understanding. But you should not trouble yourself. As a gentleman, you must be embarrassed by such a situation, I am sure.'

'Not at all. You are a refreshing change to most of the ladies of my acquaintance. I find you are an interesting person to talk to. No doubt you will want to return to London immediately.'

'Yes,' she said decisively.

'Can I be of service to you?'

'No—thank you. You have done enough.'

The meal over, with his hand beneath her elbow Alex escorted Lydia out of the room. She was startled by his close proximity and she was puzzled by her body's response to the simple sensation of his hand on her arm. They stood at the bottom of the stairs in the small hall, facing each other. Lydia's lips parted in a tremulous smile, and her expression softened.

'I am thankful you saved me from what would have been a terrible fate. I'm so sorry about your sister. You must be concerned about her—about the whole situation, in fact. It can't be easy for her having an unfaithful husband—or for you, knowing what you do about him.'

Alex was strangely touched by her concern. He felt a stirring for her that was new to him on first acquaintance with any woman—a mixture of awe, desire and surprise that this glorious creature had actually fallen for Henry's smooth ability to manipulate the situation. She possessed the animal grace of a young thoroughbred and a femininity that touched a chord hidden deep inside him. Her full lips were inviting, her drawn-up hair displaying to perfection the long slender column of her throat—white and arched and asking to be caressed. In fact, she looked like a beautiful work of art.

When she had confronted him earlier, normally he would not have reacted quite so angrily, but he had been on edge ever since he had found out that Henry had absconded to Scotland with an unknown woman. He had been on edge before that, having spent an extremely tiresome few days dancing attendance on Irene—the wilful, spoilt sister of his good friend Sir David Hilton.

He had spent the past few weeks as David's guest at his house on the outskirts of Paris, a city which David loved and to which he would escape at every opportunity. David had returned with him to London, his sister accompanying him. Alex had intended spending the day prior to him learning about Henry's escapade at his house, Aspen Grange, in Berkshire. David was a close neighbour and the two of them had planned to do some fishing. It had been unfortunate for Alex that Irene had come along. That she nurtured hopes of marriage between them was evident, for she had hounded him ever since the demise of his wife.

But Irene would be disappointed, for he had

no intention of marrying again in a hurry. He had nothing but contempt for an institution that he had once believed would bring him happiness and fulfilment, but which had brought him nothing but misery instead.

'If I were not tied up in the north on business, I would offer to take you back.'

'Please do not concern yourself with my welfare. I'll be all right, really,' she said with more determination than accuracy. 'I can find my own way.' A wistful look clouded her eyes and her lips curved in a tremulous smile. 'It feels strange when I remember that tonight should have been my wedding night. I did not think it would end like this.' She sighed, meeting his eyes. 'None of that matters any more. We will not meet again, sir, for I doubt our paths will cross in the different societies in which we move.'

Alex was reluctant to let her go. The light shone on her soft dark hair and he visualised himself touching it, loosening it from its pins, running his fingers through it, feeling it caress his naked flesh as they shared an embrace. Despite her lowly background she was not of the common kind and there was also about her a mysterious, almost sweet and gentle allure. She had the poise of a woman fully conscious of her beautiful face and figure, and his instinct de-

tected untapped depths of passion in her that
sent silent signals instantly recognisable to a
lusty, full-blooded male like himself. The impact of those signals brought a smouldering glow
to his eyes as he imagined what it would be like
to possess such a glorious creature.

'It need not be like that.' His expression suddenly changed and the lightness disappeared
from his tone as he came to a decision. 'You
strike me as a sensible young woman—and a
beautiful one—although from my experience
the two do not always keep good company.'

'What are you saying?'

'I realise that this should have been your wedding night,' he said, speaking softly, holding her
with his gaze, knowing that she, too, was the
victim of irresistible forces at work between
them. 'You don't have to be alone tonight.'

He waited for her to reply, watching her,
knowing that her reaction to his suggestion
would determine everything between them. She
looked startled by his question and for a moment held his gaze with innocent perplexity. A
sudden shock of hunger that she might accept
shot through him, but he was to be disappointed.

His words and their implication did indeed
take Lydia by surprise. What shocked her even
more in that second when it registered was her

inclination to accept his offer. She had spent most of her life in the more deprived areas of London—she was not naive and would have had to be a fool not to have known the implication of his words. Throughout the meal and the warmth that had developed between them, and the way he'd listened to her as she had told him about her work and hopes for the future, she had been quite carried away.

She watched his smile. It was a most appealing smile. Her resolve hardened automatically at the sight of it. After today she knew well enough what degree of complicity an appealing smile was able to conceal. Henry had taught her to discount any warmth she might feel for another human being. To feel that way led to weakness, which could be fatal.

Hot colour flooded her cheeks and she took a step back abruptly. 'Either I am mad, sir, or you are,' she said, keeping her voice low so as not to overheard by others drifting in and out of the hall. 'What kind of woman do you think I am? I do not want to sound ungrateful for your kind attention, but I feel that now you are either carrying gallantry too far or pitying me to the extreme.'

'I am not being gallant, Miss Brook, nor do I pity you,' he said, his eyes held by this vibrant, graceful woman who was so close he only had to raise his hand to touch her. 'That has nothing to do with it. I assure you I am completely serious.' He spoke softly, so cool, so self-assured, holding her gaze.

'Yes, I can see you are, and if you wonder at my decision to turn you down it is because I have a well-developed instinct for self-preservation.'

'Not so well developed, otherwise you would have seen through Henry from the beginning,' he murmured.

'No doubt you think that because Henry picked me up from the back streets of London I am fair game. You are mistaken. How can you suggest anything so improper? I am not a whore. I am not for sale. If you were any sort of gentleman, you would not have said what you just did.'

The savagery in her tone startled Alex. 'It was merely a suggestion. I thought that after all that has happened today you might not want to be alone.'

'I like my own company, Mr Golding. Henry has turned out to be most unworthy. If I agreed to what you suggest, I could well be uniting myself with another equally unworthy.'

Alex's jaw tightened, and he stepped away from her. So, she thought she could impose on him with her ladylike airs. But then, furious with himself, more than with her, after all she had been through that day, he understood how insulted she must feel by his improper suggestion. 'If you are going to cast doubt on my good intentions, then there is nothing more for me to do than bid you goodnight and wish you a safe journey.'

'Goodnight, Mr Golding,' she said in a shaky, breathless voice, trying to ignore the dull ache of disappointment in her chest, regretting this new turn of events that had ruined the closeness that had developed between them throughout the meal.

Alex looked at her face, drawn by the candlelight reflecting softly in the depths of her eyes and the appealing pink of her lips slightly parted to reveal shining white teeth. His conscience rising up to do battle at what he had suggested, he tried flaying his thoughts into obedience, but he could smell her perfume in the air, which weakened his resolve.

He had known and made love to many beautiful women, but he could not remember wanting any of them on first acquaintance as he wanted Lydia Brook. What was it about her that he found so appealing? Her sincerity? Her innocence? Her smile that set his heart pounding like that of an inexperienced youth in the first throes of love? He told himself that what he felt was the ache of frustrated desire, but whatever it was he could not deny that she affected him deeply. Almost without conscious thought, as she was about to turn away he found himself reaching for her.

Lydia was surprised when he suddenly took hold of her arm and drew her into a curtained alcove beneath the stairs. The light was muted, the space small, forcing them together. She gave a sharp jerk, trying to pull herself free, but his arms went around her, drawing her close.

'Please,' she gasped, lifting her head and dragging her eyes past his finely sculpted mouth to meet his gaze, suspecting he was going to kiss her. 'This should not be happening.' Raising his hand, he gently brushed her cheek with the tip of his finger, moving it down with sensuous slowness. Her skin grew warm with pleasure.

'I know,' he said, bending his head to whisper quietly against her hair, and she impulsively turned her head slightly to meet his cheek with her own. 'Just one kiss, Miss Brook. Where's the harm in that?' The contact with her flesh was electric. He raised his head, his smouldering eyes gazing down at her face as if he were memorising it, then they fixed on her lips.

Quite inexplicably Lydia's heart gave a leap of desire and, when her gaze settled on his mouth, she was lulled into a curious sense of well-being by his closeness as a rush of warmth completely pervaded her and her lovely eyes became blurred. 'Just a kiss, then,' she whispered.

'Just a kiss, Miss Brook,' he murmured in a husky whisper.

Very slowly, he lifted his hands and placed them on either side of her face. His eyes darkened as he leaned forward, and at his touch Lydia trembled slightly—with fear or with excitement, she didn't know which—but she did not draw away as he lowered his head the final few inches, and placed his mouth on her soft, quivering lips, cherishing them with his own, slowly and so very tenderly. His gentleness kindled a response and a warm glow spread over her, but also a fear began to possess her, a fear not of him but of herself and the dark, hidden feelings he aroused within her.

Suddenly his arms encircled her and she was drawn closer to his hard chest, moulding her body to his rigid contours. A flame of white heat rushed through her. She allowed him to hold her in his embrace, feeling the strength of him against her as slowly his warm parted lips, tender and insistent, continued to claim hers, moulding, caressing and possessive.

The shock of his kiss was one of wild, indescribable sweetness and sensuality, violent yet tender, evoking feelings Lydia had never felt before. She felt her body ignite as she responded eagerly, pressing herself closer still and opening her mouth to receive his. He smelled of brandy and cologne, and it intoxicated her senses. Blood pounded through her veins and her stomach tensed, but she didn't try to move away. Imprisoned by his protective embrace and seduced by his mouth and strong, caressing hands, which slid down the curve of her spine to the swell of her buttocks and back to her arms, her neck, burning wherever they touched, Lydia clung to him, her body responding eagerly, melting with the primitive sensations that went soaring through her. Nothing in all her twenty years could have prepared her for his kiss and she became lost in the joy, the heat and the magic of the moment.

A soft moan interrupted the quiet space, and Lydia realised it came from her. Suddenly her world had become exquisitely sensual, where nothing mattered but this man and what his mouth locked hungrily on hers and the closeness of his body was doing to her.

Alex held her unresisting, pliant young body close, his lips caressing her cheek, her jaw, before finding her lips once more. He was a virile and an extremely masculine man, well used to the pleasures of the flesh that were available to him. But this woman confounded him. She was pure, untouched innocence, a woman who had never known a man's intimate embrace. As her mouth fed his hunger, his body strained towards her.

When he finally released her lips they were both breathing heavily. Standing unmoving, as though still suspended in that kiss, her lips moist and slightly parted, slowly Lydia began to surface from the dangerous cocoon of sensuality where the absolute splendour of his kiss had sent her and where she had no control over anything.

Tenderly, Alex caressed her cheek with the tips of his fingers. She was utterly lovely, breathtakingly so, and he was moved by emotions almost beyond his control, wanting so very much to kiss her again, but this time with all the hunger and passion that threatened to engulf him. He told himself to slow down, to be content with what she was willing to permit, not to push her into anything, but at that moment his desire was to continue to be close to her, to savour the sweetness of her. He was seized by an uncontrollable compulsion to make love to her—reluctant to allow this glorious young woman to slip through his fingers. He cupped her face in his strong hands, gently brushing a strand of hair from her cheek and tilting her face to his.

'Don't spend this night alone. Stay with me.'

She gazed up at his face, darkened in the dim light, feeling a numbing of her senses as her desire for him took on a dangerous life of its own. There was a need in her and she couldn't understand the nature of that need. Where had it come from? All she knew was that this man was the man to satisfy that need. She wanted him. She wanted more of what he could give her, but she must not. Her own thoughts shocked her. What was she thinking? This man was of a different class, living in a different world. He might not have a title like his brother-in-law, but he was of the gentry. It seeped out of him in volumes. It spoke of power, confidence and strength—and more than a little arrogance.

'No. I really must go.'

For a moment Alex stood there, looking down at her face flushed with desire in the dim light, her eyes glazed with it.

'Why? Are you afraid of me?'

'No, of course I'm not,' Lydia said shortly, but she realised as soon as she had said it that it was a lie. Of course she was afraid of him, afraid of what she might do with him if she stayed any longer, because that was exactly what she wanted to do. To feel his lips on hers once more, to feel those exquisite feelings his lips had ignited in her.

'I must go.' She flung herself away from him

and even though her legs were trembling and her flesh was on fire she began to climb the stairs with all the dignity she could muster, knowing that he continued to watch her like some dark brooding sentinel. Never had anyone affected her like this in her whole life. The thought of giving herself to Mr Golding sent a tremor down her spine, but it no longer shocked her, the events of the past twenty-four hours having finally drained her of all feeling so there was hardly any emotion left in her.

And yet she could not put what had just happened from her mind. The feelings she had experienced when they had talked over dinner took some understanding—she had felt herself being drawn to him against her will by the compelling magnetism he seemed to radiate and the memory of his smile and how he had looked at her, how his incredibly light blue eyes had hardly left hers for a moment and the intimacy of his lazy gaze made her tremble and heat course through her body.

She told herself that to enter into any sort of relationship with a complete stranger could be both foolhardy and ruinous. But Alex Golding's suggestion in the aftermath of Henry's betrayal constituted a phase in her life that was both flattering and essential for her pride. His desire for her had aroused an equal desire in her. It was the kind of desire that was completely new to her, the kind of desire that, despite all his efforts, Henry had never been able to stir.

She tried telling herself that the two men were not in the least alike, but how could she know that? She didn't know Alex Golding.

She had a flicker of doubt that what she was about to do was foolish, but then she reminded herself that the steps she was about to take, that what would happen, would be on her terms and that afterwards she would walk away and no one would be any the wiser at what she had done.

She shivered, but it was not because she was cold. Suddenly she felt warm—far too warm. Something was happening to her. It was as if a spark had been lit that could not now be extinguished. A need was rising up inside her—a need to be close to the man who still watched her, to this stranger—to wallow in the desire that had suddenly taken hold of her, to saturate herself in this newfound passion his embrace and his kiss had awoken in her.

Chapter Three

$Alex$ watched Lydia go with a brooding attentiveness in his eyes. Left alone with a raw ache inside him, wanting more of her, the vexing tide of mortification which had consumed him since, like a mindless idiot, he had put his proposition to Miss Brook only to be rejected, began to subside. His mind was locked in a furious combat with the desire to seek her out and beg her pardon and the urge to shrug his shoulders and forget her, but he knew that was impossible.

Everything about her threw him off balance. Her mere presence stirred emotions he hadn't felt in a long time—not since... But as he was about to let his thoughts wander and resurrect the past, angrily he thrust them back into the darkest corners of his mind, unwilling to allow them to intrude into the present.

What had he been thinking of? He should not have tried to take advantage of her. He realised just how devastated she must have felt when she had discovered that Henry was married, the inexplicable anguish she must have been through. The girl was traumatised, vulnerable. After the way Henry had dealt with her she wanted someone she could trust, someone to sympathise with her situation, not some stranger who wanted to take her to bed.

With his hand resting on the newel post, he continued to watch her as she climbed the stairs, seeing her pause when she reached the top. He could sense the tension in her. After a moment she slowly turned and looked down at him.

With her heart pounding in her breast and deeply affected by her desire and aroused by his kiss, Lydia felt something stir within her—something she had never felt before. A flicker, a leaping, a reaching out. The memory of the burning kiss and the dark, hidden pleasure it had roused in her was something she wanted to experience once more. She remained motionless, looking down at him. His eyes captured hers, a lazy seductive smile passing across his handsome face, curling his lips, and against her will she felt herself being drawn towards him, knowing she should go on her way, but she was too inexperienced and affected by him to do that.

She allowed her captivated senses full rein. She was trapped and she knew it. She was mesmerised by him, like a moth to a flame, and she felt her heart suddenly start pounding in a quite unpredictable manner.

He was looking into her eyes, holding her spellbound, weaving some magic web around her from which there was no escape. There was a weakening in every muscle and bone in her body as it offered itself to Alex Golding. She felt an upheaval inside her and a melting in her secret parts. Her need flashed like a current, charging the air between them and there, in a hotel bustling with other people, her eyes bestowed on him a silent carnal promise as binding as any spoken vow.

Alex read the message her eyes conveyed. It was all the encouragement he needed. With a knowing smile curving his lips, he began to climb the stairs.

At the top of the stairs there was a corridor with closed doors on either side. Lydia entered one of these. Alex followed. The room was warm. It was not a large room, but it was comfortably furnished with everything the occupant needed—or occupants, as it should have been this night, had Henry's plans come to fruition. The curtains were drawn across the window. The air was hushed and a single candle burned on a small table beside the bed.

Alex stepped inside and closed the door behind him. Lydia stood watching him, so still she could have been a statue. In the soft glow of candlelight her eyes were huge, like those of a wide-eyed kitten, luminous and infinitely lovely. Her chest rose and fell with each breath she took as her conscience chose that moment to rear up and do battle, for what she was contemplating went beyond anything she had ever contemplated before. She trembled, her desire triumphing over her better judgement. She was more frightened than she had ever been in her life and she was both appalled and ashamed that she could even consider doing such a thing after all Henry had put her through.

Without taking his eyes off her, Alex crossed to where she stood. The darkening of his eyes, the naked passion she saw in their depths, seemed to work a strange spell on her and conquered her.

Alex's thoughts turned to what was happening between them. If what she had told him was true, that Henry had failed to coerce her into becoming his lover, it was highly likely that she was still a virgin. In which case, if he, Alex, had any scruples whatsoever, he'd walk out of that room right now. But that brief stirring of his conscience was not strong enough to deter him and, as he gazed at her lovely, apprehensive face, the feeble protest melted away.

'Whatever scruples I was born with I lost long ago. We are not children. We both know what is happening to us and we both know what this is leading to. I want to make love to you—and I think you want me, too. You might say my motives are anything but noble and decent and you would be right, but they are adult and natural. I will not force you. You have to want this as much as I do.'

Want? That word didn't express how Lydia felt, how she yearned with every fibre of her being, every pulse and bone and breath she took to take what he was offering. She did not know this man, yet the physical desire she felt for him ached inside her. The intensity of feeling between them was evident, but not easily understood, although what she did know was that it offered a new excitement, as though the future held a secret and a promise.

A small insidious voice whispered a caution, reminding her that any kind of liaison with him could bring her nothing but heartache, but another voice was whispering something else, telling her not to let the moment pass, to catch it and hold on to it. She would welcome it, glory in it, if he would make love to her here, in this room—in the same bed she was to have spent her wedding night with Henry. Alex's powerful masculinity was an assault to her senses. As if moved by forces beyond her control, she was unable to resist him, but she would not tempt fate beyond this one night.

'Tell me what it is you want,' he murmured, taking her upper arms and drawing her close. 'Would you like me to leave?'

Drawing an unsteady breath, Lydia rested her forehead against his chest. 'No—please don't go. I don't know what is happening to me,' she whispered. Raising her head, she met his gaze. 'What I feel is too strong to fight—I don't think that I even want to. My emotions seem to be all over the place.'

Watching her closely, Alex saw something move and glow a little in her eyes, and a tiny flame of triumph licked about his heart. Completely relaxed, he smiled then, that unnerving white smile that could charm and melt the stoniest heart.

'Am I to take it that my attentions are not unwelcome?' He spoke softly, his voice a caress. She nodded. 'I'm glad you don't find me repulsive,' he murmured tenderly.

'No—never that,' she replied honestly.

Alex smiled. 'You are not only beautiful and clever, Miss Brook, but mysterious also. In truth, I will do my best to please you. I am aware of the importance of what you are doing and never having had the responsibility of being a woman's first lover, I consider it a privilege—and a pleasure.'

His voice was low, with a husky rasp, and his eyes held Lydia's captive, gleaming in the dim light. The effect of his intimate expression made her heart turn over. His potent virility was acting like a drug to her senses, the tug of his voice, his eyes, too strong for her to resist. Sensations of unexpected pleasure washed over her, making her want to stay, making it impossible for her to leave. What was happening to her? She had never felt like this, but she recognised the feeling. It was happiness, a feeling she had not felt in a long time and never with such warmth, such intensity.

As if her need communicated itself to Alex,

with his eyes fastened to her lips he said, 'What are you thinking? Tell me?'

With a shaking breath she raised her eyes to his. 'I am wondering when you are going to kiss me again.'

He smiled. 'And I am asking myself if your mouth still tastes as sweet on mine as it did a few minutes ago.'

Lydia's heart skipped a beat and any resistance she might have had disintegrated in that moment. She felt herself melting, ready to experience whatever lay ahead. She was sinking into a deep, sensual spell.

Alex captured her face between his hands and turned it up to his. He gazed into her eyes, unconsciously memorising the way she looked, her cheeks flushed, soft and alluring. There was an enormous amount of subliminal sensuality in her every gesture and, seeing her bite her lower lip apprehensively with the decision that she had made, plucked a deep chord within him.

'For one night I am asking you to forget everything else. Do you not find that appealing?' he said, his light blue eyes, darkened in the muted light of the room, caressing her face. 'And my name is Alex. Do you mind if I call you Lydia?' She shook her head. 'Good. Now that is out of the way I think we should soon retire to

the comfortable bed that awaits us, where neither conscience nor Henry will intrude tonight.'

Slowly he rubbed his thumb over her soft bottom lip, but the deep green depths of her eyes
were pulling him inexorably in. Lydia shivered
inwardly, her lips parting on a breathless gasp,
and she tried in vain to see past the darkness of
his magnetic, shameless eyes. Sliding his hand
round her nape, he kissed her. It was a hard,
drugging kiss, the kiss of a starving man hope-
lessly trying to sate his hunger. His arms went
around her, and she melted against his chest,
trembling, welcoming his lips, his tongue as it
invaded her mouth.

What seemed to be an eternity later Alex put
her from him and did what he had been wanting
to do throughout the meal. Raising his hands, he
began removing the pins from her hair, with deft
fingers combing out each curl and braid until it
fell in dark shining locks about her shoulders.

'This,' he said, glorying in the tender passion
in her eyes, feeling the heat flame in his belly as
he drew aside the curtain of her hair and placed
a kiss in the warm, sweet-scented hollow of her
throat, 'is what I've been thinking of from the
moment you walked into the dining room.'

As his lips trailed over her flesh, with a gasp
of exquisite pleasure Lydia threw back her head

and closed her eyes. 'I cannot believe this is happening to me—that I am even allowing it to happen,' she breathed softly. 'I feel I must confess to having little knowledge or experience of the intimacies that take place between a man and a woman. I'm afraid that you will find me a complete novice,' she murmured. She knew she was on the brink of the unknown and her pulses began to race dangerously. 'I—I feel I am heading for something I cannot possibly know how to handle.'

'Then I think it is about time you learnt,' he replied seductively.

Again his mouth laid siege to her own, taking her lips in a fierce, devouring kiss that sent jolt after jolt of exquisite sensations rocketing through her, filling her with a fever of longing. Leaving off just long enough to divest her of her dress and undergarments with the dexterous ease of long practice, murmuring to her between kisses which he dropped on creamy flesh as each item of clothing was removed, he somehow managed to remove his own attire in the process. Lydia heard his sharp intake of breath as her body was slowly revealed to him, his eyes fastening hungrily on her naked beauty. She was gloriously lovely, and he was bewitched, helpless to resist such temptation.

Lydia was enthralled by what was happening to her—by her own nakedness and his, after he had removed his clothes unselfconsciously to reveal the muscled, well-honed body of an athlete, brown and hard and eager—and she took a moment to admire his shoulders and deep chest, matted with crisp black hair. She flushed and tried to avoid looking at his manhood, and Alex chuckled softly, charmed. Passion flared and he pulled her down onto the bed, soft and ready for them.

In the glow of the single candlelight that burnished their bodies gold, he took a moment to study her thoughtfully. Lydia felt the heat at each spot that his eyes rested on her body. He took his time, with his mouth moving lingeringly over her, and when his lips took possession of her breast she was unable to stifle a gasp. Never would she have suspected that the feel of a man's lips on such a secret part of her body could create such incredible pleasure. He continued kissing her, enfolding, caressing, gently at first and then with increasing urgency, sliding his hand down to the curve of her waist, kissing her eyes, her throat, the rosy nipples of her breasts, his fingers burning wherever they touched. No part of her escaped and her sighs and moans fed Alex's ardour, fuelling his passion.

There was a moment when, at such an intimate invasion of her body, she almost objected, to thrust him away, but he filled her with such exquisite promise as he continued to arouse her that she moved her hips instinctively against him, pressing, arching herself closer. All rational thought had flown from her head. Deep within her a spark flickered and flared. She shivered, feeling the hard strength of his body pressed to hers, his strong, knowledgeable hands moving everywhere, arousing the hunger she could not deny and a wild elation that went surging through her and singing through her blood. With an abandon that shocked her, she melted against him, responding to the need he was so skilfully building in her.

As he began to surrender to a primitive and powerful, desperate need that became a torment inside, the restraint Alex had shown so far vanished in his desire to possess the woman writhing beneath him, her hands generating sparks as they moved over his shoulders and back and down to his taut hips. The perfection of her body intoxicated him. The perfumed mass of her hair tumbled about them. He knew instinctively that, unlike all the other women he had bedded, she was sexually untutored. He gloried in her and the soft yielding body was redolent of his passion.

Tears sprang to Lydia's eyes at the fierce stab of pain when he entered her, filling her, but the few seconds of discomfort were lost in what came after. The flame he had ignited with his touch, his kisses and caresses, was too well lit. After that there was no holding back, no thought of past or future. No thought of Henry or anything else, only now, this moment, as they gave and received pleasure, moving surely towards the ecstasy that consumed them both. It was wild and primitive and growing, something so wonderful that Lydia's conscience receded completely as she unwittingly drove Alex to unparalleled agonies of desire.

Wave after wave of exquisite pleasure washed over her and she felt herself being ruled by him, possessed by him, igniting her female flesh with new life. Wrapped in the pure rapture of their union, yielding and merging with each other, their need for each other overwhelmed them and Lydia's body, released at last from its long-held virginity, became insatiable for whatever he had to offer.

Breathing heavily as they waited for the slow and powerful beating of their hearts to return to normal, when they lay spent, their bodies entwined together, the hot climactic world that had held them in its thrall began to subside. The golden glow of the single candle washed over their skin. It seemed a long time before either of them stirred. Alex shifted to his side, taking Lydia with him and drawing the quilt over them both.

Propping himself up on his elbow, Alex gazed at the incredibly beautiful young woman nestling in the crook of his arm, her hair a dark blur against the white pillows. He noticed that her eyes had taken on a peculiar deep lustre and that her skin, like his own, was damp and glowed with an inner fire. She was goodness and gentleness personified, an enchanting temptress who had yielded without reservation.

'Are you all right? Did I hurt you?' he asked quietly.

'Yes,' she whispered, her cheeks a rosy hue. 'At first. It didn't last long.'

'Forgive me. I'm not in the habit of deflowering virgins.'

She stretched languidly, her eyes soft and alluring beneath half-lowered lids. 'I found it wonderful, but quite exhausting. I'm sleepy.'

'The night is not yet over,' Alex breathed, nuzzling her ear. 'Sleep is the last thing on my mind.'

Her skin gleaming with a silken sheen, Lydia's lips broke into a smile. Feeling neither shame nor guilt, raising her hand, she slid it about his neck and brought his head down to hers, placing her mouth on his. Again they made love, slowly now and with a tenderness which was beyond anything Lydia had ever known. Amazed by her own sensuality, naive and unskilled in the arts of making love, she allowed Alex to introduce her to new fields of pleasure, teaching her how to please him, watching as he awakened her into a tantalising creature who breathed sensuality, whose body pulsated with fire.

Later, when Lydia at last succumbed to exhaustion and slept, with her hair tumbling onto the pillows, her cheeks flushed with her exertions, Alex studied her face, feeling that even if he lived to be a hundred without another sight of her, his memory would still retain every curve, every line of it. Getting out of bed, he began to dress to go back to his own room, trying not to make a noise so as not to disturb her, but she must have sensed his absence.

Opening her eyes for a moment, Lydia was confused. Reaching out her hand to the empty space he had occupied, she half opened her eyes. Still trapped in the throes of passion, she sighed, feeling sexually awakened and free of ignorance and anxiety.

'Please come back to bed,' she murmured, her voice husky with sleep. 'I never dreamed that loving someone could be like this—so wonderful.'

Hearing her remark, Alex felt his face freeze and a warning voice sounded in his mind. 'No, you don't,' he said, his tone sharper than he intended.

'Don't? Don't what?'

'Love has nothing to do with what has happened between us, so don't imagine it has.'

Bewildered by his words and the tone of his voice, Lydia opened her eyes wide. Too inexperienced to hide her feelings, her face was like an open book. She had discovered in being with him, what it was like to be violently attracted to a man without loving him. On seeing him pulling on his clothes, she sat up, disappointment clouding her eyes. 'You're leaving?' He nodded, picking up his jacket and thrusting his arms into the sleeves. 'But—but I thought…'

In a blinding flash it dawned on Alex that she might expect more from him than he was prepared to give and, if so, he must put a crushing end to it right now before she even had time to nurture the idea. 'What? What did you think, Lydia? That after one night in your bed I might be so besotted that I would offer what Henry could not give you?'

With those words, he broke the slender, fragile thread that had held them together a moment before—fragile yet invisibly binding, for Lydia would never be able to forget. Deeply hurt and bewildered by his attitude, she shook her head. 'No—no, of course I didn't.'

She tried to sound unconcerned when she spoke, but somehow it didn't sound like that to Alex. When he heard the telltale catch in her voice, it was so touching that he was moved in spite of himself and when he next spoke he gentled his tone.

'Because of who I am, I have become accustomed to being pursued by all manner of young ladies and it would not be the first time a woman has insinuated herself into my bed with marriage as her object—'

'But it wasn't like that,' Lydia was quick to point out, her chin lifting with indignation. 'I did not insinuate myself into your bed—which you know perfectly well.'

'No—you didn't, and I apologise. But if you think I feel flattered that you gave me that which you have denied Henry, then you are mistaken.'

His face had hardened into an expressionless mask, his words flicking over Lydia like a whiplash. 'You make me sound mercenary—like a schemer—when I am not,' she said, her voice trembling with emotion, for she was unable to understand why her simple words on waking should have created so much wrath in him. 'If you will recall it was you who suggested we— we…'

'I did. I admit that and you knew what you were doing, what would happen between us when you let me into your room. In time you will learn that sharing a bed with a man does not bring commitment—so do not tempt fate beyond this one night, for it would grieve me sorely to see the intimacy we have shared turn to bitterness. On meeting you I may have lost my head, but I am not going to make any undying declarations of love.'

Lydia actually flinched at the bite in his voice. She felt all the unease of her position. There had been no vows between them and, because she was a nobody and quite penniless, there never would be. Despite the tender words he had spoken to her as they made love, she wasn't going to fool herself into believing it meant any more than that. She was unhappily aware that he had made love to countless other women and that he had simply needed her tonight as he would any other.

'I did not expect you to.'

'I am glad to hear it. I despise the romantic ideal of love. I've seen enough of it in the past to know its destructive effects. Desire I understand. It's a more honest emotion. Passion and desire are easily appeased—fleeting—and easily doused.'

'Then it's a good thing not every man is as cynical as you are. Not every woman is as ambitious and devious as you seem to think they are.'

'As to that, I have yet to meet one who isn't. You knew the score when you let me into your bed. I don't need anyone in my life—and I particularly don't need the added guilt and responsibility of a naive young woman. You are to go back to London tomorrow where you belong and forget about me. That is what I want you to do.'

His cutting tone and the injustice of his words were so insulting that Lydia felt as though she had been slapped. An icy numbness crept over her body, shattering all her tender feelings for him. But it was the way he retained his arrogant superiority that was hard for her to accept. Deeply regretting the impulse to invite him into her bed, she now realised she should have stayed away from him. She felt insulted, but her wounded pride forced her head up.

'How dare you mock my feelings. What a

callous, self-opinionated blackguard you are, Alex Golding. You are right,' she said with all the dignity she could muster. 'It is time to return to reality and the sooner the better.'

He arched an eyebrow, his tone one of irony when he spoke. 'Yes, I am all those things. What did you expect—some infallible being?'

'No, not that. How excruciatingly ignorant you must find me. Just to set the record straight, I do not expect a proposal or anything else from you. It never entered my head.'

'It didn't?' He seemed genuinely surprised.

'Why, you conceited ass,' she flared. 'Cast your mind back to yesterday. I made one mistake when I agreed to marry Henry. I have learned my lesson the hard way. I will not make another. I have decided that matrimony is not for me. I will not sacrifice myself on that particular altar for any man.'

Alex looked at her long and hard, his eyes probing hers like dagger thrusts. He refused to be moved. He was a man who had made his own choices for most of his life and, as much as he would like to make love to her once more, he considered it time to leave. 'I am glad matters have been clarified between us. You knew I was not prepared to pledge eternal vows or offer you declarations of solemn love or devotion—but I do find you quite adorable and I wanted to know you better.'

'And now you do—at least you think you do. No man will ever know me that well. Looking back, I find it odd that you should have wanted to seduce me—considering the heartache I might inadvertently have caused your sister.'

'Because that's the way I am,' he stated.

His attitude to the female sex was highly critical, his opinions low, but his own popularity among them was high. He was unattached, unattainable, and he would stay that way.

'You presented a challenge. When I see something I want, I go for it. What happened between us was consensual. We each enjoyed what happened.'

His voice was low, like pure silk, and his eyes became warm and appreciative as they took in her nakedness. Immediately she pulled the sheet over her and, feeling at a disadvantage with him towering over her, keeping the bedsheet wrapped about her she got out of bed.

'You are a lovely young woman,' he uttered on a gentler note, his gaze lingering on one naked shoulder not covered by the sheet, remembering her delicious curves and how soft her flesh had been to his touch. His desire was quick to ignite. 'It is unfortunate that it has to end here.'

Lydia raised her head and looked at him levelly, noting the unleashed sensuality she saw in his expression. 'That's the way it has to be. It is what I want,' she said icily. 'I have never thought of myself as a romantic.'

'In that we are alike.'

'It is the kind of sentimental nonsense spoken only by silly young girls and idiots,' Lydia uttered with biting scorn.

'And is only for the naive,' he mocked cruelly.

'Naive I might have been, sir, but since my unfortunate experiences with Henry and now you, naive is something I am no longer. Where you are concerned I submitted to temptation in a moment that I will no doubt regret to my dying day. I was not mistaken when I accused you of being callous. Your notion of deeper feelings is nothing more substantial than mere indulgence. The only kind you seem to know about is the kind made between the sheets. I have not known you twenty-four hours, and yet to me you appear to be so insecure and disenchanted with life that I find myself feeling almost sorry for you.'

He fixed his cold eyes on her. 'Don't try to analyse me. Others have tried and failed.'

'And I am surprised they even bothered to

take the time. I was mistaken in you. Initially you gave me the impression that you were a gentleman, with a sense of honour. It would seem I was mistaken on both counts.'

'That is your opinion,' he said, torn between anger, amusement and desire as he looked down at her proud beauty and the wild tangle of her wonderful black mane tumbling down her spine as she held her head high. 'I will not change the way I live my life and I make no apologies for it, either. But I do not recall you complaining when we made love,' he murmured intimately, moving closer, his gaze devouring her face, feeling the need for one parting kiss.

Suddenly the room seemed smaller, making each aware of the closeness of the other, of the warmth, the intimacy that had existed so briefly between them. The pull of Alex's eyes was hard for Lydia to resist, but she had to.

'Do not come near me again,' she warned, unable to move away because the bed stopped her.

He laughed mercilessly, his eyes unrelenting. 'I'll risk it.'

'No, you won't!'

'Just one more kiss before I leave.'

Before she could move, iron-hewn arms went around her with stunning force and drew her against a broad, hard chest. 'Get off me,' she objected furiously. 'I don't...'

'Don't what, Lydia? You don't want me to kiss you?' He chuckled softly. With one arm about her holding her close, his free hand grasped her chin, tilting her face to his. She was just as alluring, just as desirable as she had been when they had made love. 'I think it's a little late for that.'

Lydia tried to pull away, her determination not to yield as strong as his determination to make her. 'I don't want this. I don't want you to touch me. I want you to leave.' He held her fast. She saw the burning light in his eyes, and deep within her she felt the answering stirring of longing she'd felt when he'd made love to her. She fought the weakness, not wanting to be completely at his mercy, but her body was already beginning to respond with a gross miscalculation of her will. She wasn't made of stone. She was flesh and blood, and her blood was on fire.

'I have a hankering for one more kiss before I go—one more kiss to remember you by.'

As he lowered his mouth to hers, Lydia flamed with a fiery heat that warmed her whole body. Her eyes closed and the strength of his embrace and the hard pressure of his loins made her all too aware that he was treating her as he would any woman he had an overwhelming desire for. Her world began to tilt and once again she was lost in a dreamy limbo where nothing mattered but the closeness of his body and the circling protection of his arms.

His lips caressed and clung to hers, finding them moist and honey sweet, and for a slow beat of time, hers responded, parting under his mounting fervour. And then as abruptly as he had seized her, so did he release her, so that she stumbled back from him.

In the tearing, agonising hurt that enfolded her, Lydia was ashamed at how easy it had been for him, following all his harsh words, to expose the proof of her vulnerability. 'How dare you?' she attacked. 'How dare you do that to me? I asked you to go, now please do as I ask. I do not want to see you again—ever. If you touch me again,' she added with quiet firmness, 'I will fight you with my dying breath. Now go.'

Never had Lydia been so humiliated or made to feel so worthless in her life, she told herself, whipping up her temper until her cheeks were scarlet with anger. He looked so powerful, so arrogantly self-assured that she could not believe it was the same man who had… 'I have not the slightest intention of repeating what happened between us. I will not become any man's light-of-love, fawned over today and forgotten tomorrow.'

'No? That is a shame. As long as you don't accuse me of taking advantage of you. If you regret your actions, then you should forget tonight ever happened.'

But I can't, Lydia almost shouted at him. That was the trouble. The memory of what she had done would linger far too strongly for her to discount its effect on her. Because she had only allowed herself this one night, she would have to cultivate her secrecy, but she would be haunted by the sense that she would never again know such passion, such ecstasy with Alex ever again.

'Please go.' Clutching the sheet about her naked form, she turned her back to him, waiting for him to leave.

At the door, Alex paused and looked at her. He wasn't to know that what had just passed between them had been the most humiliating event of her young life. Her head was bent forward and her shoulders slumped. She looked so young and vulnerable, he felt momentarily disgusted with himself and his conscience gave a sharp wrench. But at that moment her head lifted and she squared her shoulders. He stiffened, feeling reluctant admiration for her stubborn, unyielding refusal to cower before him.

Lydia heard him leave before turning and looking at the closed door. She hated herself, which was a new feeling for her. She hated herself more than she hated Alex Golding who had brought her to this moment. It made no difference that every kiss, every act of love had been built on their mutual need, because they had wanted each other. What mattered was that she had been a party to it. So she was filled with self-loathing and consumed with the fact that she should have known that what she was experiencing now would be the ultimate outcome of their passion.

Later, waking in his own bedroom in the hotel, all manner of thoughts raced through Alex's mind. Lydia Brook was very much a feature. Glowing and warm after their lovemaking, she had been a picture of alluring innocence and intoxicating sensuality and he had wanted her with a fierceness that still took his breath away.

He had a powerful sex drive, but he craved intensity, not variety. Lydia had provided that intensity in spades. But he was forced to question his own actions. He must have taken leave of his senses, he thought as he contemplated the irony of the situation. Here he was, one of the most eligible single men in England, and yet he had made the fatal mistake of taking to bed an inexperienced young virgin. His stupidity galled him and he cursed himself for a dim-witted fool.

But then he remembered the stunning beauty of her. She was certainly an interesting, unconventional female. When he had watched her walk into the dining room he had seen she was beautiful, dignified and ladylike in her demeanour, but he now knew that beneath the facade of serenity and gentleness she was also sensual and provocative. They had been incredibly sexually attuned to each other and she had satisfied him completely.

He could easily fall in love with her and that troubled him, for he would not allow that to happen. Having been shackled to a difficult woman for three years of his life, he had no wish to sacrifice his freedom just yet—if ever. But if he saw Lydia again, how long would it be before he found himself wanting to share his life with her in every way? How long before she betrayed him with another man? He'd been there once and had no mind to travel down the same road twice.

Besides, if Lydia Brook thought her virtue of such little importance that she could sacrifice it without a qualm and with a virtual stranger, then who was to say she would not do so again whenever she felt the need to look elsewhere for sexual fulfilment?

But no matter how hard he tried, he could not deny that she had stirred his desire as no other woman had succeeded in doing for a long time, so, remembering with a surge of remorse the harsh words he had said to her, furious with himself and unable to leave things like this between them, he was up early the following morning to speak to her before she boarded the coach for London.

Having no wish to see Alex, Lydia didn't go down to breakfast. She had arranged for her baggage to be taken to the coach and didn't leave her room until it was time to leave. She was about to climb inside the coach with the other passengers when she was surprised to see Alex striding towards her. He was wearing a dark brown jacket and buff-coloured trousers, and his neckcloth was expertly tied. His jaw was set with cool purpose and there was a confidence emanating from every inch of his tall frame.

She watched him approach, wondering how he could look so utterly casual after the things they had done to each other. But then, he probably made a habit of making love to every woman who drew his fancy, so in all probability it had meant nothing to him at all. He smiled, and she wished he didn't look quite so nonchalant, not when she was struggling to appear normal in the aftermath of their night together and their acrimonious parting.

'I'm glad to have caught you before you left.'

She looked at him frankly, openly, and with a dispassion so chilling that he was intensely moved by it, yet he sensed that beneath it all was heartbreak and dejection. Seeing this and remembering the joy of her, he experienced another wrenching pain of unbearable guilt and a profound feeling of self-loathing. He looked at her for a long time before speaking again. His light blue eyes, in stark contrast to his dark hair, intently studied her face, bathed in the light of the early spring sun. She was so poised, so still.

'You look pale,' he said quietly.

'My state of health need not concern you.'

'But it does. I feel that I am responsible.'

'Please don't flatter yourself.'

'I don't. It was not my intention to insult you and I could not let you leave Gretna without trying to put things right between us. I owe you an apology. It was wrong of me to say what I did. If it makes you feel any better, I am deeply ashamed of myself.'

'Ashamed, Mr Golding!' Lydia exclaimed

with a hint of sarcasm, stiff with pride and anger, the humiliation and the hurt she had suffered at both his and Henry's hands still all too fresh, too real. She had been insulted and sorely wounded and she was determined not to make it easy for him. 'Yes, you should be. As for apologising to me, I think it's a little late to withdraw all that you said to me—what you insinuated.'

'Nevertheless, I do apologise—and I shall not be happy until you tell me I am forgiven. I quite understand how upset you must have been.'

'I doubt it,' she replied coldly. The coach driver climbed up on to the box and asked for everyone to board. 'Excuse me. I have to go.'

'Miss Brook, if there is ever anything I can do...'

'I don't think there is anything you can do for me, Mr Golding.'

'Even so, the offer is still there. And Henry...'

'What about him? I fully intend to forget him. In fact, I intend to put this whole sorry episode behind me for good. Whatever connection existed between Henry and me—and you—is severed. I will chalk it up to a bad experience.'

'Then I wish you well, Miss Brook—and I sincerely hope that you achieve all you set out to do.'

Taking a step towards the coach, she paused

and looked at him. There was a burning intensity in her eyes. 'Oh, I shall. Despite this unfortunate interlude in my life my ambition remains the same. No power or persuasion will deter me.' On that remark the only course that seemed open to her was a dignified exit, which she attempted to make, adding, 'I think we've said all we need to, Mr Golding.'

Before he could answer she turned away, but she did so slowly, deliberately, so as not to betray anything that he might take as an adverse reaction to their altercation.

'Before you leave, there is something that we should take into account.'

She turned her head and raised an eyebrow at him. 'Oh? And what might that be?'

He held out a card. 'Take this, in case you should find yourself in, shall we say, a delicate condition. If that turns out to be the case, I would like to know. It is as well you know where to find me.'

Lydia stared at him uncomprehending, momentarily at a loss for words. That a child might be the result of their night together had not even entered her head. 'I—I had not thought...'

'Clearly,' he murmured. 'Please take it.'

She did as he asked. 'If that should turn out to be the case, then it need not concern you—

indeed, I'm surprised that you would even want me to contact you.'

'What makes you think that?'

'I am sure you have no wish to see me again after today, any more than I wish to see you— especially after you condemned me in so cruel and harsh a manner.'

'For which I have already apologised. Do not for one minute think I would abandon you should you find yourself with child.'

'Do not feel you have a duty towards me. I would not want that—to hold you through some obligation that would make a mockery of what we shared last night, however brief it was.'

His expression hardened. 'And I told you not to confuse physical desire with love.'

'I don't,' she replied coldly.

'Do not think that just because we shared a bed—because I made love to you—it means that you touched my heart. However, should you find yourself with child it would change everything.'

'It needn't. I realise that this would complicate matters for you and, to avoid any future embarrassment, I am telling you to do what you have to do, Mr Golding. Forget about me and, if there is one, the child, too. I would not want anything from you, I can promise you that.'

'My obligation would be towards the child—

unless, of course, you had it adopted. But please don't do that without contacting me first.'

Lydia stared at him as if he had struck her. Alex saw the pupils of her eyes dilate until the green had almost disappeared. 'Clearly you do not know me at all,' she said, with so much anger in her voice that every word was clipped. 'That is precisely the kind of arrogant assumption I would expect you to make. But you could not be more wrong. No matter what my circumstances are, if I were the poorest and meanest creature on God's earth, nothing and no one would ever persuade me to part with my child. I've told you I want nothing from you. Now go on your way, Mr Golding. I promise I shall not come looking for you in the future.' Having no wish to say anything further, she turned from him once more and climbed into the coach.

Alex's jaw tightened, his eyes burning furiously into her back, while feeling a passionate surge of relief and thankfulness that she had spoken as she had. With all the passengers aboard the coach the driver closed the door. With a curt bow of his head Alex turned and walked away.

Chapter Four

As Lydia settled into her seat, isolated in her own private misery, swamped with self-retribution and tortured by memories, she tried to sort through her muddled thoughts. The whole episode from leaving London with Henry and what had transpired when she had met Alex Golding had left her numb. She gave fleeting thought to the point he had made that she might find herself with child, but it was too dreadful to even contemplate.

She had always sensibly believed in the teachings of her mother, that it was a sin for a woman to give herself to a man in carnal lust outside wedlock and that she must learn to exercise the strictest discipline over the demands of the flesh—even though she herself had not adhered to her own teachings when she had taken up with Alistair. Indeed, Lydia's ideals had always dictated that for her there would be no frenzied coupling with a lover, that any attachment for her would engage body and mind, but not the heart.

But that had been before she had met Alex Golding, a man who had broken through her resistance—a man she hadn't wanted to resist. Only for a moment had she paused to consider what she was about to do. Before then she would have been appalled that she could ever contemplate such behaviour, but when the memory of Henry had flashed into her mind and how he had brought her near to ruin, she had thrust all such thoughts from her mind. Life just had to go on. *She* must go on and if she could find oblivion for just one night in the arms of Alex Golding then she had welcomed it.

Never having been affected by lust before, never having desired a man as she desperately desired Alex Golding, all she could hope was that given time it would burn itself out. She accused herself of being a shameless wanton, soiled and used and unfit for any gullible male who might one day come along and want to marry her. She had broken all the rules that had been made to protect young ladies from experienced men like Alex, rules that governed the moral code of a decently reared young lady.

After a while, having put off thinking about Henry, she now did so. Over dinner Alex had asked her if she'd loved Henry. She grimaced inwardly. She had told him that she didn't even know if that kind of love existed. She had been fond of him and had always eagerly awaited his visits, when he would take her to Greenwich to walk on the Heath and sometimes they would take a boat on the river. She had enjoyed his company and his easy devil-may-care attitude toward life. So she had accepted his proposal of marriage, thinking that perhaps the kind of love others spoke of might develop in time.

Lydia had often wondered what life would have been like had her mother married Alistair— but she couldn't, of course, since she was still married to Lydia's father. Not that her mother would have gone back to him. That part of her life had ended when he'd walked out on them. They were living in Coventry when he'd deserted them on a wet morning, heading for London and never coming back. But Lydia's mother would never describe it that way. *Blessed* was the word she used, and good riddance. They were both better off without him. Lydia had come to believe that, too.

There was a rumour that he had been arrested for some felony and sent to Botany Bay to serve his sentence. They never did find out the truth of it—until six weeks ago when Lydia received a letter. It had been forwarded from the man who had taken over her deceased grandfather's parish in Yorkshire, but it had originated in Australia. This confirmed the rumour. Her father had indeed been a convict, had served out his sentence and was coming home.

To Lydia this man was a distant, fearful figure and the thought of meeting him, of knowing him, filled her with dread. Whenever thoughts of her father came to mind they were unwelcome and the only way to deal with them was to make them go away. Contempt was what she experienced; contempt and a cold anger were the only safe emotions she could harbour towards him, for the man who had abandoned her and her mother. These thoughts and emotions had taught Lydia to run as far and as quickly as her mind and will would take her.

As the coach travelled south, tormented by weariness and the cramped conditions she had to endure, she welcomed her discomfort, for it prevented her dwelling on thoughts of Alex, whom despite the angry words she had flung at him, had made a lasting impression on her naive and trusting heart, and his loss was as fresh to her as the void inside her. She had no outlet for her emotions and the emptiness inside her was so total that it eclipsed everything. With that thought she finally slammed a door on his image, for she knew otherwise it would never let her rest again.

Before Lydia had left for Scotland, Alistair had moved his business from the less salubrious area of Bethnal Green to a three-storeyed spacious building in Covent Garden. The working conditions of the seamstresses he employed were better than could be found in some of the other establishments. He was shrewd in business and had a viable enterprise catering for a better class of customer. He sold a wide variety of ready-made goods—clothing for tradespeople and the middle class, but some were more specialised when material would have to be cut and made into the appropriate style which the customer required.

On arriving at the premises Lydia left the bustle of the street and let herself into the shop. The building was large with rooms at the top to accommodate some of the workers. After four days of travelling in a coach she was relieved to have arrived in London. As soon as she had left the coach, having no wish to find fresh lodgings and hoping Alistair would let her have her old room back, after arranging at the coaching inn to have her baggage collected later, she had come directly to the shop.

The cream and pale green decorations were fresh and it was pleasantly furnished, but it lacked that certain something which to Lydia would be an essential part of her own business. She would add velvet chairs to match the decor where customers could sit and discuss designs and fabrics in their desire to dress well and to drink the tea she would provide.

Emily Hunter, an attractive fair-haired well-mannered young woman whose job it was to receive customers and work on garments when the shop was quiet, looked up from sorting through a box of gloves on the counter when the door opened. On seeing who had entered she smiled her welcome, her face rosy with delight.

'Why, this is a surprise, Lydia. What are you doing back in London? I thought you would be a married woman by now and halfway to America.'

'So did I, Emily. Let's just say it didn't work out. No doubt my reputation will come in for a bit of a battering, running off to Scotland like I did with Henry, but there's nothing I can do

about it now. I will tell you all about it later.'
She was not yet ready to explain her reason for
returning to London.

'I'm so sorry,' Emily said sympathetically.
'What will you do?'

'Work—which is what I have always done.'

'Are you back for good, then?'

'Until my circumstances change and I can
start up on my own,' she said, more determined
than ever to open her own establishment when
she could find affordable premises and afford to
buy stock. She was impatient to have independence. 'If Alistair will have me back, that is.'

'Of course he will. You're the best thing that's
ever happened to him and he knows it.'

'I expect I shall have some grovelling to do
first—he'll enjoy that. Where is he?'

Emily raised her eyes to the ceiling. 'Upstairs.
I only hope you coming back will put him in a
better mood. He's been out of sorts since you
went and he hasn't been able to find anyone to
replace you. He's nothing but an overbearing
bully,' she said, careful to keep her voice low.

Lydia smiled. 'My mother used to tell me it
was because he is a perfectionist.'

'And she adored him as I remember.'

'Yes, she did—and in his own way he adored
her, too. I know he didn't show it, but her death

affected him deeply. Behind his bluster and harsh manner he does have a certain charm—when he chooses to employ it, that is.'

'There's been no pleasing him since you left. I think he's missed you and will be glad to have you back.'

Lydia climbed the stairs to the large workroom. She stood in the doorway and watched the familiar scene and smelled the equally familiar smell of the bales of fabrics—silks, satins, cotton and linens, all attractively patterned—stacked on shelves. Dressmaker's dummies in various stages of fittings stood like effigies of real people around the room.

Over the years Lydia had developed excellent needlework skills, mastering the skills of cutting and fitting. The desk where she had worked long hours on the sketches for her designs was in a corner of the room by the window to catch more light, while the centre of the room was taken up with an enormous square table on which designs and fabrics were spread out. Seamstresses who stitched the garments worked in a room on the top floor and some of the work was put out to be made by needlewomen in their homes.

Some of the women working in the room raised their heads and looked her way, their eyes opening wide with surprise on seeing she had come back, some smiling their welcome, others merely nodding their heads slightly to acknowledge her, but they did not stop their work.

Alistair was carrying a bale of cloth to the table. He wasn't aware of her presence so she took a moment to observe him. He was a tall man, slender in build. His face was thin and deeply lined, his once-brown hair now almost white, making him look older than his fifty years. His eyes were pale and close set. They missed nothing.

He was a hard master who would not hesitate to discard any time wasters or any woman whose work fell short of his expectations like he would any troublesome baggage. Alistair hadn't wanted her to marry Henry and certainly not to go and live in America. The way he went about his work two weeks before her departure told her how agitated and infuriated he was by her decision and what it would mean for him to lose his best skilled worker. But behind it all, having known her since she was a child and because of the close and loving relationship he had had with her mother, she knew he was concerned for her.

But she'd had to go. Henry was offering her an opportunity that might never come again— and then there was the letter from Australia...

She hadn't told Alistair about the letter.

Glancing towards the door and seeing her standing there, he set the bale down and sauntered towards her, studying her coolly.

Lydia saw a hard glint in his eyes, but behind that hard glint she saw relief—relief that she had come back. He tried to give her the impression that he didn't care, but she knew differently. She was well thought of by the clients and it wouldn't have done much to enhance his reputation as a man with his workshop under control when she had left. He knew full well that she had come to ask for her job back. She was confident that he wouldn't refuse. After all, with her amazing talent for design—as her mother had possessed before her—and the fact that her creations brought Alistair splendid returns, she was a valuable asset to his business he couldn't afford to turn away. Her gaze was clear and steady as she waited for him to speak.

'Well,' he drawled after a moment, moving closer, 'what have we here?'

Lydia's hands clenched in the folds of her skirt. Lifting her chin, she looked at him directly, not to the point of haughtiness, but to let Alistair know that she still had her pride. She would not be subservient. 'What you see, Alistair. I have come back to work—if you will have me.'

'And your husband?'

'There is no husband, Alistair. I—changed my mind.' She wouldn't give him the satisfaction of telling him the true reason for her return to London, of the humiliation she still felt, knowing she had fallen into the hands of a married philanderer.

He nodded slowly, digesting what she said and making his own conclusions. 'If you say so. I only set eyes on him the once, but it was enough to know you and him were worlds apart. Men of his ilk know their places in the social hierarchy and generally keep to them. You'll have plenty of time to feel the consequences of failing to do so.'

Lydia smiled thinly. 'If you say so, Alistair,' she said, determined not to be drawn into an argument. She needed the work.

'You're not the first woman to be taken in when a man shows interest in their talents— and I'm not talking about their skills with a needle and thread. Some have left me and when it hasn't worked out wanted to come back. If they're lucky and I'm in the mood, I take them back. I knew you'd be back if I waited long enough. I didn't expect you to be back quite so soon, though.'

'You haven't set anyone on to replace me, I

see,' she said, preferring to ignore his acerbic comments and glancing towards the empty desk.

'Not yet.'

'So—can I come back, Alistair?' she asked, smiling softly and knowing he would say yes. 'I think you need me.'

Alistair's gaze ran over her, taking in the challenge her eyes laid down and the beautiful woman she had become. Something passed behind his eyes—perhaps the acknowledgement that she spoke the truth.

He nodded slowly. 'Try to contain your euphoria. If I take you back, you will learn to toe the line. You will try not to agitate me—which you tend to do.'

She laughed, tempted to lean towards him and give him a kiss, which she decided against. That would be taking gratitude too far. 'I will try very hard not to.'

'Damn your impudence,' he said on a softer note. 'I hope you will not think of leaving me again. That would be thoughtless of you.'

'Be assured, Alistair, I have no plans to go anywhere in the *immediate* future. So—does that mean I can have my room back?'

With a low grunt he nodded and strode back to the table. 'I will honour your dear mother's wishes and allow you to keep a roof over your head. You know what you have to do. Get on with it.'

Lydia allowed herself to exhale and walked towards her desk. Alistair was right. She knew very well what she had to do and, as she picked up her quill and dipped it into the ink, it was as if she had never left.

She could almost feel her mother looking over her shoulder, guiding her as she had all her life. The strain of finding herself alone with a young child explained so much about her mother—her focus on her daughter throughout her childhood and her determination that she would experience the best that she could give her, her single-minded protection of her when at thirteen she was old enough to begin her apprenticeship as a seamstress. It wasn't the kind of work she'd wanted for her daughter. Lower middle-class girls generally gravitated towards dressmaking, but with long hours and small wages it was by far an unenviable occupation.

She could not change that, but she had made sure her daughter was the most proficient. It helped because Lydia was willing to learn. Her mother taught her lessons other than needlework when they had finished work, often late into the night until exhaustion took over. There was a small table where Lydia did her arithmetic and grammar exercises, and learned enunciation, diction and pronunciation.

Alistair had recognised her mother's talent and that she had passed it on to her daughter. It would have been foolish of him to let her go elsewhere, to let someone else get the benefit of her exceptional skills. The only contact her mother had had with her parents was when her father died, leaving her a small legacy, which she'd put away for Lydia's future.

Lydia worked hard on her return. She had no sooner climbed into bed than it was time to get out again. Two months on from her return to London, there had been no further contact from her father. She was relieved by this, but she felt he had not gone away and that as soon as he arrived in London he would lose no time in seeking her out. Did he know about the demise of her mother? It was doubtful. She now accepted that she could not escape him so she was resigned to wait.

Her plans for her future were firm in her mind. Working for Alistair, she was never going to accumulate enough money to start her own business. The money would have to come from somewhere. She was twenty years old and she told herself now that she was done with working for Alistair. Considering the difficulties she would encounter on setting up her own dress shop, she was anxious for the next part of her life to begin. Indeed, she was so impatient to do so that she was determined to get the money she needed from somewhere.

The hour was late and Lydia was working on one of her own creations in her room when Emily came to say goodnight before turning in.

'I've seen some empty premises just off Bond Street that would be perfect, Emily. The rent is exorbitant, but if I am to cater for the clientele I have in mind then it is vital to have premises in the fashionable part of London. It also has a small but adequate living accommodation. I've even gone as far as to arrange with the agent to let me look inside. The trouble is that I need finance if I'm to open my own shop—to purchase the stock and fitting out the shop.'

'The bank might be able to help you.'

'Do you think they would loan me the money I need?'

'I don't know and neither do you unless you try. If not, I suppose you could try money lenders.'

'I don't think so, Emily. They would rob me blind with the exorbitant interest they would charge.'

* * *

Later that week, Lydia and Emily managed to work it so they both had a little time off together to look at the premises Lydia had found. The agent unlocked the door and let them inside the empty shop. As soon as Lydia saw it she knew this was it. This was what she wanted. With its double-fronted bay windows it was perfect.

It had been a haberdasher's and Lydia was impressed with how spacious and clean it was. The showroom was large with a counter and cupboards. Two decent-sized rooms leading off could be used for fitting and general use. Up above there was a large workroom with space for the storage of stock, and there were also three small rooms under the eaves for accommodation.

Lydia could see herself living and working there. It was perfect. Emily agreed with her and should Lydia be fortunate to raise the money she would be more than willing to leave Alistair to come and work for her.

'I can't let you do this alone, Lydia. It's all so exciting.'

Lydia's heart warmed to her friend. 'But I won't be able to pay you much at first.'

'I'll get by. *We'll* get by. I do believe in you—besides, I have a little money put by, too. I also sew well—Alistair said so, which is praise indeed. I just want to be part of this and I refuse to let you do it alone. You need friends around you and that means me.'

Lydia had faith that taking Emily with her would benefit both her and the business. She was clever and had the ideas and the wherewithal to make their dreams into realities.

So, wearing a dress she had made—a pretty pale blue muslin dress with a tight-fitting bodice, a full skirt and edged with white lace at the throat—and a wide-brimmed bonnet on her head, Lydia stepped along the street to discuss business with the manager of the bank where she had a small account. She knew she was taking a chance, but it was a chance she had to take if she wanted to get anywhere.

It was a warm day in midsummer and the sun was shining from a cloudless sky, which she hoped was a good omen.

Reaching the bank, she stepped round an elegant midnight-blue open carriage and four matching greys, unaware that the gentleman who it belonged to had come out of the bank and was seated inside. Her mind was so occupied with the task ahead of her and her heart beating fast with apprehension and excitement that she failed to notice how his eyes followed her inside and that he sat back to wait for her to emerge.

Lydia had to wait ten minutes before she was told the manager would see her. She was ushered inside where Mr Pemberton, the manager, met her at the door.

'Miss Brook, come and sit down and tell me what I can do for you.'

Lydia perched stiffly on the edge of the chair in front of the desk and waited until the impeccably dressed Mr Pemberton was seated across from her before she spoke. 'I intend to open my own business and would be grateful if your bank would grant me a loan. I have found sound premises just off Bond Street where I would like to set up as a dressmaker. I do know the business and I am confident I can make it a success.'

Mr Pemberton looked taken aback. The appearance of a beautiful young woman wanting to do business was unprecedented. Despite her effrontery, he listened to her as she outlined her plans. He admired her determination and ambition and he was impressed by her enthusiasm. But she did not imbue him with enough confidence despite her high expectations.

'I have made a list of everything that I will need and how much it will cost,' she said, delving into her bag to produce her carefully drafted list, but she stopped when he came directly to the point and said,

'That won't be necessary, Miss Brook. I am sorry to have to tell you that I cannot grant you what you want.'

'Oh,' she breathed, looking across at him, thinking that he wasn't sorry at all. She sat perfectly still in her seat, her hands clutching the bag on her knee, her face pale but composed. 'I see. You—cannot help me?'

'What do you have in the way of collateral?'

'Collateral…? I—I am sorry…what…?' she stammered, not having thought of this.

'You have to have collateral to set against a loan.'

'I—have a small account here at the bank, but nothing else of value.'

'The money in your account is a small sum and not nearly enough. If the bank were to loan you the amount you need, should you be unable to meet your obligations, as your creditor we would be forced to call in the loan.'

'But I have no intention of failing, Mr Pemberton. I intend to make my business a success.'

Raising his eyebrows, he pursed his lips and shook his head. 'We don't know for definite that will happen. Unfortunately, you lack the necessary wherewithal. I am a banker, Miss Brook, in the business of making money. I must also tell you that I have never approved a business loan for a lady before and I am hesitant to start with you. You must forgive me therefore when I tell you that there will be no loan forthcoming.'

'I see.' She rose. 'Thank you for seeing me and giving me your time. I am much obliged, sir.'

Utterly deflated, Lydia left Mr Pemberton's office with her head held high. Once outside she paused and bowed her head, allowing no one to witness the collapse of her courageous facade.

Standing beside his carriage, Alex watched Lydia leave the bank. It was two months since the events in Scotland. He had frequently thought of her during that time, wondering what had become of her. It was only when they had parted that the full reality of what he had done took over. He told himself he'd been a fool in taking her to bed. He had been unfair to them both, but he could not deny that the memory of their coupling had had a profound and lasting effect on him. He remembered the passion of her. It was still there in her. That was what was so mesmerising. There was something about her that reached out and touched him in half-forgotten obscure places.

He was amazed to think so mystical a woman could be made up of such simple, soft and warm human flesh. He had known from the start that she could never belong to him and he had accepted the fact as a permanent condition and that come daylight they would go their separate ways. But that night she had cast a lethal spell over his life that could never be broken.

Encased in disappointment, Lydia was unaware of Alex as she walked past him. He noted that the excitement had left her eyes and the spring that had been in her step before she entered the bank was absent as she moved slowly along the pavement, seemingly uncaring of the direction in which she was heading. Instructing his driver to wait, Alex went after her, slowing his long stride when he was almost upon her.

'Miss Brook?'

The words reached Lydia only faintly through the mist of her anxiety. On hearing her name she paused and slowly turned to face the man approaching her. The sun was in her eyes and too bright for her to see clearly, but there was something familiar about the way he moved. He was very tall, with the same dark hair and taut grace, the same air of cool self-possession as Alex Golding. Blinking hard, she told herself that she was losing her mind, that it was her imagination playing tricks on her. But she sensed it was him. It was as if some tangible, powerful force told her so. She even recognised the elusive, tangy smell of his cologne, borne to her on the warm breeze.

The closer he came, on trembling limbs she stood and waited, her heart pounding with dread as she recalled the manner of their parting. Suddenly, the busy thoroughfare and the people who flowed past her seemed to melt away and Lydia was stunned as she looked at the man she had not expected to see again. He looked so handsome in a black morning coat, striped trousers and a pristine white collar and black satin tie. She remembered the feel of him close to her, the heat of his body, the scent of him, the feel of the pulse beating in her throat, the dizzying moment when he had entered her. She remembered that nothing had mattered then but the wanting and the satiation. Swallowing hard, she resisted the pull of memory.

The sunlight moved off her face. Her lovely eyes were liquid bright, their sadness so deep Alex felt the breath catch in his throat, but when she recognised him the sadness evaporated to be replaced with hostility. Her head lifted imperiously and her shoulders squared, her manner saying quite clearly that she had not forgiven him for his harsh words on their parting in Scotland.

He smiled crookedly, but made no move towards her, instinct telling him he'd be best served to keep some distance between them for the present. 'So,' he said, 'you do remember me.'

'Yes, I do. I would like to say I do not know you, but we would both know it to be a falsehood. I am hardly likely to forget our last encounter.' Feeling the heat of his gaze, she waited for him to move closer, her hands holding her reticule in front of her. Until that moment she had thought she remembered exactly what he looked like, his well-chiselled features stamped indelibly in her mind, but what she saw now did not resemble what she remembered of him. Everything about him exuded brute strength and his pale blue eyes bore down into hers with cynicism, his jaw set and ruthless.

As she waited for him to speak again, she saw no sign of the passionate, sensual side to his nature, of the man who had held and kissed her with such tender delight. He moved closer, his penetrating stare relentless.

'I see you are still angry with me.'

'I have not forgotten the things you said to

me,' she replied with cool civility. 'But I've lost all desire to quarrel with you.'

He laughed shortly, the severity of his features softening. 'I'm happy to hear it. To what do we owe this temporary truce?'

She frowned, averting her eyes. 'I have more important things on my mind just now than remembering that awful time in Scotland.'

He cocked his head to one side and studied her troubled features. 'It is two months since then. Are you with child?' he asked bluntly.

Lydia's cheeks burned with the frankness of the question. 'No,' she uttered sharply. 'No, I am not, so you can set your mind at rest on that matter. I assure you, Mr Golding, your relief cannot be greater than my own.'

It was exactly the reaction Alex had expected from the proud beauty who had caught his attention in Scotland. 'I am relieved to hear it,' he said on a more gentle note, his expression grave as he looked down at her troubled face. 'And my name is Alex, remember. Considering our previous meeting and what transpired between us, don't you think it's ridiculous to call me Mr Golding?'

'You are right. I did blame you entirely for what happened in Scotland,' she said quietly. 'But after much deliberation I've come to see things more clearly. The truth is that my actions when I agreed to have supper with you and consented to what happened later were foolish. I behaved like a shameless wanton and I cannot in all honesty blame you for thinking that's what I was.'

'And how do you know what I thought?'

His voice across the distance that separated them and the way he was looking at her did strange things to Lydia's heart. 'I was certain that was what you felt.'

Alex stepped closer. 'Then you were wrong. I thought you were not only a lovely young woman, but so refreshingly different from all the other women of my acquaintance.'

'I—I didn't know.'

'The simple fact was that I couldn't resist you, Lydia. All I could think about was getting you to myself then and there and having you melt in my arms. I did not have the scruples to ignore that ignoble impulse.' He had wanted her then and he wanted her now—this remained unsaid. It was evidently still there; the bond that had developed between them in Scotland continued to pull them together.

Lydia stared at him. He captured her eyes with his. She was aware of a treacherous warmth slowly beginning to seep through her body.

'Whatever it is that is troubling you, I'm a good listener if you would like to talk about it.'

She continued to gaze up at him. With his back to the sun his face was all angles and planes and shadows. His expression was firm, his eyes glittering and faintly troubled. 'Talk? To you?'

'Why not?' he murmured, looking down into her huge, clear eyes, which were steady and direct.

'It isn't your problem.'

'Then I'll make it my problem.'

She looked deep into his eyes. He really did seem disposed to listen.

'Share it with me, Lydia,' he persisted gently. 'Hasn't anyone told you that a trouble shared is a trouble halved, that two can bear a cross more easily than one?'

Lydia smiled. A softness entered her eyes and a haziness that suggested tears. 'Yes. My mother—once.'

Alex was relieved to see her smile and her shoulders relax a little. It was a start. 'So, what is it? I might be able to help.'

Her smile disappeared and she sighed despondently, shaking her head. 'I don't think anyone can help me. I've just been to the bank to ask the manager for a loan to enable me to open my own dressmaking business and he refused to entertain the idea.'

'I see. It is not the only bank in London.'

She looked at him frankly. 'It might as well be. The mere fact that I am a woman is against me.'

He nodded. 'There is a disparity between the privileges accorded to the sexes—which is unjust, I agree.'

'I had no idea it would matter so much. Men have such a hold over the world of business. I thought that with the account I have at the bank it would stand as collateral. Before I came here... I—I thought...' She fell into a momentary silence, her eyes fixed some distance a long way beyond the bustling street.

Alex looked at her in surprise, holding his breath for her to continue. But coming abruptly back to earth, she only said harshly, 'I beg your pardon. I should not be telling you this. You could not possibly understand.'

'I understand more than you realise. I have not got to where I am now without my share of pitfalls along the way. When we parted in Scotland I told you that if there was anything I could do to help you I would do so. Do you remember?'

Lydia was stirred despite her earlier hostility

by the depth of sincerity in his voice. Silence fell once more between them. Alex stood very still, but it seemed to Lydia that his broad shoulders leaned towards her. She nodded slowly, looking at him with fresh interest and collecting her thoughts. Her mind worked steadily along as practically, logically, an idea formed and enlarged in her brain. From the very beginning she had suspected Alex Golding of being a wealthy man. Suddenly it seemed so simple. Distrustful and very much on her guard against men's wiles after what had happened in Scotland, such was her need to forge ahead with her plans that she was tempted to find out how much sincerity was in Alex's words.

'Just how serious are you about helping me, Alex? Would you lend me the money to start up my business?'

'I would be happy to talk about it.' He watched her eyes narrow slightly and he guessed that her quick mind was beginning to understand that he might be about to offer her a way out of her predicament. 'Do you have premises for the business you wish to open?'

'I have seen some premises I could rent that would be just perfect for what I want.'

'That's a start. I have my coach outside the bank. Why don't you show me?'

'I will have to collect the key from the owner first.'

'That shouldn't be a problem.'

Driving away from the bank, they were unaware that they were being observed. Accompanied by her maid, Irene Hilton was in a carriage that stood across the road from the bank. Instantly, she had recognised Alex's carriage and frowned, her pencilled black brows drawn together like wings, her eyes darting to the occupants and fastening on Alex's companion.

She had watched closely as he handed the unfamiliar woman into his carriage. Her eyes narrowed and glittered as they followed the other carriage down the street, but not before she had seen how Alex looked at the woman. Her heart leapt in dismay on seeing the warm smile he bestowed on her. Resentful and wishing he would look at her that way, she took refuge in anger, a fierce glint lighting her eyes. With jealousy ripping through her, her face turned an ugly red, then paled as every vestige of blood drained out of it.

She was curious. Who was that woman? The beauty of her face shone out of her and her figure attracted the eye. Going about without a maid told Irene she belonged to the underclasses. But there was something in her face when she looked at Alex, a spark of something between them, a connection that she, Irene, would not countenance, not when she wanted him for herself.

Alex was an attractive man who exuded sex appeal and masculine allurement. These traits were a lethal combination, but when one added his enormous wealth and the power he wielded, it made him irresistible. He had visited her brother in France and she had welcomed him like a lover. But she had got nowhere. He had been polite, with a ready smile and always willing to accompany her with her brother to parties and to dance with her, but he showed her no more attention than he would any other woman.

Now she was back in London and in his company once more, she had high hopes that she would succeed where she had failed in France and she would not allow any upstart to thwart her plans. When Alex's carriage was about to turn off towards Bond Street, she instructed her driver to follow it.

They had no difficulty obtaining the key for the premises. Alex crossed the threshold after Lydia, his gaze sweeping round the empty room with a great deal of interest. Lydia could hardly contain her excitement and enthusiasm as she pointed everything out to him. Caught up in her project, she could not stop talking. When she at last fell silent she glanced at him. He was standing perfectly still by the counter, studying her with those strongly marked eyebrows slightly raised. Something in his expression told her he was waiting for her to continue selling herself.

With her hands clasped tightly together at her waist, she moved towards him, an earnest expression on her face as she tried to convince him she knew what she was doing.

'I know the trade. I've been involved in it all my life. I am a good seamstress and I have experience in design. My customers will be middle-class ladies who require practical wear and fashionable ladies who wish to be elegant—and perhaps order the occasional ball gown.'

Alex leaned against the counter, folding his arms in front of him. 'To be successful it will take a shrewd business head. Do you have reliable connections and where will you buy your fabrics?'

'I have my sources for the fabrics I shall require—Alistair allowed me to accompany him on occasion, introducing me to the owners and people of note. I will search out other warehouses and factories for what I need and employ people to find what I want further afield—and to keep expenditure low I will buy end of rolls, fabrics that have not sold or are flawed in some way. I know draymen who will deliver the heavy rolls to the shop.'

Alex listened to her carefully. Her knowledge and enthusiasm had him in thrall and, as he listened, he noticed how animated she became, how her eyes shone and her brow wrinkled with displeasure when she thought he wasn't listening. She wore her determination like chainmail—such was the result of having ambition in a world dominated by men. He laughed lightly and apologised for becoming distracted by her expressive face, but he did not tell her how lovely he thought her eyes were. He promised he would give her his undivided attention.

When she fell silent, he said, 'It's a big step to take—a risk.'

'I know, but I have to do it. I have nothing to lose.'

'If it's a success—which, with your acumen and experience in the trade, I am sure it will be—if you need advice when it comes to savings, investments and insurance, I will be happy to give you all the assistance that I can.'

Lydia looked at him. He was watching her intently. 'Are you saying that you are willing to invest in my enterprise?'

'I know when and where to invest my money. I make investments all the time.'

'But do you ever invest in people?'

'If I am interested.'

'And if you consider them worth the risk.'

'Exactly.'

'But it is a loan you are offering and not an investment. Your only return will be the interest on the loan.'

'That is true. When I do make an investment I always expect a good return.'

Lydia tilted her head to one side, eyeing him quizzically. 'And—not only a financial one? I think I would be wise to ask exactly what you are expecting from me in return.'

He raised an eyebrow, a small smile quirking his lips. 'Interest on the loan I would give you. What else?'

'What else, indeed! You know exactly what I mean, so do not pretend you don't.'

He gave her a lazy, devastating smile, teasing amusement glinting in his eyes. 'You read me too well, Lydia. I think you and I could have a very delightful arrangement.'

Tilting her head to one side, she frowned. 'You jest—at least, I hope you do.'

He looked at her a long moment and sighed. 'Of course I'm jesting. I would not suggest you become my mistress should you fail to repay my loan. I'm sorry, Lydia. I'm not being very subtle, I fear. I behaved very badly towards you in Scotland. I wouldn't blame you if you wanted to slap my face.'

Startled, she shook her head. 'I don't—although I'm not saying you didn't deserve it.'

'I did. I want to help you get started—it will go some way to making amends. Interest on the loan will suit me for the time being.'

She eyed him warily. 'For the time being? Please explain to me what you mean by that?'

He laughed. 'There may come a time when you fall behind on your repayments. If such a thing occurs, then I shall have to reconsider the terms of our agreement.'

Lydia continued to give him a sidelong look. He was teasing, of course, but the undercurrent between them was pleasurable, she had to admit. His familiarity was nothing new to her. She knew well how seduction worked—she'd experienced it herself. It gained definition from casual encounters, a knowing look, a touch, a heat on the flesh, a hungering look, and to see and to know desire. She already knew how easily she could be carried away by Alex Golding's ardour, which would lead him to behave in an unspecified way. She had experienced the dan-

gers of getting too close to him, for she would
be unable to resist him if he plied her again with
his particular brand of persuasive seduction. He
could steal her will away with no more than a
kiss.

'Ours will be purely a business arrangement,'
she told him evenly. 'Although what we did in
Scotland did happen, it must not influence what
happens from now on.'

'You do remember how it was between us,
don't you, Lydia?' he murmured.

'Yes,' she replied, her heart hammering like
a captive bird. 'I imagine that when a woman
gives herself to a man for the first time, it is not
something she could forget.'

'No, I don't suppose it is. You are an amazing
woman, Lydia Brook, and I know how much this
venture means to you. You are about to give of
your talents to women all over London. It will
give me joy seeing you succeed and knowing I
was part of that.'

'Thank you, Alex,' she said, taking a step
away from him. 'I assure you, I shall try hard
not fall behind on my repayments. I will make
a point of it.'

'Neither of us has anything to gain by pre-
tending that night in Scotland never happened.
What I felt when I saw you outside the bank

earlier proved it isn't over between us. I remembered you, Lydia. I've thought about you often and I know you've remembered me.'

Lydia averted her eyes. Affected by the things he had just admitted to her, she was unable to deny that what he said was the truth. 'No, I haven't forgotten. How could I?'

'I'm glad.'

He smiled slowly and raised a dark brow as he considered her flushed cheeks and soft, trembling mouth. Reaching out, he gently touched her cheek with the backs of his fingers. 'You are a woman, a very beautiful woman any man would desire to have in his bed—as I have already experienced to my pleasure. But I feel I must assure you that that is where it ends. My behaviour towards you will be that of an honourable gentleman personified. As you said— ours will be a business arrangement.'

She stared at him. Despite what he said, she felt an invisible trap closing slowly around her. There was a quiet alertness in his manner, like that of a wolf, its strength ready to explode, but docile for the moment. Something in his eyes made her heart quicken. She felt it so strongly, it was as if her whole body was throbbing suddenly and in her head her thoughts were not orderly—just odd, strong responses. And in her breasts—how could just one look from him reach her breasts? Yet it had—it was making them desperate to be touched and it was all she could do not to reach for one of his hands and place it there.

And the sensation moved on, lower, sweetly soft and liquid—small darts of pleasure travelled as if on silken threads to her stomach and inner thighs. Oddly feeling no grudge against him, surreptitiously she looked into his eyes. The effect of that warmly intimate gaze was vibrantly, alarmingly alive, and the full import of the risk she was about to take made her stomach quake. She knew that if she wanted his help to open her shop, she really had no choice but to accept his offer of a loan.

Chapter Five

Reading what was going through her mind, Alex laughed triumphantly. 'Fear not, Lydia. I shall not take advantage of you in your moment of weakness,' he promised, drinking his fill of her lovely face and comely shape. 'I can only hope that my act of mercy will in due course reap its own rewards—of the monetary kind, of course.'

Lydia glanced at him sharply. His manner was one of ease, the gaze of his penetrating light blue eyes unsettling. He really was the most lethally attractive man she had ever met and she was determined not to be drawn in by him a second time. Swiftly, she raised her defences and smiled at him.

'Oh, it will,' she replied sweetly. 'Every penny.'

Alex smiled appreciatively. 'There is that, but there is no reason why during the time we spend together we cannot be civil towards one another.'

'It is the least I can do.'

'You asked me why I am doing this. Yes, I will see a return on my loan, but that aside it is also because I believe in you and I have every confidence that you will succeed. I admire you for your independence and what you are doing— pursuing a lifestyle of going against the grain. I admire your resolute determination to become what you intend to become despite your situation.'

He wanted to impart the lessons he had learned himself from a difficult life. He wanted to tell her that it was not the circumstances of one's life experiences that were important, but what one gained from the outcome. But he did not say this since this wasn't about him. So, instead he said to her, 'You are at a turning point in your life. You are determined to prevail in a world which is foreign to you. Even then it will be tough, establishing yourself in the competitive world of fashion. You will encounter many hazards.'

'I do realise that. There are numerous dressmaking establishments in London and competition is always a healthy thing. Making clothes for people to wear immediately is expanding, I know, but my aim is to specialise in made-to-measure garments.'

'For someone who has spent her life as a seamstress, you are a clever young woman. You never try to hide the fact that you have a mind.'

'I have my mother to thank for that. As the only child of a minister of the church in Yorkshire, having been educated by a governess, she could not afford to give me that luxury so she educated me herself after she had finished her work for the day as a seamstress. Not only did she teach me to read and write and mathematics, she taught me the social skills to get on in life when—or perhaps I should say if—I became a woman of means through my own endeavours. Although I am sure I will find the rules of social etiquette and convention tiresome in the extreme when faced with such situations.'

'Your mother must have been a remarkable woman.'

'Yes, she was. She was the one constant in my life. She believed in the purpose of education. It was important to her.'

He smiled. 'She puts me in mind of my grandfather. He was the one who insisted I had a good education and paid for it, for which I shall be eternally grateful. I recall you telling me that your mother was close to your employer, Alistair. How did you feel about that? Did you mind?'

'No, not if he made her happy—and I believe he did. She—couldn't marry him.'

'Would she—had she been free?'

'Yes, I think she would.'

'And what of you, Lydia?' he asked, speaking softly, holding her with his gaze. 'Instead of forging yourself a niche in the competitive world of fashion, would you not prefer a home with husband and children? I know it's rude to ask, but I think you and I are beyond the point of social niceties.'

Had the question come from someone else Lydia might have minded, but from Alex Golding there seemed to be a capacity for understanding that superseded idle curiosity. 'I enjoy what I do. Besides, I believe I'm not the sort of woman men marry.'

'I beg to differ.'

'Oh, but it's true. I have to earn my living. I'm too busy to think of such things.'

'Nevertheless, you are a refreshing alternative to the women I am acquainted with—most of them vacuous young ladies with pushy mothers keen to make a prestigious marriage for their darlings.'

She glanced at him. 'What about you? What was your wife like? Blanche, you said her name was.'

His face took on a sombre look. 'She was beautiful and she had breeding and brains. But I never had a moment's happiness with her—no peace.'

'Why?'

'She wasn't a devoted wife. Our marriage was a fraud. The house was always full of her friends and she—had lovers. I couldn't stand the life of deceit any longer. I was on the point of divorcing her when she was killed—along with her current lover—in a carriage accident on her way back from Newmarket.'

'How awful for you.'

'Yes, it was—at the time.'

'And—your sister? Was she very angry with Henry when he got home?'

'I underestimated Miranda. Yes, she was angry. In fact, to teach him a lesson, she has been living with me here in London.'

'Oh, my goodness! Are you saying that she has left him?'

'Not exactly, although understandably it has had some effect on their relationship. Miranda is with child. It is important that they get through this. She will go back to him when he is fully chastened. Until then he has promised to remain at their home in Surrey and not to venture anywhere near London until she goes back to him.'

'Under the circumstances I cannot say that I blame her. I can only regret the part I played in bringing it about.'

'You weren't to know. Had it not been you it would have been someone else.'

'I suppose so, but that does not absolve me completely. Have you told her what Henry intended where I was concerned?'

He nodded. 'Yes, but not who you are. If it makes you feel any better, she thinks his treatment of you was abominable.'

'It doesn't—not really.' On a sigh she turned towards to the door. 'I should be getting back. My time off is limited and Alistair will wonder where I have got to.'

'Now that it is agreed that I loan you the money—once you have made a list of your immediate needs to get started—there will be papers to sign, protocols and procedures to be followed.'

'Yes—thank you.' Taking some paperwork from her reticule, she handed it to him. 'I made a list of what I will need to furbish the salon and the stock I will have to purchase to give to the manager at the bank.'

Taking them from her, he cast a brief eye over them. 'Perfect. I will have my secretary draw up the documents immediately.'

As they left the premises, Alex, who dealt with business ventures and legalities on a daily basis, wondered at the absurdity of offering to loan Lydia the money for her business—which was like a drop in the ocean to him, but a fortune to her. He had made up his mind in that first moment when she had told him she required a loan to champion her. He knew he was looking at a fighter and that she would succeed. One of the wealthiest and most influential men in the city, he could have gone into the bank and persuaded the manager he would secure a loan for Miss Brook, but that would mean that if the bank took over her affairs, he would lose contact with her.

What he knew was that now he had found her again he didn't want to lose her. He, who had never needed anyone, found his very soul crying out for a girl he scarcely knew, a girl who, when he had last seen her, had every reason to despise him. He was quite bewildered by the emotion he felt for her. He couldn't really describe what he felt because he didn't have any words, but offering to loan her the money she needed was simply an excuse to see her again.

He did not know what he intended to do beyond that.

* * *

Alex deposited Lydia as she requested several yards away from Alistair's establishment—she had no wish to have him see her get out of a gentleman's carriage and bombard her with questions. She would tell him when the time was right, when everything was arranged for her to begin work on her salon.

Having given her a roof over her head, if anything, he deserved her honesty. She couldn't just walk away. But she wasn't looking forward to telling him and she felt a twinge—it was like a piece of string tugging at her conscience, a piece of string that might unravel if she pulled too hard. It wasn't guilt she felt, for she didn't think she had done anything to feel guilty about, but she knew that after leaving Alistair to marry Henry, even though he would not show it he would be hurt that she was to leave him so soon after her return, if at all.

She did not go inside immediately. She stood and stared after Alex's carriage, smiling in acknowledgement of a future that had suddenly expanded beyond anything she had dreamed. Yet, she thought, her smile turning into a frown, there was something nagging at her in a corner of her mind, for even though she had been happy to accept his loan, she was not comfortable about it and would rather have got it from the bank.

She wondered who Alex Golding really was. Despite having spent a night in his bed and knowing his body as intimately as he knew hers, she knew practically nothing about him. She knew that his sister was married to Henry and that they lived in Surrey. But who was Alex Golding the man? She knew what he did, that he was a businessman and that he was very wealthy. She knew he was prepared to loan her the money to start her venture, but why had he done so? Why was he really doing this?

She had been with him for the past two hours. It had been like a dream as she had showed him the premises. He had listened attentively as she told him how she would run her business, how many seamstresses she would employ and the class of customer she hoped to attract. But she was still no wiser as to who he really was. Why lend her the money when he didn't know her— not really? Was he such a philanthropist that from the goodness of his heart he was prepared to loan money to a woman who was a seamstress by trade, a woman who had inadvertently almost wrecked his sister's marriage?

The feeling that in her dealings with that particular gentlemen she would be wise to proceed with caution swept over her. Because of the threat he posed to her emotions, to her life, she felt the first stirrings of regret that she had accepted his offer of a loan.

Two weeks later when the premises were secure, Lydia decided to give Alistair her notice. Everyone had finished for the night and gone home. She was alone in the workshop.

'Alistair, I have some news,' she said, slipping off her chair at her desk and going to stand across the large work table facing him. 'I have decided to open my own establishment.'

His head shot up from what he was doing. 'You're what?'

She explained, glad that he listened and did not interrupt until she had finished.

'But—it is quite ridiculous,' he snapped.

Lydia bristled, her chin coming up. 'Why is it ridiculous? How can you say that? Is it because I am a woman?'

'Women don't go into business.'

'Well, that is what I am about to do.'

'Where? Where will you work from?'

'I have rented premises just off Bond Street.'

His eyes opened wide. He looked at her hard and then he lowered his head as he proceeded to fold a square of fabric in front of him. He was clearly disturbed and trying hard to hide his feelings. It was somewhat gratifying to Lydia to realise how much he hated losing her. Yes, he would miss her expertise and her usefulness. Her skill and ingenuity had repaid him a thousandfold. He was going to find it difficult to replace her in the workplace, but she also knew he would miss her on a personal level.

'I'm sorry, Alistair,' she said gently. 'You knew I intended to leave some time.'

He nodded. 'When?'

'Two weeks. I have much to do before the opening.' She didn't mention that Emily would be coming with her. Emily wanted to tell him herself.

There followed a time of great excitement. Lydia did not see Alex, but in a letter he told her that the loan was secure in her account. Lydia lost no time in moving into the premises with Emily. She hadn't told Emily that Alex had loaned her the money. On her return from the bank when Emily had asked her if she had been successful, Lydia said yes, she had. Emily assumed the bank had granted her the loan and Lydia let it go at that.

They sorted out their accommodation at the top of the building before setting about improving the shop to Lydia's taste and ordering stock. Decorated in soft cream and pastel-green hues, the salon was smart and bright and well ventilated, the atmosphere pleasant. Lydia introduced an aura of comfort and luxury, with fashion magazines on a polished round table and green-velvet chairs where customers could sit and browse. In the window, shawls, an array of fans, gowns, bonnets and purses were artfully arranged. Upstairs in the workshop shelves were stocked with rolls of fabrics—linen, cotton, gingham, silk, satin and luscious velvets.

Everything was being readied for the opening of the shop and the sooner the better. Emily was a godsend. Along with two experienced seamstresses Lydia had known for some time who were eager to find new employment and hopeful of bettering themselves, they worked round the clock at the various tasks. She knew she couldn't possibly set herself up as a first-rate house who drew their clients from the upper echelons of society, but she did hope to attract wealthy clients. She didn't employ enough seamstresses on the premises and some of the dresses she would have to send out to be made up by freelance needlewomen in their own homes.

Two days before the opening Lydia was in the workroom, leaning over the large square table on which her designs were spread out. Emily, who had been sorting out the drawers behind the counter, came up to tell her that a gentleman was asking for her below.

'What does he want, Emily? I'm busy with—'

'I told him that and he says that he understands, but he won't keep you long.'

Lydia went down to the salon. A man stood with his back to the door, gazing around the shop. Immediately she knew who it was. When she entered he looked directly at her. Lydia stared at him. Her throat became dry and her whole body tensed. Without turning her head, she said, 'Leave us, will you, Emily.'

Emily looked from one to the other and returned to the workroom.

'Hello, Lydia,' Samuel Brook said softly, his gaze seeming to feed on her features, not having seen her since she was three years old. 'You know who I am?'

'Yes,' she said firmly. 'I have not seen you since I was three years old and I have only a vague memory of you, but I know very well who you are. I never thought to see you again.'

'No, I don't suppose you did.'

Although he was soberly dressed, Lydia noted that his clothes were of good quality. Of average height, he was thin and gaunt. His skull could be seen through his sparse hair. His skin reminded her of leather and it was patched with scales from too much exposure to the sun. His face was drawn. His eyes watched her, clinging steadfastly to her face with something like hope in their depths.

This was her father, she told herself—the bogey man of her past, the man who had cast such a giant shadow over her life she had desperately tried to escape by agreeing to marry Henry and live in America. Looking at him now, she knew she had nothing to fear from him. He was forty-two years old and yet he looked like an old man. His frailty made her reluctant to get angry with him. With one hand he held himself upright and steady with the aid of a cane and sheer willpower, but it looked to Lydia as if it cost him a tremendous effort. He was diminished by infirmity, brought on by the harsh and brutal life of a convict in Australia.

'Please,' she said, indicating a chair. 'Do sit down.'

He did so gladly. They sat facing each other.

'This establishment,' he said. 'It is yours?'

'Yes. I rent the premises but the business is my own.'

'You have done well for yourself.'

'Not yet as it is brand new, but I hope it will prosper. I did not have enough capital to begin with. I've had to borrow more before I could set everything up. We open in two days.' She was filled with questions, with the whys of almost everything that had defined her childhood. But in this short time they were together she only asked him a few of those questions and as she did so she tried to read his face. 'But what of you? You—have been in Australia I believe,' she said tactfully.

He nodded. 'For my sins—for seven years.'

'What was your crime?'

'Petty theft. I stole seven shillings to feed myself.'

'And for that you were condemned to seven years in a penal colony—for every shilling you stole you gave one year of your life? How long did it take for the vessel to reach Australia?'

'The voyage took nine months.'

'I cannot imagine how horrendous that must have been.'

He nodded. 'Yes,' he said hoarsely as memories assailed him. 'Many didn't survive—and some who did could not endure the harsh conditions of the penal colony. They never saw home and loved ones again.'

'When were you released?'

'I was given my certificate of freedom four years ago.'

'Four years? Why did you not return to England then?'

'I considered joining the free settlers as many emancipated convicts were doing, but after spending some time in the interior I decided to return. In Australia—the worst that could happen did happen.'

'And yet despite all that you survived.'

He nodded. 'A man can adapt to anything. He can learn to survive because as long as the will to endure remains, the body and the mind adjust to do the same. But one does not undergo such alterations to one's life and walk away from the damage without being affected by it.'

'My mother found that out,' Lydia remarked, unable to conceal her bitterness over his treatment of her mother. 'That day when you left us was long ago. It left a tarnished memory, like a piece of old unpolished silver, but it eventually faded. She had no use for it any longer and moved on with her life.' Watching him, he looked terribly sad. 'So much has happened in the intervening years. When you deserted us in Coventry we came to London. She met someone—Alistair. He helped her by giving her work—he helped us both.'

'They were close?'

Lydia nodded. 'I think they would have married—had she been free to do so.'

Her father nodded, thoughtful. 'Your mother was a woman of exceptional beauty. It was natural that she would meet someone else. What can I say? I am so sorry.'

Lydia stoically ignored the mistiness she saw in his eyes and heard the unutterable sadness in his voice as she tried to harden her heart. 'If you think I will forgive and forget what you did simply because you say you're sorry, then you are wrong.'

'I understand and for what it's worth I cannot blame you for feeling bitter. It's no less than I deserve.'

'Why did you desert us? For what reason?'

He was silent for a long, considering moment. 'I have no excuse. I could not find work in Coventry—which as you know was where we went to live after we were married. Your grandparents did their utmost to discourage your mother from marrying me—they did not consider me, a printer's apprentice—or a printer's devil as we were called—suitable for their only daughter, but she was determined and defied them.'

'Yes, I know. According to my mother, my grandparents were strict disciplinarians. As an only child it was not easy for her.'

'She was a fine seamstress when I met her. She took in sewing—which, after you were born, she was able to do and take care of you at the same time. Sadly things went from bad to worse between us. There were many arguments. I decided to try my luck elsewhere—always believing that the grass was greener and all that. I was young, weak and foolish. I should not have left her. Eventually I came to London, where I hoped, eventually, to begin my own printing business. I was desperate by then. I had no money and was unable to find anywhere to live. I wanted to find work and then send for you and your mother, but before I could do that I was arrested for stealing.'

'I see. It's a sorry tale. What you did to her was unforgivable. You hurt her deeply—but you did not destroy her. She would not allow you to do that, but I was so young when you left. I kept asking her where you had gone, when you would be coming back—it was not easy for her to explain it all to a child.'

'No,' he said, unable to conceal his regret, 'I don't imagine it was. In Australia I had plenty of time to consider what I did, to rake over the sad debris of my life. It was the shame of my life when I left her—and you. I've waited for this moment for more years than you can imagine. I

hoped your mother would still be alive. I wrote
to her in Coventry and sent letters to her parents' address in Yorkshire several times. When
I did not get a reply I assumed she no longer
cared about me. How she must have reviled me.'

'Yes,' Lydia said frankly, 'she did. I never
met my grandparents. They died within months
of each other several years ago. Mother never
received your letters. If my grandparents kept
them from her that was wrong. Perhaps they may
have gone astray. Whatever happened we will
never know. They never forgave her for marrying you and I cannot pretend otherwise to salve
your conscience, but she was proud and when
you left us she would not go back to Yorkshire.
The letter informing me that you were returning
to England from Australia—we knew nothing
about your imprisonment although Mother did
hear a rumour of your being sent to Australia
at one time, but we never did find out the truth
of it—was forwarded to the address where my
mother worked here in London.

'I went to the establishment where she worked
here in London. The man—the owner—told me
where I could find you.'

'That would be Alistair. Did you tell him who
you were?'

He shook his head. 'No, but now I know what

he was to your mother, no doubt I left him wondering. When he spoke to me his eyes held speculation and not surprise.'

'Yes. Alistair is sharp—perceptive. He will know.'

'Lydia,' he said, his voice husky with emotion, 'do you think that some day you might forgive me for what I did to you and your mother?'

Lydia was pierced by his question, as if it penetrated her spirit as well as her flesh. She looked at him. His eyes were both proud and beseeching. 'I don't know.'

He drew a deep breath and nodded. 'If I could undo what I did to your mother, and to you, all those years ago, I swear to you I would do it.' With an effort he got to his feet. 'I will leave you now. I will not encroach on your time any longer. I—I just wanted to see you. You are a lovely girl, Lydia—a credit to your mother.'

Lydia stood and watched him cross to the door. 'You are not well. Where are you staying?'

'I have found lodgings here—in town. I'm looking for a small property to buy—somewhere I can be comfortable to end my days.'

'Will—will I see you again?'

He turned and looked at her, meeting her eyes directly. 'Would you like to see me again?'

She thought about it for a moment. She was

overcome by so many confusing and contradict-ing emotions right at this moment that she found it difficult to analyse her feelings. He was not what she had expected. If she was to continue seeing him, that meant healing the breach in the wall that surrounded her heart, allowing com-passion to enter it.

She nodded. 'Yes, I—I think I would.'

He smiled in relief. 'Thank you. I'm glad. If you need any further assistance with your business, I have money to spare. I will call on you again and we will talk. We must proceed slowly—one step at a time.'

'Yes—one step at a time.'

From the moment her father left her Lydia carried on with her work without thought. Her father's intrusion into her life gave her compli-cations she did not want right now, so she thrust them to the back of her mind.

Having been told by Lydia about her father and taking note of her pallor and quietness since that encounter with some concern, Emily sug-gested they take a walk in the park to put some colour into her cheeks.

'We're ready for the opening,' Emily said. Not giving her time to argue, she handed Lydia her bonnet. 'Some time away from the shop will do you good.'

It wasn't until they strolled over the rolling green park that Lydia felt as though she could breathe again. It was good to get away from the confines of the shop, where brooding on the situation with her father preyed on her mind.

As it was the fashionable hour the park was full of people, drawing all classes of a pleasure-seeking society. The ring was crowded with mounted riders and elegant carriages. Some people strolled and some gathered in clusters to gossip. Rosy-cheeked, excited children played all manner of games. An abundance of multi-coloured flowers in beds and borders added a vivid splash of colour to the park, and the grass was like soft green velvet. Dressed in their finest, the two girls attracted many admiring glances.

What Emily was saying drifted away into the depths of Lydia's mind, the words disjointed and coming to her from a distance when her eyes fell on a carriage, its occupants being a man and a woman. It was the same gleaming midnight blue carriage she had ridden in with Alex on the day she had gone to the bank. Alex saw Lydia walking across the grass and instructed his driver to halt. He had appeared too suddenly for her to prepare herself, so the quickening of her heartbeat and the heady surge of pleasure that beset her was evident in her eyes and her quick intake of breath.

His gaze passed appreciatively over her. Dressed with tasteful simplicity in pale blue silk, the material so fine, the colour so light as to be almost white, she was a vision of elegance and grace. Her bonnet was of the same pale blue, wreathed in white and tied beneath her chin with a broad silk ribbon of a deeper blue. Under it her hair, taken back in a chignon, shone rich and dark.

They looked at one another across the days that had passed since they had parted, when Alex had offered to lend her the money for the shop. His eyes were warm, filled with a velvet-textured softness. He was dressed in a brown coat, and nothing else he wore of contrast other than the snowy white of his cravat. His dark hair was smoothly brushed and the familiar scent of his cologne assailed her. She could feel his seductive power reaching out to caress her.

'Mr Golding,' she said politely. 'This is a surprise.'

He smiled, seeming to be unable to tear his eyes from her. He noted her pallor and the blue smudges beneath her eyes. The last time he had seen her she had been a young woman with a purpose in life. Now he sensed her withdrawal and that something was wrong. 'A pleasant one, I hope.' He turned to the young woman by his side. 'Miranda, I would like to introduce you to an acquaintance of mine, Lydia Brook. She is to open a dress shop shortly. Miss Brook, may I introduce my sister, Lady Seymour.'

Lydia bowed her head politely. 'How do you do, Lady Seymour. It is a pleasure to meet you. And this is a friend of mine, Emily Hunter,' she said, taking Emily's arm and drawing her forward. 'She is also an excellent seamstress and is assisting me with the opening and afterwards.'

Emily bobbed a little curtsy, a stunned expression on her face on being introduced to two such important people.

Holding a brown-silk parasol decorated with lace, Alex's sister was a young woman with a fair complexion and thoughtful, greyish-blue eyes. Her hair was dark brown and arranged in ringlets which bounced delightfully when she moved her head. She was extremely pretty, with a vivacity and freshness to her manner, and she was all smiles, for who could resist such a lovely and well-mannered young woman her brother had halted the carriage to acknowledge. She seemed to be assessing Lydia with interest and when her eyes ceased to regard her so seriously her lips curved in a wide smile.

'How exciting,' Miranda exclaimed. 'And when do you expect to open your shop, Miss Brook?'

'Salon,' Emily was quick to say. 'It's not a shop, it's a salon.'

Lady Seymour laughed. 'My apologies. I stand corrected. Salon it is.'

'It hardly matters,' Lydia said. 'Salon or shop—we sell the same things.'

'Of course it matters,' Emily argued lightly. 'Salon sounds much more interesting and appealing than a shop. Very grand, in fact.'

'Of course it does,' Lady Seymour agreed. 'Are you to open soon?'

'The day after tomorrow,' Lydia provided.

Lady Seymour's eyes widened. 'As soon as that—and yet here you are taking a walk in the park. Goodness!'

'We have been working non-stop for the past month. We are as ready as we can be, with just a few finishing touches to take care of. We thought it would not do any harm to take an hour off.'

'Quite right, too.' Lady Seymour glanced at her brother, a quizzical look in her eyes. 'You have known Miss Brook long, Alex?'

'Several weeks,' he answered without hesitation. 'We—met through a mutual acquaintance.' Unable to resist, he glanced at Lydia briefly just as she looked at him. He caught her gaze and held it frankly, sending her a faint, conspiratorial wink which went unobserved by his sister, but not by the sharp-eyed Emily.

'I see,' Lady Seymour said. 'Well, Miss Brook, you have aroused my interest—and more than a little curiosity. I am interested in fashion. Did you make the dress you are wearing?' she asked, her gaze appreciative. 'It must be the latest thing.'

'Yes. I design and sew all my own clothes.'

'Which is a fitting advertisement for your work. It is such a lovely gown—the colour most unusual. I want a new morning gown so I may find my way to look at what you have on show in your salon some time very soon. If I like what I see then I will happily pass your name on to my friends, too.'

'Thank you. I would appreciate that. I do not think you will be disappointed.' As Lydia said the words she could not help feeling that should Henry's wife become a client of hers, then it could provide her with something of a dilemma, not to mention an embarrassment, which was something she could do without. But she liked Alex's sister. She exuded a vitality and good humour and a jaunty self-confidence she could not help but admire.

* * *

As the driver snapped the reins smartly over the backs of the high-stepping horses taking his passengers on their way, Miranda glanced at her brother with some curiosity. 'I see Miss Brook has taken your fancy, Alex. You always did have an eye for a pretty girl,' she teased.

'Miss Brook is no ordinary young lady, Miranda.'

'Owing to the fact that she is a working girl she has no silken chains to bind her to her family, which puts her on a different plane to most of the young ladies you are acquainted with.'

'And that fact alone is why I find her a refreshing change, Miranda.'

'Clearly,' his sister said, smiling at him. 'You—like her, don't you?'

He sighed and nodded slowly. 'Yes—yes, I do.'

Miranda smiled. 'I think I shall pay a visit to Miss Brook's *salon*. If she is as good at her work as you say she is, then I may place an order.' She settled back against the squabs, eyeing her brother with a good deal of interest. 'Tell me more about Miss Brook, Alex. Is she the woman Irene saw you with in your carriage a short while ago, leaving the bank?'

Alex glanced at her sharply. 'What are you talking about?'

'Irene saw you together. She asked me who the woman was. I told her I really had no idea— which was quite true at the time. Was it Miss Brook you were with and, if so, what is your connection, Alex? Come,' she said with quiet cajoling laughter in her voice when her brother threw her a belligerent look. 'You know how I hate secrets. I always manage to wheedle them out of you in the end, so do tell.'

Emily watched the carriage go, a stunned expression on her face. 'My goodness, Lydia. How did you come to know him? He's the most handsome man I've ever seen—and rich by the looks of him. Are you going to see him again?'

'I will have to, Emily.'

'You should. Men like him are few and far between.'

'I thought that when I met Henry and look what happened there. Henry is Mr Golding's brother-in-law. He is married to Mr Golding's sister—the lady we have just been introduced to. As a matter of fact, Emily, I—met him in Scotland. After finding out what Henry was up to he came to Scotland to stop the wedding before Henry committed bigamy. I let you assume the bank granted me a loan to start my business. I'm sorry.'

'You mean it didn't?' Emily frowned, clearly bemused. 'I don't understand. Then how? Who did?'

'Mr Golding lent me the money,' Lydia informed her quietly. 'I am to repay him in instalments—with interest, of course.'

Emily eyed her quizzically. 'But? I do sense a but.'

Lydia sighed and nodded. 'It means I am beholden to him—indebted to him.'

'Of course you are if he lent you the money. Don't you want to see him? A man who looks like that?'

'I know. It's a dilemma.'

'It needn't be. I don't mind telling you that if he had looked at me the way he looked at you I'd give you some strong competition for him. Grab him, Lydia—although I suspect girls like you and me are too inexperienced to take on a man of Mr Golding's ilk. I imagine he eats women for breakfast. Men like him are few and far between—and rich to boot.'

'That is precisely what he is—a very wealthy man. I am a seamstress—way out of his league— hardly worthy of him. A woman like me can only ever have one kind of relationship with a man like that and I will be no man's mistress.'

'Of course you are worthy of him. Don't do yourself down, Lydia. It's what you are that is important, what you are inside, not who you are and where you come from.'

Lydia smiled. 'That may be so, Emily, but Mr Golding means nothing to me except as a means of obtaining the loan for my shop. I have no intention of becoming involved with him romantically or in any other way.'

Emily rolled her eyes and gave her an exasperated look, but she did not pursue the subject. In the space of time since meeting the gentleman, Emily considered Lydia's denial of him. She noted the total absence of her normal warmth and correctly assumed her friend's current attitude of proud indifference was a facade to conceal some sort of deep hurt. She strongly suspected Mr Golding was the likely cause of the problem.

'His sister seems nice. Do you think she meant what she said and that she'll visit the salon?'

'Perhaps. I don't know, Emily. We'll have to wait and see.'

'Her custom would be not only welcome, but beneficial. If she is satisfied, then she may well recommend us to her rich and titled friends. What a boon that would be.'

'I suppose so,' Lydia replied, her mind beginning to drift to Lady Seymour's brother. 'It would certainly help pay the rent.'

It was the evening before the opening. Everything was ready. In the workroom Emily was putting some finishing touches to a hat she wanted to put on display in the window. Lydia was out in the street in front of the shop. It had already drawn a good deal of interest, with people stopping to enquire when it was opening.

It had been a warm, sunny day and Lydia hoped it would be the same tomorrow. Sighing deeply, she folded her hands at her waist, feeling somehow that after all the hard work they had put into it, her business would succeed. But her mind had been elsewhere since her father had re-entered her life. Beneath her calm exterior she endured a nauseating turmoil of conflicting emotions and distress. Deeply troubled by their meeting, she was strangely saddened to have seen how his seven years as a convict had affected his health. She was also regretful of the years she had missed not knowing him.

Across the street, having climbed down from his carriage, Alex took a moment to watch her.

Her shining black hair, doing its best to escape from its arrangement, curled about her brow and ears, giving her a youthful look. Attired in a dress of dark blue that clung to her breasts and small waist, he admired her regal poise and outward beauty, but he was far more intrigued by her inner attributes, her unmistakable presence that made her stand out so clearly in the slowly shifting throng on the street.

She was looking attentively at the contents of the bow windows but, sensitive to her mood, he felt she wasn't really seeing the elaborate display. He had enough experience with women to know when one was upset and on the verge of tears. When they had met in the park he had sensed that all was not well with her. He was curious. After all her hard work getting everything ready for the opening, why the dejection? He thought that perhaps he should leave before she turned and saw him, but he hesitated, torn between an urge to avoid a scene involving an upset female and a less understandable impulse to offer her some sort of strength and support.

The latter impulse was by far the stronger and won.

As she continued to stare at the window display, Lydia was oblivious to Alex—to everything except the bewildering emotions she had felt since her meeting with her father that had almost sent her spiralling out of control. She had veered between a kind of lethargic helplessness to sudden bursts of angry energy that resulted in a frenzy of mindless activity as she prepared for tomorrow's opening.

The swift plunge from the excitement that had gripped her since she had moved into the premises to the grim truth of her father's return that she had feared for so long had affected her deeply and left her bewildered and unprepared to know how to deal with it.

Aware that someone had come to stand beside her, she turned, her heart doing a little somersault when she saw the identity of her visitor. His unexpected arrival stirred hidden pleasures and emotions and for the moment every emotion and every thought was lost to her. All she could think about for the moment was being with him again and how happy that made her. Just when she had thought she might get over him, that he no longer affected her, he appeared again and all her carefully tended illusions were shattered. The depth of her feelings for him continued to shake her and shock her. His eyes, warm and appreciative, did a quick sweep of her face. Immediately, the touching sadness Alex had witnessed a moment earlier was wiped clean from her face and replaced with a smile.

'Well?' he asked. 'Is everything in readiness for the opening?'

'Yes—at least I sincerely hope we haven't overlooked anything.'

'Not you. I am sure you have everything planned down to the last, minute detail.'

'I do hope so.' She sighed deeply. 'But I can't help being apprehensive.'

'That's understandable. But I have every faith in you. You will be a success—how could it not be with your determination and your will of iron you have clearly inherited from your mother?'

An unforgettable smile curved her lips. 'Yes, she might have something to do with that. Why are you here, Alex?'

'I have to go away in the morning and I didn't want to leave without seeing you and wishing you well tomorrow.'

His words warmed Lydia. 'Thank you, Alex,' she said, her smile bright and amenable. It was the effect he always had on her. 'How long will you be away?'

'Two—three weeks at the most. You know I am a businessman and a number of speculative ventures have come to my attention. I am interested in investing in several companies in

France. Arrangements have been made for me to meet some prominent businessmen over there.'

'And it is important that you go there in person?'

'Absolutely. I wish to know the real position of the companies I am to sink my money into, to be sure in my own mind that they will not fail to meet their liabilities. If they do, and my investments collapse, then I will only have myself to blame.'

'I know very little about business on the scale you speak of. You are very astute.'

'I have to be.'

'Yes, I can see that. I hope you have a safe journey.'

'Lydia, when I saw you yesterday, I sensed you were troubled about something. Is everything all right?'

He made a close study of her until she stirred uncomfortably beneath his scrutiny and looked away. It had nothing to do with her business and everything to do with her father's reappearance in her life and the obvious fact that he was an ill man, but that was not Alex's problem.

Alex stared at her profile, at the brush of thick ebony lashes shading her cheek. 'Would you like to tell me what is wrong?'

Lydia was tempted to tell Alex the truth. She

thought about it, but then decided against it. So she told him it was nothing more serious than the opening that worried her—which, in part, was true, feeling she would have to reveal too much if she told him about her father, everything that remained private and unacknowledged and needed to stay that way until she had sorted things out in her own mind.

She did it with such spurious indifference that Alex wasn't fooled in the slightest, but he chose not to pursue the matter as she clearly wasn't ready to talk about it.

Chapter Six

'It is very quiet. Hopefully it will not be so tomorrow and you will find yourself inundated with clients,' Alex commented.

'I sincerely hope that will be the case,' Lydia said, focusing her attention on the window and the publicity for the opening ensured by a conspicuous display of goods.

'Although being the end of July, London is quiet. The aristocracy desert the town at this time of year for their country estates, so they can indulge in country pleasures. They will begin to drift back in the early months of next year and by May the whole round of frivolity will begin again.'

'I don't think that will affect my business,'

she said. 'Will you be one of those deserting London?'

'I do not follow the same routine. I am a businessman, after all. I do not spend half the year in idleness persecuting dumb animals.' Raising his eyes, Alex noted the impressive name of the shop, clear and distinctive, painted in large gilt letters over the doorway.

'Lillie's.' Alex looked at her in puzzlement. 'I'm curious. Why did you choose Lillie's?'

'Lillie was my mother's name. To own her own shop was what she always wanted. I vowed that if ever I opened my own establishment that was what it would be called—as a tribute to her. I owe her a great deal.'

'That is a lovely sentiment, Lydia. I am sure your mother would be very proud of you.' He eyed the window display with interest. 'I see the items you have placed in the window have their prices clearly marked. Is that wise?'

'It was my idea. I am hoping that the pass-ers-by will be so impressed by the quality and range of goods in the window that it will ex-cite them and tempt them inside—and hopefully buy something.' She looked at him, noting his frown, and sighed. 'You don't think it's a good idea, do you?'

He grinned down at her. 'Being a mere male,

I am hardly in a position to offer a qualified opinion.'

'Oh, I know the fact that high-class clientele prefer to purchase their clothes at well-appointed premises run on the lines of a French couture house—the establishments that do not advertise and are recommended by word of mouth, which I would like my own establishment to become eventually, when I am in a position to think about expanding the business—but until I have enough funds behind me and have established myself, which will enable me to make the transition, this is how it will be.'

'You are ambitious. I wish you all the luck in the world, Lydia.'

'Besides, there are numerous smaller establishments that are used by society ladies to purchase garments to be worn on social occasions not considered grand enough to merit the considerable outlay required for an outfit from an exclusive dressmaker.'

'I see you have it all worked out.' He admired her brightness, her intelligence and cleverness and her determination to be more than a seamstress. He also admired her sheer perseverance in mastering the challenging task of how a business should be run. 'Where are your employees?' he asked, looking beyond the glass windows into the interior of the shop. 'I imagined they would be rushing about putting the finishing touches on things.'

'With everything prepared for the opening I gave the two girls I am employing the afternoon off while it is quiet. I'm hoping that we get sufficient orders so they will be busy in the coming days helping me complete them.'

'And the young lady you were with in the park yesterday?'

'That was Emily. She's retired to her room to do some sewing of her own. It was lovely to meet your sister. She…seems nice.'

'She is. You made quite an impression on her. I expect she'll visit your salon.'

'She may not be so amenable if she were to know who I really am. I hope she never finds out—how we became acquainted, I mean. She would never forgive you. She would feel herself cruelly betrayed if she knew of it.'

'By Henry?'

'No. By you—a brother she clearly adores. For her sake, I hope the truth of it never comes out. The scandal of having her husband's dirty linen aired in public would discredit them both. I'm still angry that he made bets amongst his friends and that I was so smitten with him as to do anything he suggested. Is it possible that you can dissuade her from coming to the shop?'

'Why?'

'Come, Alex, I should not have to spell it out. I am sure you'll be able to think of something to stop her. I…can perceive the trouble it could cause. I would not feel comfortable selling clothes to the wife of the man I almost married bigamously. You must understand that.'

Alex nodded. 'I'll see what I can do. I have no wish for you to be distressed over this.'

'I am not distressed—nor am I likely to be,' she told him with a trace of indignation and amazing candour. 'For the duration of our… arrangement,' she said, for want of a better word since she was unable to describe what it was that held them together other than the loan, 'I would be obliged if you would restrain your ardour and do not behave as you did in Scotland again.'

'But if I did, you would be tempted, wouldn't you?'

Alex's smile was infuriating, and the warm sensuality of his voice almost stole Lydia's breath. If he was trying to destroy her resistance, he was succeeding admirably. At that moment some indefinable alchemy made them extremely aware of each other, and their eyes became caught in that age-old way of lovers.

Lydia's vulnerability was laid bare for him to pierce the guard she had resolved to keep on her emotions.

'I can feel it in your response to me, Lydia, so do not try denying it.'

'Am I so predictable?'

'You are to me.' He was speaking softly, his eyes perusing her beautiful face. 'I would like to promise you that whenever we meet I shall try to keep my ardour under control and my hands to myself—but there will be times when desire overwhelms me.'

'We have no reason to meet,' she told him bluntly. 'I will make my payments to the bank. I suspect you are a busy man and that your accountant takes care of such things.'

'That is what I pay him for,' he said, keeping his gaze fixed firmly on her face. Reaching out, he pushed a tendril of hair away from her cheek. His hand lingered there. The skin of her cheek felt warm beneath his fingers. They moved down to her lips. How could they feel so soft? 'But that will not prevent me from seeing you on occasion.'

Lydia looked at him, her eyes wide with shock that he was being so familiar, but there was also something else, something that reflected what she was feeling. A wave of longing and anticipation swept over her. Desire was in her eyes and in the warm breath against his fingers. It was in her stance, poised like a young animal about to flee.

'If the occasion arises, then I suppose I must,' she replied quietly.

It had not escaped Alex's notice that they were attracting curious glances from passers-by. He suddenly felt exposed standing there with her on the street. 'Let us go inside.'

Lydia knew that if they went inside there would be no talking. His mere presence in a confined space would seduce her into his arms and they would end in a frenzy of desire and that would lead to catastrophe.

'But…don't you have to be elsewhere?' she tried.

'I'm on my way to meet an acquaintance at my club in St James's Street. It's nothing that can't wait.'

To Alex's relief she did not argue. He followed on the soft swish of her skirts and the scent of her perfume that drifted in her wake. Everything was in order in readiness for the opening. The sweet fragrance of fresh flowers artfully arranged in vases was inviting. Sauntering past rails of ready-made outfits on padded hangers, he looked about him and smiled and nodded his approval.

'Very nice,' he murmured. 'Were I a lady I would certainly be tempted to come here to be dressed by you.'

They stood facing one another, intensely aware of each other—how could they not be? The air was sultry and warm, the atmosphere charged with tension and something else each of them clearly recognised.

Lydia was wide-eyed and uncertain. Her gaze took in the sheer male beauty of him, of his darkly handsome face and the saturnine twist to his firm lips, his wide, masculine shoulders and narrow waist. In all her life she had never known a man like him and was at a loss to understand him. 'You don't know me or what I am capable of achieving, Alex—not really.'

Holding her gaze, he moved slowly to where she stood, scrutinising her intently, his eyes drawn to her mouth. His hand touched her chin, tipping her face up to his, and he smiled into her eyes, wondering not for the first time what went on behind her tranquil exterior and those liquid bright green eyes. She was truly lovely, like a delicate flower. He felt a rare peace when he looked into her eyes.

'You are a strange young woman, Lydia

Brook, I grant you,' he murmured, focusing his eyes on a wisp of hair against her cheek. Without conscious thought he tucked it behind her ear, feeling the velvet texture of her skin against his fingers. She stood perfectly still as he ran the tip of his finger along the line of her chin and down the column of her throat, to her collar. 'Suddenly I find myself wanting to know everything there is to know about you—what you are thinking, what you are feeling. You are still a mystery to me.'

Hypnotised by that seductive voice and those mesmerising light blue eyes, Lydia gazed at him with a combination of fear and excitement. Brushing his hand away, she tried to relax, but in the charged atmosphere between them it was impossible. 'In the short time we have known each other, haven't you learned anything about me?'

'I have learned some things. I have learned that you are no prim and proper miss and that you like making love to strange men in hotel bedrooms—'

'Alex, please!' Lydia said, aghast, her face heating. 'Please stop now. It wasn't like that and you know it.'

'No? Are you saying that you didn't enjoy making love to me?'

'No—yes... Oh, behave yourself. Now will

you please stop tormenting me about my…slip of propriety.'

His eyes darkened. 'I like reminding you. I like seeing you get all flushed and flustered and hot under the collar.'

She glowered at him. 'Now you're making fun of me.'

'I know.'

Unable to stay cross with him, knowing he was teasing anyway, Lydia smiled. 'Then stop it. What do you want from me, Alex?'

He studied her, bemused by the sheer perfection of her. She was graceful and as slender as a wand, and he wanted her. More importantly, he knew, as an experienced man of the world, that she wanted him, too.

'I want to talk about us.' He was slow to answer her question, but it did not take her by surprise.

'There is no us.' She swallowed hard, the blood pounding in her temples. 'I—I really do think you should go,' she whispered.

'Is that what you want?' His eyes were beginning to glint with a wicked light. 'And if I wish to remain? If I want to find out if what we experienced together once can be repeated between us again, as good as it was before, would you mind if I stayed?' he asked with a question-ing lift to his brow.

'I—I don't know,' she said, her heart be-ginning to pound in helpless anticipation. She no longer had any idea what she wanted. Her thoughts were irrational and the feelings slip-ping through her body made her melt inside.

Searching the depths of her glowing green eyes for a moment, seeing the pupils large and as black as jet in their centres, Alex smiled. 'Shall we find out?'

Lydia took a step back and turned away from him. She could still feel his fingers on her flesh, touching her with such tenderness. That simple act stirred her desire and began to spark the pas-sion that had lain dormant between them for far too long. How was it possible for him to make her body come to life like that? It was nothing to do with experience or practised technique, it was instant. Emotionally it would seem they were perfectly matched, as if something deep within each of them reached out to the other—like a strong magnetic pull drawing them together.

'You are a beautiful and very desirable, intel-ligent young woman, Lydia, but right now it is not your intelligence I am thinking of. I think you know how I feel about you.' He would have had to be made of stone had he not felt aroused.

Her very flesh demanded that he touch her. He put his hand on the back of her neck, his fingers using gentle pressure. She shivered and turned to face him.

Drawing her into his arms, he kissed her then. She didn't resist. Everything else about her life receded, leaving her open only to the present moment. Once again she felt that melting sensation low down inside her as his mouth made sensuous movements on her. The fact that she was in danger of falling under his spell once more did occur to her, but she wasn't thinking rationally and she wanted more of what he had made her feel when they had shared a bed.

Slowly, he released her and, taking her hand, seeing the open door to a room which Lydia used as her office and sitting room, he drew her inside and away from the windows. She didn't object. She knew she should do so, but she wanted his kisses as much as he wanted hers and all the cautions that were prodding uselessly inside her head were ignored. Her traitorous body was remembering how long it had been since he had held her, how good it had felt, and how insignificant it was to resist when they could share their desires—with no strings attached.

Closing the door and turning the key in the lock, Alex drew her into his arms. He became lost in the exciting beauty of her, knowing his masculine desire had already changed from desire to something else, although what it was he could not put a name to just then. A sharp, wonderful ache tore through him as he kissed her lips, parting them, his tongue caressing hers before lifting his head and then sliding his mouth down the long, graceful line of her neck, gentle, harmless, with the merest whisper of a caress.

Raw emotion had robbed Lydia of any kind of reason. She was aflame, her body responding to his lips and the caress of his hands like an explosion of raging thirst. She returned his kisses as if nothing in the world existed for her but him. Briefly releasing her lips, he drew her down onto a *chaise longue*, holding her in a state of bemused suspension, before fastening his mouth on hers once more, kissing her with a demanding fierceness he was unable to control, her lips tormenting him in their intimate sweetness.

Sliding the palms of her hands up his chest, feeling the hard muscles through the fabric of his coat, the rise and fall of his breathing, Lydia wrapped her arms about his neck, clinging to him as an ache and a rush of warmth and joy spread through every part of her body. The sensations were familiar and welcome, but not extraordinary, since she had experienced the same feelings in Scotland.

Alex slid his fingers into her hair, uncaring that it had become loose from its pins. He deepened his kiss before tearing his lips away from her soft mouth and trailing kisses along her jaw and throat before recapturing her lips and pressing her back against the cushions. Her fingers curled round the lapels of his coat, her mouth opening wider beneath his. Taking her hands and lacing his fingers with hers, he placed their hands above her head as she relaxed and yielded her body to his as he continued to kiss her. Releasing her hands, he slid one of his own along her ribs, moving higher to cup and caress her breast. Pleasure surged through his body and he wanted to tear away the clothes that were a barrier to her hidden delights.

Raising his head, he saw the pleasure in her eyes, and somewhere deep inside him he felt the stirrings of a desire that made him draw in his breath. He wanted her so much he couldn't bear to think she would deny him now. The hot, sweet scent of her whipped the blood in his veins.

Lydia saw that the heavy-lidded light blue eyes looking down at her were beginning to smoulder.

With his lips against hers, he murmured, 'I

wish I could take you to bed.' His long fingers began to unfasten the buttons down the front of her bodice. When she raised her hand to halt him, he laughed raggedly.

'Do you forget, Lydia, that I have seen you naked before? You have a beautiful body—so why the reticence now?'

'I can't—not here. Someone…' Before she could continue, Alex had seized her lips once more.

When she wound her arms about his neck Alex's heart constricted with an emotion so intense, so profound, that it made him ache. He felt his wits slipping as she arched her body into his. Each move she made brought him exquisite pleasure. Her breath was sweet against his throat. Dear God, she was so warm, so womanly, long and slender, but curving against his body, doing whatever she could to get even closer. His male body rejoiced in it, for it told him he held a warm and willing woman in his arms.

In a tangle of clothes, buttons and hooks, of seeking hands and eager mouths, their restraint finally broke. Lydia moaned with joy as his mouth touched her breasts and so lost was she in the desire he was so skilfully building inside her that she scarcely noticed when he eased her body beneath his own. As he entered her she expelled a breath at the exquisite sensation of her body opening to him like a flower. Not holding back, she strained towards him with trembling need, each instinctive, demanding thrust pushing her closer to the edge.

Alex, unlike Lydia, did hold back, for he wanted her to experience as much as his body would allow before he lost control and his need for her became raw hunger, his body craving hers with a violence he could scarcely believe. Filling her again and again with masterly precision, straining to come closer still, he forced the beautiful, writhing creature beneath him to the brink of total surrender.

Lydia forgot everything and allowed herself to be carried away ecstatically by this vastly superior power, expressing her feelings with every fibre of her being as he led her along paths of sheer, exciting incredible torment and she became lost in incoherent yearnings as their passion became all consuming.

When their passion finally exploded in a burst of extravagant pleasure, in languid exhaustion and bone-deep satisfaction, they lay close together, breathless from exertion, clinging to the fading euphoria. Closing her eyes, Lydia nestled against his broad chest, wanting to enjoy their closeness while it lasted. Her happiness at that moment was greater by far than anything she had experienced before.

Contentment stole over them both, lapping gently. They trembled with the rapture of their union, the passion which Alex had known with no other woman. He watched her open her eyes and smiled down at her.

'You are exquisite. How do you feel?'

She gave him a slumberous smile, the smile of a woman totally fulfilled by her man. 'Wonderful,' she breathed. 'It was very special. Thank you.'

He stroked the hair from her smooth brow, his eyes warm and serious and very tender. 'My pleasure, Miss Brook.'

She sighed against him. This man who had just made love to her was exactly the same man who had made love to her before, but this time there had been something different about him. He had taken her not just sexually, but with a deeper, infinitely more alluring need—something profound.

Suddenly there was a noise from up above in the workroom, as if an object had been dropped. Sanity returned. Lydia gasped with alarm.

'That will be Emily.' In a flash, she had thrust Alex away from her and scrambled to her feet, hurriedly replacing the clothes that had become discarded, her trembling fingers fastening buttons before turning to an amused Alex and assisting him into his coat. 'Quickly. You should go before she comes down. I really wouldn't know how to explain your presence—and what we were doing in here,' she said, hurriedly tidying her hair and smoothing her skirt with her hands.

Alex grinned down at her, cupping her face between his hands and gently brushing her lips with his own. 'I don't think she would need any explanations. One look at your face and she will know. As much as I would like nothing more than to go on kissing you and making love to you all day, I think that I should release you while I still can. But worry not. I'm going. It is not my wish to cause you embarrassment in front of your employees. But I shall be back very soon—when you have opened your shop and had time to take stock of things. I think we have much to offer each other, Lydia. We will come to some kind of arrangement.'

A coldness came over Lydia. She knew what he was suggesting and it did not include marriage. His mistress, yes, which, after what had just happened between them, she found exciting and she was ashamed that it presented some temptation. But she would not be tempted. She knew that what Alex felt for her was basic, the kind of trick the human species played upon people to propagate itself. But this knowledge didn't lessen the intensity of what she felt for him, what her body was experiencing. Desire had planted its insidious seeds inside her in Scotland, when seduction had been brought to a satisfying conclusion—and it had happened again today.

But she was no fool. She did not want this. She did not want him to be romantic. She could not believe that he cared for her in that way when it was only a facade to get her back into his bed to sate his desire. He was an important man in a world she could not even begin to imagine. He did not love her. He never would, but from the pain in her heart she knew that she was in definite danger of falling in love with him.

He had been married once and despite the death of his wife he had told her it had not been a happy marriage. He would not be in a hurry to marry again. He wanted freedom, no encumbrances. But she would not enter into a torrid love affair with him. She would have to consider very dispassionately before she entered into that kind of relationship with Alex or any man.

But nothing in her experience had prepared her for what he had done to her, or the emotions he had aroused in her, triggering off an explosion of sensuality, the like of which she could never have imagined, prompting her to respond in a way that astounded her. She asked herself why she had allowed her emotions to become involved—why had she succumbed to his persuasion yet again and allowed it to go so far. And he looked so pleased with himself, like a proud and beautiful peacock who already believed the less colourful peahen bowed to his wishes.

This gave her added determination and strength and she gathered her emotions to her in a tight knot of pride.

'I think it is time you left, Alex. My head is in a turmoil and I cannot think straight.'

'You don't have to. I'll take care of that.'

'I—I can't discuss it with you now. I have much to think about before tomorrow.'

He kissed her lips before he turned from her. She stared at his back as he left the shop, still feeling the tingle of his touch on her cheek, her throat, and the gentle throb of her lips. She would have had to be insensate not to feel the pleasure he could give her and the stirrings for him that she experienced when they were together.

Only it could not continue. She must find the strength and the will to resist him, but where he was concerned her body refused to listen to reason. Perhaps she should ask him not to come to the shop again, not to take her in his arms and do to her what he had done today.

But what was she to do with the loan he had been so ready and so generous to give her hanging over her like a heavy cloud?

On the crossing to France, Alex had plenty of time to muse on his relationship with Lydia. When they had parted in Scotland he had made up his mind that she could never belong to him and had accepted that fact as a permanent condition, but meeting her again—finding her even more ravishing than before—and making love to her again, had cast a spell over his life that could never be broken. He could not wrest himself free of her. She was under his skin and in his blood and there was an end to the matter.

In the past, sexual encounters he had looked for had to be hot and brief, with no regrets and no expectations. With Lydia it was entirely different. Having been as close as it was possible for a man and woman to be, he only wanted more, which amazed him because she possessed—would possess for ever—the ability to enable him to put behind him the ugly memories of his marriage.

Already he missed her. How well he had

come to know her. He was a man burning with a single need to possess one woman. He was unable to banish her from his mind, from his dreams, knowing she was the catalyst that set his blood aflame until his desire for her seethed. How could he let a woman affect him so? He could still feel the warm weight of her body in his arms, tantalising his senses. He could recall the delicate fragrance of her flesh, the taste of her on his lips, and see the luminous green eyes that had gazed into his with such engaging, trusting candour.

It was her green eyes that were brought to mind when he was buying a gift for Miranda in Paris. The moment he saw the diamond and emerald necklace with matching drop earrings, imagining how Lydia's eyes would enhance the glow of the emeralds, he knew he had to buy them for her.

The morning of the opening, dressed in smart dark blue dresses with white trimming, nervous and full of anticipation, Lydia and Emily were in the shop early to make sure everything was in order. It got off to a quiet start, but by mid-morning a constant stream of ladies came in and they were kept busy. Some came to look and browse among the racks of ready-made outfits, others bought small items—

embroidered gloves, painted fans, shawls, decorative purses and reticules, a new bonnet and ribbons, lace collars and cuffs and artificial flowers to perk up last year's dresses and hats. Some were happy to sit and gossip and sip tea and browse through some of Lydia's designs and the fashion magazines neatly placed on tables.

Emily had a way with her when dealing with the customers. Even though their friendship was of long standing, Emily had an enviable ability to charm and sweet-talk the customers into purchasing something that Lydia admired.

At the end of the day they were exhausted but well pleased at the way everything had gone and as the week progressed they had orders for gowns to be made exclusively.

She was surprised when Alistair came—to take a look at the competition, he said. After looking around and taking stock he went, but not before telling Lydia her mother would have been proud of her and wishing her well. She watched him go, glad he'd found the time to come and see her.

Determined not to think of Alex, Lydia immersed herself in her work. It was agreed among her customers that she was a clever dressmaker, her designs fresh and original, her salon welcoming and comfortable, and the staff polite. She had more than enough to do and there was plenty of sewing to occupy her free time. But she could do nothing to prevent him stealing into her thoughts and dreams when she closed her eyes at night.

Her father called to see her one week after the salon had opened. It was a Sunday, so the shop was closed. Lydia let him in and took him into her office. Over tea he came straight to the point of what he had in mind.

'I want to ask you about your business. How did the opening go? Well, I hope?'

'Yes,' Lydia replied with a smile. 'Better than I hoped, in fact. We have orders that will keep us busy for weeks.'

'That is good. I'm pleased for you. I remember what you said about having to borrow money to begin with.'

He was watching her intently and she had a notion he knew what she was going to say. 'I wanted so much to start out on my own. It was what my mother wanted. She left me a little money, but it was not nearly sufficient and I could never hope to save enough from the amount I was earning working for Alistair.'

'Do you mind telling me who loaned you the money? The bank?'

'No. I tried, but was refused.'

'Perhaps I could be of assistance.'

Lydia looked at him in astonishment. 'You? How?'

'I am not a poor man, Lydia—far from it. I told you that when I had served my sentence I went into the Australian interior. I had listened to reports of gold finds and decided to do some prospecting of my own. I went to Bathurst in New South Wales. I was lucky. Within days, there in the bottom of the pan was the precious metal I had heard about. They were good days, Lydia. I was practically surrounded by gold. There was a fortune to be made by the early diggers. When I left Australia hundreds of people were descending on the country from all over. So you see I have not done too badly out of being sent to the other side of the world.'

'Goodness! How exciting that must be— panning for gold, which I have heard about both in Australia and California.'

He smiled. 'It was and I would take it as a privilege if you would allow me to help with your venture.'

'Oh,' she said quickly, 'that is good of you,

but of course I couldn't possibly. I have already borrowed money…'

'I was not talking about loaning you more money. You are my daughter. I find myself in a situation I could not even have imagined when I was a young man. I have more money than I know what to do with. Let me invest in your salon, Lydia. After all, when I am gone what I have will be yours.'

'But…I don't want it. I cannot accept it.'

'It would give me immense pleasure to provide for you.'

'Please— You cannot— I mean, I wish you will think no more of it. It is out of the question.'

He looked at her sadly. 'I see that what I have done to you and your mother runs too deep to be forgiven. You do not accept me as your father.'

'We…cannot rewrite the past.'

'No, but I can make amends for it. If I can. Wouldn't you want to do the same?'

'I understand why you want to, but I want to live my life being true to myself. What you want to do now you have found me is to live your life being true to my perception of you.'

He thought for a moment about what she said. 'I think we'll have to agree to disagree on this. Both of us will have to wait and see how things turn out. I sincerely hope things can only get better between us on a personal level, but I beg you to consider my offer.'

'But—forgive me—I do not know you. This is only the second time we have met since I was a child and you offer me this.'

'I have thought long and hard about it. My decision to make you the offer was not made on the spur of the moment.'

'I may prove to be a poor investment and you could lose all your money.'

'It is a risk I am willing to take. Besides, if you are anything like your mother, then I have every confidence in your ability to make it a success. Will you at least think about it?'

'I don't have to. Since we opened there has been a good deal of interest—and orders. I am sure it will give me a profitable return in the future and enable me to pay off the loan I've already taken out. It is most generous of you to make the offer of financial help and I thank you for it, but I cannot accept it. It would be like taking your money for what you did to my mother.'

'So it is a matter of pride that stands in your way.' He smiled sadly. 'You are so like your mother. You know, Lydia, I am beside myself with contrition. I do so want a chance to right the wrong I did. It has been on my conscience ever since I left you both. Answer me this. Would it help you become a success more quickly were I to invest in your business?'

'Well—yes, of course...' she stammered.

'Then please take it. I have no one else to give it to. I would feel that I have made some recompense for my past actions. Did Alistair loan you the money?'

'No. It—it was a friend.'

'I see. Have you made any repayments on the loan?'

'No, not yet.'

'Then accept my offer and you can repay the loan in full and be financially independent. Do not let that foolish pride of yours get in the way. It's no good to God or man. I can't take away the past, but I can do my best for you in the future. Promise me you will consider it.'

'Yes,' she said. 'Yes, I will.'

When Samuel Brook parted from his daughter she was in a dilemma. What was she to do? She was torn between accepting her father's offer and abiding by the arrangement she had made with Alex. She knew that where Alex was concerned she had become bound in a situation that could only end in heartbreak for her. To let her father into her life and accept his offer to invest in her business could be the answer to her quandary.

She had already decided that any communication she had with Alex in the romantic sense must end. It could not go on. He could banish her reason by taking her in his arms and kissing her senseless, playing on her heartstrings like a musician plucked on the strings of a violin.

Undecided, she sought out Emily, who was in the workroom attaching an extra flounce and lace to the skirt of a dress a lady was to collect the next day. Sunday was supposed to be a day of rest, but they had orders to complete and the only time to catch up with them was on the Sabbath. It was a good situation to be in and Lydia was satisfied that things were going better than she had expected. In fact, if trade continued to expand then she would have to consider taking on another apprentice.

When she told Emily what her father had offered, that he wanted to invest in the salon, the other woman put down her needle and clapped her hands, her face alight with joy.

'But that is wonderful. Think about it, Lydia. You will be able to employ more workers and expand in other ways.'

'Don't be too ecstatic, Emily. I only told him I would consider his offer.'

'No, but you will. Just think of the future—what it will mean.'

Lydia did just that. Perhaps her father's appearance and his offer to invest in the business would turn out to be a godsend. She did pause to wonder what her mother would have said about it—no doubt she would have sent him on his way and told him not to come back. But Lydia wasn't her mother and, looking into the future and seeing her dreams come to fruition, she knew she could not turn her back on his offer.

When next her father called and she told him she would be happy for him to invest in the salon, on seeing the genuine pleasure that shone in his eyes and the bustle and excitement that followed, she was gradually convinced she had done the right thing.

The problem was how she was going to tell Alex when he got back from France. It was something that could not be put off. She knew that she might never see him again once she paid him back as he'd have no reason to visit her. She would never forget those passionate moments they had shared—in fact, the prospect saddened her. But her mind was made up.

It was a Monday afternoon when Lydia prepared for her visit to Alex's home. She dressed herself in a full blue satin skirt with a tight-fitting boned bodice. Over this she donned a short matching jacket with a wide collar and neatly pinched waist. Adding a touch of light powder to her cheeks and securing a matching hat atop her carefully curled hair, she took a hackney cab to Belgrave Square. She knew this to be Alex's town residence from the card he had given her in Scotland.

It was not really proper that she visit his home. She had already visited the bank with her father to sort out the financial aspect of her business and to cancel Alex's loan and pay back what she had spent—with interest—but she really wanted to tell him herself, face to face.

As soon as she stepped down from the cab she felt that she had entered a different world. She stared at the splendid white-stuccoed mansions—townhouses for the country gentry and aristocracy—with awe. She had known that Belgravia was one of London's most fashionable residential districts, but she had not imagined it to be so grand.

She was nervous as she climbed the steps to the impressive oak door and it was a moment before she found the courage to ring the bell. She heard it sound somewhere within the house and after a short time the door was opened by a servant meticulously garbed in black with just a white collar to relieve the severity. In middle age his bearing was dignified and he had a superior air about him. His face was impassive, his eyes assessing as they passed over her.

'Yes?' he said.

'I have come to see Mr Golding,' Lydia said, clutching her purse in front of her to keep her hands from trembling. 'If he is at home, that is. I know he's been away in France. Has he returned?'

He nodded. 'He's not expecting you.'

'I'm afraid not, but…'

'It's all right, Albert,' a female voice said from behind him.

A woman emerged from the shadows. Lydia recognised her as Alex's sister—Henry's wife.

'Why, Miss Brook. How lovely it is to see you. Please, do come in.' Ushering her inside, she turned to the servant. 'It's all right, Albert. Please tell my brother Miss Brook is here to see him—although he might be a while,' she informed Lydia. 'He's ensconced with a business associate at present—has been for the past hour.'

'Oh, I see. I—I do not wish to interrupt, Lady Seymour. Perhaps I should come back at some other time…'

'I wouldn't hear of it and I know he'll be disappointed if you don't wait. And my name is Miranda. Lady Seymour sounds far too formal.'

'Then you must call me Lydia.'

'I will.'

'He—he did say he had to go away for a while—to France.'

'He wasn't away as long as he expected. Come into the drawing room. I would so like to hear how your salon is going. Well, I hope. Have some tea sent in, please, Albert.'

'Yes, it's going very well. Better than I had expected.'

'That's wonderful—really. I'm so glad. Come, let me take your coat.' Lydia quickly removed it and handed it to her, taking a moment to look at her surroundings as Miranda went to deposit her coat on a chair.

Lydia was completely overwhelmed by the beauty and wealth of the house. Standing in the centre of the black-and-white marble-floored hall, she looked dazedly about her, wondering if she had not come to some royal palace by mistake. She wasn't to know that compared to Aspen Grange, Alex's home in Berkshire, this house was considered to be of moderate proportions. A curved staircase rose to the upper reaches of the house and, craning her neck, she was almost dazzled by the huge chandelier suspended from the ceiling, dripping with hundreds of tiny crystal pieces.

'I'm so glad you've come today,' Miranda said, coming to stand beside her. 'Any later and I would have missed you. I've decided to return to Surrey tomorrow—to my husband.'

Lydia's heart skipped a beat on being reminded of Henry by his wife. 'He…is not here with you…in London?'

'No. Alex thinks the country air will be better for me than the air here in London. I—I am with child, you see,' she said with a quiet confidentiality.

'Yes, Alex told me.'

Miranda looked surprised. 'He did? Oh—I see. When?'

Lydia could have bitten her tongue, but she could not retract the words. 'He—he called at the salon before he went to France. I hope you don't mind him telling me.'

She smiled. 'No, of course I don't. It's early days. Anyway, here we are.' Having reached a closed door, she paused. 'We have a guest. Come and meet her. She's staying with her brother in town, Sir David Hilton. He's a close friend and neighbour of Alex. Irene is in London for an indefinite period.'

Lydia smiled, looking at her with interest. 'You are close to your brother, I think.'

'Yes—I adore him. I cannot hide the fact that he's an exacting man, who insists on the highest standards from all those he employs and the people he does business with. He has a brilliant mind and a head for figures that shames me. He drives himself hard, demanding too much of himself—and others. But he can be charming, when it suits him. You probably know he was married—his wife died rather tragically. They didn't get on.' She laughed when she saw Lydia was quite taken aback by her forthright manner. 'It's all right—I know, I always talk too much, but it was no secret to anyone who knew them.'

Entering the drawing room, Lydia blinked at the extravagance and unaccustomed luxury. Her uneducated eye was unable to place a value on the beautiful things she saw, but she was able to appreciate and admire the quality of the beautifully furnished room. Now Lydia knew who Alex Golding actually was. She saw what comprised his background, the wealth, the trappings of a world so very different from her own that they might have come from different planets.

In that moment, the enormous difference between them became emphasised. She saw all these things as extensions of the world in which

Alex lived, one where Alex Golding had never known labour in the way the people she had been acquainted with all her life had laboured. Seeing his luxurious home only reinforced Lydia's decision that she was doing the right thing. Everything she saw marked the gulf between them, a form of Rubicon that, in her mind, she could not cross.

Chapter Seven

At the warmth and sincerity of Miranda's greeting, despite Lydia's history with Henry, she felt
at ease. This good feeling lasted only a moment.
One look at the beautiful young woman Miranda
introduced her to—whose nose was long and
straight and perfect for looking down—made
Lydia's heart sink. It only took her moment to
realise that Irene Hilton, who was perhaps two
or three years older than herself, was unlike Miranda in every aspect. Lydia did not care for her.
There was something malicious about her.

It was plain to Lydia that Miss Hilton was
confident and assured of her place in the grand
sphere of things. With her attractive looks, an
abundance of shining fair hair, the dark-lashed
deep blue eyes and skin like clotted cream, she

had been blessed with every physical advantage a woman could wish for. And just a few minutes in her company were enough to tell Lydia that she knew it.

As Lydia settled herself opposite this aloof woman, Miss Hilton's austere gaze settled on her in a cool and exacting way. Impersonally, her eyes raked her with a single withering glance as if she were some beggar who had the temerity to come calling on those who were better off, deciding then that she was of the lower class and had no social credentials to recommend her. Immediately a wall of antipathy sprang up between them and Irene seemed bent on putting her at a disadvantage from the start.

'So you are the woman Alex has taken under his wing,' she remarked, her tone lightly contemptuous. Her lips stretched tightly in a practised smile, giving Lydia a flash of sharp white teeth from between her parted red lips.

There were hidden connotations behind the smile and Lydia was not quite sure how to read them, but whatever the meaning behind it, Lydia knew it would not do to get off on a bad footing with this woman. Puzzled, she looked at Miranda, a look that said how does she know?

'I'm sorry, Lydia. A few weeks ago Irene saw you in Alex's carriage driving away from the bank. Irene mentioned it to me and I told her I had no idea who you were. When we met in the park that day, being the busybody that I am, I asked Alex a few impertinent questions. He told me what had transpired between you and the bank manager and how he had stepped in to help you.' She had the grace to look contrite. 'I did tell Irene about it. I'm sorry. I should not have been so indiscreet.'

'Please—don't worry about it,' Lydia said tersely, having credited Alex with more discretion. Looking at Miss Hilton, though, she gritted her teeth, longing to slap this woman's impertinent face, but common sense prevailed. There was nothing she could do about the knowledge Alex had imparted to his sister, but there was nothing like a smile and politeness to confuse a foe or charm a friend, and Lydia's lips curved graciously. 'He has not taken me under his wing, Miss Hilton, but he has certainly been generous enough to give me a temporary loan—on a proper business footing, naturally.'

Irene gave her an arch look. 'Naturally. I can imagine how difficult it must be for someone in your position to find the necessary funds to begin a business. How fortunate you were to be acquainted with Alex—and to have him pay for it all.'

Lydia stared at her, trying not to succumb to her rudeness. Irene Hilton was supposed to be a lady or at least pretend that she was, whereas she, Lydia, brought up in some of the meanest streets of London where she'd soon learned to fight and fend for herself, had no such pretensions. This woman's father might be a gentleman whereas her father was a ne'er-do-well. But if life had taught her one thing, it was how to defend herself, and if Irene Hilton ever did anything to threaten her she would be sorry. Her heart thudded painfully, but she must show no concern or distress. She must smile and pretend her rude remarks were nothing to her. This woman did not know—nobody knew—what was between her and Alex Golding and she had to keep it hidden.

'I was indeed fortunate,' she said as she eased the stiffness in her jaw and forced a smile to her lips, her voice quiet and controlled.

'And is it business that brings you here today to see Alex?'

Lydia met her gaze directly. 'What else would it be, Miss Hilton?'

'What else indeed. So, you have opened a shop—a dress shop. Goodness! How awful for you. I cannot imagine what it must be like having to wait on hordes of women like that.'

If Irene hoped to see a flicker of emotion pass across Lydia's face she was disappointed, for Lydia continued to smile—even though Irene made it sound as though Lydia had opened a house of ill repute. 'On the contrary. I design and make the gowns—with the assistance of the seamstresses I employ. I assure you I enjoy what I do and would not have it any other way.'

'I see,' Irene said stiffly. Having not managed to get a rise out of Lydia, with a slight nod and look of boredom, she picked up a magazine and moved away to sit by the window overlooking a terrace. She made no further attempt at conversation, clearly considering Lydia of no consequence.

With an exasperated glance in Irene's direction, Miranda seated herself on the sofa opposite Lydia, a small table between them on which a maid entered and placed a tray laden with the tea Miranda had ordered.

'Take no notice of Irene,' she said quietly, picking up the teapot and pouring the steaming beverage and milk into two matching china cups and handing a cup and saucer to Lydia. 'She called in the hope of seeing Alex. She was disappointed and more than a little vexed when he disappeared into his study to discuss business with an associate. I feel he'll keep the gentleman for as long as possible in order to avoid her.'

'Little wonder she didn't take my arrival too kindly. It is important that I speak to Alex today, but I don't expect I shall detain him long.'

As they sipped their tea they talked at length and Lydia found herself chatting to this friendly, engaging young woman as she had never talked to anyone before. Not only did she have a kind heart and a caring nature, she was also a woman of great energy. She was the sort of woman who conversed and laughed compulsively—the sort of woman who would be easily hurt. Her eyes sparkled as she listened with rapt attention to all Lydia told her of her business. She was genuinely interested and full of admiration for what Lydia was doing.

'I can imagine what an exciting time this must be for you—wonderful and colourful, too, particularly when compared to my own often boring life. I envy you your freedom to do as you please, Lydia. It can't have been easy for you, but your determination to overcome obstacles that might had prevented you from achieving your goal is to your credit.'

Lydia laughed. 'I haven't—at least, not yet. I have a long way to go before I achieve the kind of success I'm aiming for.'

'That may be, but I am full of admiration for what you do—to take the reins of your life and your destiny. It must be so fulfilling. I do believe that if there were more women like you, you would change the world, if possible, whereas I shall continue doing as I do now with nothing new on the horizon.'

Taken aback by the intensity of the declaration and the fiery flash of passion in her eyes, Lydia smiled, part-friendly, part-quizzical. 'But…you are to have a child. That in itself is fulfilling.'

Placing her hand on the lower part of her abdomen, Miranda brightened, a softness entering her eyes. 'Yes…yes, it is…or it will be.' She bit her lip, lowering her gaze. 'I hope that when the baby comes, Henry will be happy about it.'

Lydia looked at her sharply. Guilty at the part she had played which had clearly driven a wedge between this lovely woman and her husband, and hating the deception, she placed her cup and saucer on the tray. 'Why do you say that? Is there some doubt that he won't be?' she asked tentatively, uncomfortable with the turn in the conversation, but unable to avoid it.

'Of course he will,' Miranda was quick to assure her. 'It— It's just that…well…I shouldn't really say this, but Henry does not always behave himself, which is why, after his last indiscretion with an unknown lady, I've come to London and left him in Surrey. I hope that after some time apart he will have missed me and promise to behave himself in the future.'

'Yes,' Lydia said quietly. 'I hope so, too.'

At that moment the door opened and Alex strode in. Lydia rose immediately. He looked straight at her, his firm mouth curling slightly at the corners, his eyes suddenly alive with interest. He was one of those men who always managed to move with an air of assurance, looking as if he would fit in anywhere. She thought it had to do with breeding.

'Lydia! You take me by surprise. What brings you to my home?'

'I'd rather not say…just now,' she replied, glancing at Irene Hilton, who had put down her magazine and got to her feet when Alex came in. 'I apologise for seeking you out at home, but there is something I have to say to you. It…is important.'

'I see. Then please step this way where we can speak in privacy.' Opening the door, he stepped aside to let her pass, casting a look at his sister and a quietly fuming Irene. 'Excuse us, ladies.' With that, he crossed the hall with Lydia and admitted her to his study, closing the door firmly behind her. Alone with her, Alex was faced with whatever reason Lydia had for coming to speak to him. She seemed nervous.

Lydia found herself stepping into a room dominated by a large mahogany desk littered with papers and ledgers. In front of it were two comfortable leather chairs and high bookcases stocked with leather-bound volumes lined the walls. Above a white marble fireplace was an ornate, gilt framed mirror. Portraits and English landscapes and exquisite miniatures adorned the walls. Sunlight streamed through the windows and her feet sank into the thick dark blue carpet. This room was a typical representation of its owner. It was all so suitable for someone of his stature.

Suddenly Alex appeared behind her, his arms going around her and drawing her back against his chest. Her heart did a somersault when he bent his head and placed his lips on her neck. 'Have you any idea how much I have missed you?' he murmured.

Lydia leaned into him, her body crying out for him while her head was saying something else. Closing her eyes, she savoured the moment, memories of their last encounter still fresh in her mind. She desperately wanted to remain in the haven of his arms and seek solace from the turmoil of her emotions, but she must not. She must be firm with herself.

'Please, Alex,' she said, gently but insistently disentangling herself from his arms and turning to face him. Taking several steps away from him, she was determined to put as much distance between them as she could for her own self-preservation. 'I have something to say to you and I cannot do that if you persist in kissing me.'

With a sigh, Alex reluctantly moved away from her. 'Very well. There is nothing I want more than to kiss you senseless, but I suppose I can wait. Please sit down,' he said, indicating a chair set by the hearth. 'I'm somewhat curious as to why you are here. Whatever the reason I am glad to see you.' A lazy, devastating smile passed over his features as he took the chair opposite her, crossing his long legs and steepling his fingers in front of his face, his eyes doing a slow sweep of her body so that Lydia could almost feel him disrobing her.

'I see you have made the acquaintance of Irene. Did she endear herself to you, by the way?'

'I am not truly acquainted with her,' Lydia replied, her face rosy from his embrace and her heart beating a wild tattoo in her chest. 'Apart from a few choice words on my arrival—and she did not endear herself to me in the slightest. Her manners leave much to be desired.'

A slow smile curved his firm lips. 'I'm sorry. She does tend to be outspoken.'

Lydia shot him a hard look. 'Outspoken? I am not simple, Alex. She does not like me and I know rudeness when I hear it. I think she considers me less than civilised. She certainly needs a lesson in manners. Are you going to marry her? Because if you are I advise you to reconsider.'

He chuckled. 'Heaven forbid! Good Lord, no! Irene is the sister of my closest friend. We have known each other since I was at university with her brother. She is both sophisticated and clever.'

'And cold and dispassionate and difficult to please, I imagine,' Lydia concluded drily. Realising that she had been too forthright with her comments she was immediately contrite. 'I'm sorry,' she sighed. 'I shouldn't have said that. It's just that women like Miss Hilton are anathema to me.'

'Don't be sorry. Now, enough about Irene. I would like to hear how your shop is going. Tell me why you are here. You said it's important.'

For a moment Lydia shrank from telling him the reason for her visit, but then she reminded herself that after what had passed between them so far, and what she had seen of his home today, she had to end it. Best she did it now. Her face took on a youthful dignity as she looked steadfastly at the proud and powerful Alex Golding, this man who had made such a big impact on her life in the short time she'd known him.

'Yes—yes, it is.' She sat forward, perched on the edge of the chair, as if poised for flight. A troubled shadow crossed his face and she realised that he knew perfectly well something was wrong. 'I—I have come to tell you that I have no further need of your loan, Alex. I know it is a little late to be deciding this, but my financial circumstances have changed for the better recently. Indeed, I have been to the bank and asked them to return the money to your account—with any interest owing, of course.'

Alex wasn't smiling any more. He stared at her incredulously, as though she had changed into a different creature. His eyes hardened and his brows snapped together in an ominous frown. 'What the devil are you saying? Why? Why do you no longer need the loan? You have only been in business a couple of weeks. Is it going so well that you can already afford to return the money you needed to start with?'

His eyes burned more fiercely beneath the

black brows, and Lydia's heart beat faster as she read the huge disappointment in them. 'I have told you...I—I no longer need it.'

'You have found another source?' he asked sharply.

'Yes—someone who wants to invest in my business.'

'Do you mind telling me who it is?'

'Suffice to say that it is someone who has my best interests at heart.' She was reluctant to tell him it was her father. Alex would be bound to question her about him. After working up the courage to come here today and with her heightened emotions, the last thing she wanted was to discuss her father and his motives for helping her. Alex was watching her, scrutinising, wondering.

'I see,' he said coldly. 'You never cease to amaze me, Lydia. Do you mind telling me why my money is suddenly so repugnant to you?'

She bristled at his mocking tone. 'It is not. Please don't think that.' She sighed, wanting so much to reach out to him, but keeping her hands clasped tightly together in her lap. 'Alex, please don't make this difficult for me.'

'That is not my intention. Is it Alistair who has offered to invest in your venture?'

'No. He wouldn't—not that I would accept

it if he did. Alistair and I have gone our separate ways.'

'Which is what is happening to us—if you have your way. Is it your wish to alienate yourself from me?'

She paused—a heartbreaking pause—before she gave him her answer. 'I have to. I must. My association with you has brought me nothing but trouble.'

'Really? You were willing to take my money when it suited you.'

'For which I shall be eternally grateful. But I no longer need it.'

'For the time being, let's forget about the money. I am more concerned about what it will mean for us—for the closeness that has developed between us.' He watched her carefully, his impassive face concealing a simmering anger as he waited for her answer. He did not have too much difficulty reading her expression and he could see her features were tense with some kind of emotional struggle.

Taking the bit between her teeth, Lydia took a deep breath, her face becoming hard, her expression closed, her green eyes fixed steadily on his. Half of her wanted to disappear, leaving behind this unbearable tension. The other half wanted to go to him and beg him to take her in his arms. Never had she felt more wretched, for what she was about to do was the worst thing she had ever had to do in her life.

'There can be no us, Alex. Before you went to France you spoke of some kind of arrangement. I have given it a great deal of thought and I don't think I was mistaken when I assumed the kind of arrangement you intended. I'm afraid that kind of arrangement does not suit me.'

His face changed as her words and their implication hit him, but if he was startled by what she'd said he did not show it. His eyes became fixed to her face and gleamed like molten fire. 'And may I ask what kind of arrangement you assumed?'

'That—that I become your mistress.'

Alex's expression became pale with anger, which gradually became visible in every feature. He did not speak as he shrugged himself out of the chair and brought himself erect in one fluid movement. He turned away from her, straight and proud, and Lydia could almost feel the effort he was exerting to keep his anger under control.

'I see,' he said at length, turning suddenly to face her, on the verge of losing the struggle within himself. His pale blue eyes had gone hard between the narrowed lids, his face like granite, and he spoke with chill precision.

'Your assumption was not correct, Lydia. Nothing was further from my mind. But was the prospect of becoming my mistress so abhorrent to you?'

'Yes— I mean, no,' she replied, confused as to how to answer his question put so directly. 'The times we have spent together will remain close to my heart, but in all conscience I could not be any man's mistress. My work—the shop—is important to me. If I were to form any kind of relationship with you, it would distract me from that. I cannot—after all I have done to start up on my own—allow that to happen.'

There was such finality in those words that Alex was momentarily at a loss to know what to say. He could see by the implacable set of her chin and the way her face was set against him that coming here today was not a decision she had taken lightly. His face hardened into an expressionless mask, his eyes probing hers like dagger thrusts.

'Damn it, Lydia! You are the most independent, self-reliant, stubborn woman I have ever met,' he said tightly. 'Can you tell me why, all of a sudden, I—as well as my money—have become repugnant to you?'

'You—you haven't.'

'No? Then what am I supposed to think when you back out of the agreement we made?'

'You mean the loan?'

'What else? As far as I am concerned it is the only agreement we made. Do you know what a man thinks when he goes away and returns to find the woman he made love to telling him she no longer needs him or his money?'

Lydia shook her head.

'He thinks,' he said dispassionately, 'that perhaps someone else has taken his place in her affections—if not her bed.' He spoke with biting scorn and gave her a look that chilled her. 'Am I right, Lydia?'

She stared at him in disbelief before fury lit her eyes and her cheeks flushed red.

He smiled thinly. 'You are blushing, Lydia,' he said in an awful voice. 'Is it guilt you feel? Have I hit upon the truth?'

'No, you have not,' she said, springing to her feet and glaring at him. 'It is because I am furious. How dare you say that to me? Please credit me with a little more sense. Your accusation is both unjust and unfounded. But if I did have someone else, then it has nothing whatsoever to do with you. I am my own person, Alex, and I shall live and work as I please without interference from you.'

Alex's stunned expression after her outburst was replaced almost instantly by one of relief and puzzlement. 'I apologise. I should not have said what I did. But you cannot blame me for wondering.'

'Then don't. Have you so little faith in me, Alex? After all that has happened between us you have such a high opinion of me you were willing to think I would blithely sleep with another man while thinking of you. That you could even think me capable of such base conduct is... is deplorable. Now I think I should leave.'

'Not until this is settled between us.'

'It is settled. There is nothing else to say.'

She tried to walk past him, but his hand reached out and stopped her.

'Damn you—you cannot do this.'

'Yes, I can,' she replied wretchedly, trying not to look at him, at his blazing eyes. He was too powerful, too close and far too masculine. She was fighting tears, struggling to keep her voice under control. His penetrating eyes were reaching into her mind, searching her heart.

Her face was a pale emotionless mask as she turned from him and crossed to the door. She felt a terrible pain inside and tears she was too proud and too angry to shed nearly choked her. She could feel his eyes burning into her. Her heart and mind felt empty, and she was chilled to the bone, and even now, when she was desperate to escape him before she broke down, she had to ask herself why it should hurt so much and to question what was in her heart. She opened the door.

Alex was torn as he watched her. In the beginning he had been driven by lust to possess her. Now he felt a protectiveness so profound that it shook him to the depths of his being and, looking back, the sweet memory of her response to him touched him deeply. She was as open and generous in her lovemaking as she was in every aspect of her life. He could succumb to the temptation of a beautiful woman as easily as the average man, but he had never experienced anything like what he was beginning to feel for this woman.

He could not let her walk out of his life.

'Marry me, Lydia.'

The three words exploded across the room and hung in the air between them. It was all Lydia could hear. She had not seen the question coming and she gasped with the shock of it, her eyes wide and staring and stunned. 'What?' she whispered. 'What did you say?'

'I said marry me.' Even as he repeated the question, Alex couldn't believe it himself. His resolve not to enter into a marriage with anyone after his one disastrous marriage to Blanche seemed to have gone the same way as his brains, his patience and his self-control. 'I'm sorry. My proposal seems to have taken you by surprise.'

This was true. In disbelief, very slowly she turned to face him, unaware that on the other side of the partly open door Irene Hilton had appeared out of nowhere, like a spirit materialising from thin air and stopping to take in the proceedings taking place between the occupants in the study.

Shaking her head very slowly, Lydia took a tentative step back to Alex. There came a temptation so powerful as to be almost irresistible, the temptation to accept, to cast herself into his arms and allow herself to be carried away to wherever it was he wanted her to be, without further thought. Yet because of who he was and everything that was happening in her life to hold her back, her pride restrained her on the very edge of yielding.

'You cannot mean that. You do not know what you are saying. How can you ask me that? How can you be serious?'

'I have never been more serious in my life.'

'But you can't be. You don't know me—not really.'

'I know enough—all I need to know.'

'No, you do not,' she countered, angry that

he was doing this to her when, after much soul searching, she had resolved to end it now. Something had gone dreadfully wrong. Everything was rushing at her too fast, surrounding her in a confusing welter beyond comprehension. Her head spun giddily and she felt faint, but she had to make the effort to get through this.

'You know what happened in Scotland...with Henry...that I was prepared to marry him—to go with him to America.'

'It is forgotten.'

'No,' she cried in earnest. 'Not by me. Not by Henry. Don't you see? Marrying me would destroy your relationship with your sister because you could not hope to keep what happened secret from her. She would be shocked if she knew that not only had I been prepared to marry Henry, but that I had also taken her brother as my lover.'

'Do you think I don't know that?' he uttered fiercely. 'I love Miranda dearly and the last thing I want is to cause her unhappiness.'

'I like your sister. I could not bear her hatred. Henry is weak. If you were to make me your wife, how long do you think it would be before it was discovered?' She sighed, averting her eyes, knowing as she spoke that if she agreed to marry Alex it wasn't Miranda's anger, hurt and disappointment she was afraid of, but her own feelings and emotions where he was concerned. 'Suddenly it all seems so difficult.'

'It needn't be. It was not your fault. It can be explained. None of that matters. I cannot, will not, let you go.'

She looked at him standing before her. He looked so cool and so completely self-assured. Why did he want to marry her? Did he need her? He certainly didn't love her and she wasn't foolish enough to succumb to that illusion.

'Yes, you will, because whatever your feelings are where I am concerned, you neither need me nor love me,' she said, voicing her thoughts aloud. 'You ask me to marry you as if you are discussing a business arrangement—without feeling or emotion. I am not so naive as to believe the reason you have proposed is because you have suddenly fallen in love with me.'

'You must know that I have come to have a high regard for you and a strong and very passionate desire and affection for you.'

'Desire and affection are all very well, Alex, but wonderful as it is, it is not enough—not enough to provoke this absurd compulsion to marry me.'

'Is it a proper proposal you wish to have? Would you like it if I were to kneel?' he asked in a demanding voice, annoyed that she was being so obstinate.

'Certainly not,' she bit back. 'It would be quite ridiculous.'

'Dear God, Lydia,' he said, thoroughly exasperated, his handsome face working with emotion, for he was not a man who liked to plead. 'What *do* you want?'

'Nothing. Absolutely nothing. I am not marriage material, Alex,' she said vehemently, desperate for him to understand. 'I am not of your world. The odds are against us—the obstacles between us unsurmountable. We have been lovers. To believe we could ever be more than that is madness.'

'I disagree.'

Lydia looked at him. She saw the purposeful gleam in his eyes and drew a swift breath. This had come unexpectedly, taking her wholly by surprise. Of course she could not possibly accept what he was offering. She shied away from delving too deeply into the exact nature of her feelings for Alex. After everything that had happened to her in the past weeks, she had little faith in trying to judge her own emotions. But she did care for him—very much. There was no use denying it.

'And then there would be the gossip. Would

it not concern you to know what others would say and think?'

He cocked a sleek black brow, speaking sardonically. 'I long since ceased to worry about other people's opinion of me. And where you are concerned,' he said on a softer note, a warm intimacy creeping into his voice, and his incredible gaze passing over her in a manner which caused her stomach to quiver despite her resolve to stand firm against him, 'I would imagine the notoriety of being married to me would generate a great deal of interest among the elite of London society. If nothing else, it would certainly benefit your business.'

Lydia flushed, bristling at the very idea. 'Don't be conceited, Alex. I can do without that kind of notoriety. But since you mentioned it, what about my work? As your wife, would I be allowed to continue?'

'It can be discussed.'

'There is nothing to discuss.'

'I am a wealthy man, Lydia. You would have no need to work.'

'But I *want* to work. I happen to *like* working—I love what I do. For the first time in my life I am independent of others and I am already beginning to enjoy the feeling.' She was adamant. 'I will not give it up.'

'You don't have to—at least not altogether. Something can be arranged.'

She stared at him in stupefied amazement. 'Arranged? Oh, no, Alex. *I* will decide what I will do with my future. It is my life. I do not belong in your world.' She threw her arms wide to embrace the room. 'You have all this. I could never be a part of it—or be the wife you would want me to be.'

'Now it is you who is being absurd. I am just trying to protect you.'

Lydia's voice was like splintered ice as she straightened her spine. 'Protection? Is that the only reason you can come up with for asking me to marry you? Or are there other reasons— because you feel sorry for me, perhaps even pity me? Do you honestly believe I am so desperate for a husband that I would say yes to an offer like that?' Pride caused her to lift her chin and calmly meet his ruthless stare. 'No, Alex. Absolutely not. I will make my own way. I don't need anyone else—and I certainly don't need a husband whose sole reason for marrying me is to protect me, although I cannot imagine from what.'

'The protection I speak of is the protection of a husband for his wife. I want nothing more than to help you.'

Lydia stepped back. She did not want to hear any more for she could feel her weak woman's body straining towards him, yearning to give in, to lean against his strong lean body. Her heart contracted with pain. She wanted him so much, more than anything she had known since she had been old enough to understand reason, and yet when she left this house, she would never see him again.

Alex watched her, an ironic twist to his finely chiselled lips in an otherwise expressionless face. He wanted to shake her. Why did she hold herself aloof from him? He believed that behind the bright expression and glib speech about independence the real warm, passionate Lydia who wanted him was still to be found. What was it that had driven the girl he knew away and replaced her with this woman who was determined to keep him at arm's length?

'Am I so unattractive a prospect, Lydia, that you prefer to look elsewhere?'

His voice was so cool that she lifted her chin in hot indignation. 'I believe it is the privilege of a woman to act as she chooses and in this instance I have done so.'

He faced her with challenging eyes. 'You have made your feelings quite clear—blatantly so.

And you are quite right. It is your privilege and prerogative to do as you please.'

Lydia glanced at him with two stormy eyes. 'I'm glad you finally understand. Since you have done me the honour of asking me to be your wife, I will do you the courtesy of telling you why I have returned your loan and about the person who has invested his money in my business. Perhaps then you will understand one of the reasons why I cannot marry you—and you will be relieved that I turned you down.'

His eyes narrowed. 'Why? Tell me.'

'It is my father.'

Alex was surprised. 'Your father?'

'Yes. I did not tell you before because there are unsavoury things about his past I did not wish to discuss with you.'

'I did not realise you even saw your father.'

'I haven't—not since I was a small child. He has only recently come back into my life.'

'I see. Can I ask where he has been?'

She looked at him directly, having no wish to miss his reaction when she told him. 'In Australia. He was a convict, Alex—a criminal. He was sent to Australia for seven years for stealing seven shillings to feed himself.'

Alex looked neither shocked nor surprised. He took a moment to digest what she divulged, then he said, 'I see. What was his profession before he was sentenced?'

'He was a printer.'

'A printer turned convict. If he has been in Australia for seven years, where did he get the money to invest in your shop?'

'After he had served his sentence he remained in Australia. He knew there had been several gold finds so he went to see for himself. He was successful—with gold sitting just beneath the surface. After making his fortune he returned to England. It was because of my father—of my fear of meeting him again—that in foolish desperation I agreed to marry Henry. He was offering to take me away to America—far enough away for me not to have to see him.'

'I sensed there was something in the past you were running from when we first met. Why did you fear him? Did he do something to hurt you?'

Lydia swallowed hard. 'He callously abandoned me and my mother to our fate when I was three years old. He caused her so much grief and unhappiness that I told myself I could not forgive him. She tried to get over it—good riddance, she would say—but deep inside her she never did. When things went wrong with Henry, I knew I could not run away any more. But my father—the man I now realise I had no reason to fear, a man who is much debilitated by his years as a convict—is not how I imagined him to be and he is finally to be a part of my life.'

'Is that what you want?'

'I knew that if he came back I might stop hating him.'

'And in doing so you would betray your mother.'

'Something like that. I thought if I could put as much distance between us I wouldn't have to face it. So there. Now you know.'

'And now? You have forgiven him? Can you forgive him for what he did?'

'I have asked myself this. I have also asked myself if I am responsible for him now. What do I owe him beside the fact that I am alive because of him? But having lived my life with my mother—how she loved me, what she did for me, all that we did together and what I now have—these things have defined me, have made me what I am. I will never change. So you see, Alex, because of the life I have lived and a father who...' She sighed. 'Think about it—the daughter of a seamstress and a father who's an ex-convict... Who am I to think I can move in a society graced by nobility and men of your ilk? I cannot be part of your world, Alex, the kind of world you inhabit. It will always stand between us.'

'You do me an injustice. I don't judge people by their parents—my own were not paragons of virtue. Far from it. Had it not been for my grandfather I would not be where I am today.' The sudden bitterness in his tone caused Lydia to glance at him sharply, but he did not expand on this any further. 'What you have told me is no cause for shame.'

'Shame? I don't feel shame. What I feel as someone who has seen struggle and grinding poverty for as long as I can remember is perhaps sorrow—regret—for the loss of a normal childhood.'

'Despite how we are now, we are not so different, you and I. We have more in common than you realise,' he told her obliquely.

Alex understood more than she comprehended the nature of her struggle and what forces within her held the world at bay while she concentrated all her efforts of succeeding in what she wanted to do. Yes, he understood this in an intellectual sense. It was the emotional sense he was finding difficult to process.

'No one can go back into the past to make things different however deeply ingrained it is in us. But we cannot allow our past to become a barrier to the future.'

'That is not what I am doing,' she protested.

'No?'

'No. How would you know that?'

Alex could tell from her voice that a tightness had come into her throat. As guarded as she was, there were moments when they were together that she would let her feelings escape. This was one of them.

'Because I recognise in you something that is also in myself.'

She shook her head in a fierce movement, as if to quell the weakening emotion that was rising within her and to negate all that was left unspoken between them. 'Forgive me if I don't believe that. How could you possibly? Now please excuse me. There is nothing more to be said. I would like to leave.'

She turned from him, but Alex reached out and gripped her arm, moving closer, his mouth tightening, determined not to let what was between them end like this. He towered over her, his face dark and threatening, his overpowering physical presence and his intention catching Lydia off guard.

'Before you go, tell me that this is what you truly really want—for our ways to part, never to see each other again?'

'Yes, it is,' she replied, her heart beginning to beat frantically as she tried avoiding his shrewd, penetrating eyes.

'Then dare to look me in the eye and tell me,' he demanded, looking at her, the sunlight slanting through the window, bathing her in light, her heavy mass of black hair beneath her hat accentuating the almost transparent whiteness of her face. Her eyes were large, dark and impelling, drawing him in.

'Yes,' she said at last, reluctantly. 'It is what I want.'

'And tell me that you don't want me to touch you, to kiss you ever again. You see, Lydia, I know how easy it is to make you forget everything, to make you behave with such wanton abandon.'

Before Lydia could protest, Alex dragged her against his chest, his hands unyielding as his mouth swooped savagely down on hers. A fierce, silent, merciless struggle went on inside Lydia as she tried to free herself, but Alex was in full possession of his strength and she felt herself weakening slowly, knowing she could not hold out against him as a blaze of excitement leapt through her, her reaction a purely primitive one.

Avidly, like a man starving, Alex crushed his lips over hers. It was a kiss that devoured them, setting them both aflame, and he felt her trembling with helpless surrender against him, the heat from her scented body acting like a drug to his senses.

Lydia could feel the heat and vibrancy of his body with every sinew pressed against hers. She couldn't breathe and was unable to resist temptation. She responded eagerly, pressing against him, the woman in her reaching out to the male in him. She forgot everything as his hand left her waist to cup the gentle fullness of her breast, before rising and stroking the back of her neck, sweeping her whole body in one long, shuddering caress.

Alex held her pliant body close as she strained against him. The logical conclusion to her enthusiastic response was to lay her down, to satisfy them both as they had done before, but her rejection of his offer of marriage, her resolve to put an end to this madness that consumed them both whenever they were together, resurrected his sanity. As quickly as he had swept her into his arms, he released her, thrusting her away from him with an abruptness that left her senses reeling, her eyes unfocused from the pleasure her flesh still felt.

After their intimate contact, Alex was almost overwhelmed with a mixture of pain and pleasure, finding her supple young body more than capable of arousing him, her mouth moist and warm, her breath so sweet that it drove him beyond all thought. His strategic attempt to weaken her into submission had rebounded on him with a vengeance. He had only succeeded in driving himself almost insane as he came close to losing the battle for control.

'I apologise for my barbaric behaviour, but when you remember during your long, lonely nights how it felt to have me hold you—to kiss you—and how willing your body was to respond, I am certain your desire will be sharpened with remorse. You may deny me all you like, but the speed with which your body is aroused whenever I touch you proclaims stronger than any words how much you want to be with me as much as I want to be with you.'

Helplessly Lydia stared at him, her cheeks flushed and her lips soft and trembling, feeling an unfulfilled need inside her that made it impossible for her to deny that what he said was true.

'This is not the end of us, Lydia,' Alex said, his voice low and determined in the silence that surrounded them. 'You cannot put me from your life so easily. I will not let you.'

'You have to,' she said quietly, her voice quivering slightly as she tried to bring her body under control. 'I have made up my mind. Do not make it more difficult for me than it is already. Please don't think badly of me, Alex. Let us part as friends.'

'Friends? What we have goes beyond that. I could fall in love with you,' he said. 'But I don't think we can be friends.'

'Then it seems we cannot agree.'

'Damn it, Lydia. Don't do this. Believe me, I am not a man to beg and if—'

'Don't threaten me, Alex.'

'I'm not,' he bit back, white-lipped with anger, his eyes glittering across at her. 'To hell with it, then. When I decide to marry I'll find someone more amenable to a proper offer of marriage. Someone who will—'

'I'm sure you won't have any difficulty doing so.'

Alex's face was expressionless. His eyes were blank, a glacial blue emptiness that told her nothing of what he felt. He spoke only seven words.

'I think you have said quite enough.'

She stared at him across the distance that separated them, memorising his face. She never wanted to forget the light blue of his eyes, his dark hair and the rebellious lock that drooped over his forehead, the hard curve of his jaw and the firm line of his lips. His eyes clouded and she saw in their depths the same churning conflict she felt in her heart.

'Then there is nothing more to be discussed. Goodbye, Alex.'

Without another word she left him, picking up her coat and leaving the house, her eyes blind with unhappiness, so she did not see Irene Hilton melt into the shadows.

In tight-lipped, rigid silence, biting back his fury, Alex watched her go, his gaze lingering on the sway of her hips, the proud tilt of her head. She was lovely, no mistake, and he couldn't believe she had refused him. He had looked into her green eyes and seen something proud and stubborn—and something wounded.

He was tempted to go after her and demand further explanation as to why she had refused his offer of marriage—an offer not made lightly. He had taken himself by surprise, for had he not sworn to himself that after one disastrous marriage he was unwilling to repeat the experience? But he decided against going after her. Setting his jaw, he turned on his heel and went to his desk. He'd be damned if he would plead with her further.

Chapter Eight

Seeing Lydia leave the house looking extremely upset, both curious and concerned as to why she had not come to say goodbye, Miranda sought out her brother. He was not in his study but in the garden. He stood with his hands behind his back, looking at the garden but seeing nothing. His expression was hard, his stance like that of a man being stretched beyond endurance by an internal struggle. It was plain that what had occurred between him and Lydia had not gone well. She went and stood beside him.

'What happened, Alex? It is obvious that your meeting with Miss Brook did not go well. Does it have anything to do with the loan you have given her?'

'You might say that. She told me that the

agreement we made in the beginning no longer stands.'

'Oh—I see. Does she not need it any more?'

'No. Her father has suddenly reappeared in her life and offered to invest in her enterprise.'

'And you are upset by that? Why, Alex? Is it because she will no longer be beholden to you?' Miranda watched the face of the man she had known the whole of her life—a brother she adored. Apart from a muscle clamping in his jaw, it didn't flinch.

'The last thing I want is for her to feel beholden to me in any way.'

'Then why did she leave looking so wretched? I don't understand, Alex.'

Alex looked at his sister's face with dispassion. 'How can you? In truth, Miranda, I don't understand it myself. She has gone. I doubt our paths will cross in the future.'

'But it is plain to me that you care for her. How can you discard her so completely?'

'I haven't discarded her. Lydia has discarded me.'

'Clearly this has upset you. Perhaps you should go and see her…'

'I strongly suspect I am the last person she would want to see.

'There's something else, isn't there? Something you are not telling me. Whatever happened that has upset the two of you has nothing to do with her returning the loan, has it?'

'Forget it, Miranda. It is not your concern.'

By no means done, Miranda placed her hand on his arm, looking up at his granite features, seeing a muscle move spasmodically on the side of his jaw. 'I am your sister. No one knows you better. I have not seen you look at a woman the way you look at Lydia Brook in a long time. If your feelings are of an…an affectionate nature, then you should do something about it. That Golding pride and quick temper of yours is a bad combination—you are bringing a lot of grief upon your own head. That is something you should consider.'

Alex's body went rigid and he stared at her in disbelief. 'Miranda! How can you tell me to go and see her when she rejected my proposal of marriage? Yes,' he said fiercely when he saw surprise and shock enter her eyes, 'I asked her to be my wife. She turned me down. I will not go and see her with a begging bowl in my hand. It is over.'

Miranda returned to the house, leaving Alex in a tormented silence.

Lydia had had a particularly busy day and she was feeling unusually tired. Her head ached and her back ached and she couldn't wait to take the weight off her feet. Writing down the day's sales and fresh orders in a large ledger on the counter, she was alone in the salon and about to close for the day when the door opened and a woman entered. Her stomach plummeted on seeing Irene Hilton. Her wide dark blue taffeta skirts rustled like a gentle breeze as she swept in.

Lydia inclined her head slightly in greeting. Irene looked at her for a moment in silence, a smug, superior smile on her face, her eyes settling on her with deadly coldness before doing a slow sweep of the salon and the racks of clothes, her expression one of distaste.

'Miss Hilton,' Lydia said calmly. 'You take me by surprise. I did not expect a visit from you. Please—look around. I will be happy to assist you should you need any help or advice. You might learn something.'

Irene smiled thinly. 'I doubt seriously there is anything I could learn from you, Miss Brook,' she replied, casting another casual glance around her.

It was open warfare. Both of them knew it.

'If I ever need advice,' Irene continued to drive her point home, 'you would be the last person I would seek out to ask for it.'

'Then please do not insult me with insincere

smiles. If it won't pain you too much, I would be obliged if you would tell me why you have come here. I do not think you can have anything to say to me that I want to listen to—unless you wish to purchase a new gown, or a hat, perhaps.'

Irene's eyes glittered, growing steady with anger. 'No, it will not pain me to tell you why I have come here and believe me, Miss Brook, there is nothing in this establishment that I could possibly want.'

Lydia's eyes opened in mock surprise. 'No, I didn't think there would be.' Instinctively, with that feminine intuition that recognises what is in another woman's mind, she knew Irene Hilton had her own agenda where Alex was concerned and was about to tell Lydia, who she saw as a threat, to keep away from him.

'I've come here to stop you making a fool of yourself.'

Lydia looked at her with distaste. The sheer gall of the woman made her draw in her breath. How dare she come here, trying to undermine all Lydia's confidence? 'Really? And how am I likely to do that?'

'With Alex.'

His name came between them like an axe falling. Lydia raised her brows in mock surprise. 'Alex? Really? If I have intentions where he is concerned, do I have to be wary of you, Miss Hilton?'

'Something like that.'

'What has Alex said?'

Her eyes gleaming with calculated malice, Irene studied her with unhidden scorn and when she spoke her voice was low and intense.

'Nothing—not to me, anyway. It's what I overheard.'

Lydia stared at her, sensing she was about to impart something unpleasant. She was right.

Irene looked at her squarely, smugly. 'It's about you—and Henry.'

Lydia tried hard not to show her alarm, but she was horrified that Irene Hilton had somehow found out about Scotland—and her relationship with Alex. 'Henry?'

'Come now, Miss Brook. You do know Henry—Alex's brother-in-law—Miranda's husband and soon-to-be father of her child.'

'I know there would be no point in denying it.'

'None whatsoever. You see, I overheard you speaking of it with Alex—how you were willing to marry Henry, and run off with him to America. How you and Alex became lovers—and I found your father's transgression particularly interesting.'

Apart from a hardening of Lydia's eyes, her expression remained unchanged. 'Goodness! It's amazing what one hears when one listens at keyholes.'

'Isn't it just.'

'I do not deny any of it—I had no idea Henry was a married man when he made overtures to me.'

'What concerns me is what Miranda will make of it—should she find out, of course.'

'I understand what you are saying. But you are her friend. Why would you want to hurt her?'

'I don't. If you swear to keep away from Alex, Miranda will be none the wiser—although she does have a right to know what her husband gets up to during his time away from her.'

Lydia looked at her, stunned. It wasn't so much the threat that appalled her, it was the hatred and terrible malevolence behind the words. 'You really are contemptible. I am not the kind of person to be either threatened or cowed.'

Irene glared at her. 'If you don't heed my warning, I will see to it that the scandal of what you did with Henry will ruin you and your business before it has hardly got off the ground. I will do all in my power to make things unpleasant for you. Do I make myself clear? Keep your hands off, if you know what's good for you. Alex

Golding belongs to me. I make no secret of the fact that I would do anything for him and I will not see it all ruined just because you briefly titillated his senses.'

Lydia felt the cruelty of it all. She understood then just how possessive Irene Hilton was over Alex. Because Alex did not reciprocate her feelings, Irene was blaming her.

'Since you eavesdropped on our conversation, you will know that I have no intention of going anywhere near Alex—not now or in the future, Miss Hilton. But I cannot stop him seeking me out if he has a mind to.'

'If he does, then you will send him on his way—otherwise…'

'Don't threaten me,' Lydia breathed, trying to control the anger in her heart, which was soaring by the minute, threatening to overwhelm her. 'If Alex doesn't want you, then I am sure you have brought his rejection on yourself.' She went to the door and opened it. 'Now please leave. I have work to do.'

With her arrogant nose elevated to a lofty angle, Irene swept past her. She turned back and shot Lydia a venomous glance before she could close the door. 'I hate you for this,' she spat.

'Hate me all you like, Miss Hilton. I cannot

say that I care one way or another—and it will not change a thing.'

Through the glass, Lydia watched her walk away, feeling sick inside and more than a little confused by the bitter altercation. But she also felt a worrying disturbance of something she didn't fully understand.

Lydia was to have Alex's child. Her world was about to fall apart. How could she have let it happen?

She knew she had been feeling unwell of late. She had put it down to all the hard work she had put into opening the shop, but when she became plagued by bouts of nausea and dizziness, especially early in the morning, she had reason to suspect the worst—that she might be with child.

Disbelieving and shocked, she was completely unprepared for this sudden explosion into her life. It was a nightmare, one she would wake up from soon, but it soon dawned on her that it was no nightmare. It was tenacious, terrifying reality and when her suspicions were duly confirmed she was devastated.

Her face became pale and drawn, her mouth tense. Consumed with pain, fear and confusion, she could not sleep, her predicament and how it would affect her future causing her to lie awake night after night worrying, pondering over what she should do—and whether or not she should tell Alex.

Isolated in her private misery, adamantly she refused to think about him, but despite herself a tremor of remembered passion and bittersweet memories sometimes coursed through her. Despite the unfortunate condition she found herself to be in, the continuation of that desire he had awoken in her still confounded her.

Over the following days she threw herself into her work—it helped to distract her mind from the self-loathing that tasted so bitter in her mouth. Whenever she thought of Alex, sadness threatened to overwhelm her and she became prey to a terrible depression. Fate was against her and nothing and nobody was going to help her. She had to help herself. But what could she do?

The one consolation to her at this time was that business was good and she had much to do. Emily took charge of the customers and the two girls in the workroom had plenty of work. Fortunately, they were efficient and could turn their hands to any task. Extra work was let out to workers who came each morning to bring finished garments and to see what was required that day. Lydia oversaw everything. She spent a great deal of her time at her desk creating new designs and assisting Emily in the shop when required.

Emily, never one to hold back, having noted Lydia's pallor and the dark shadows beneath her eyes, asked her what was wrong when the shop was quiet.

Standing in front of the counter sorting a box of beautifully embroidered handkerchiefs, swallowing hard and taking a deep breath, Lydia told her.

Emily was visibly shocked. 'Goodness! I knew there was something going on between the two of you.'

'But it isn't,' Lydia was quick to reply. She sighed when Emily gave her a 'I don't believe you' look. 'Well—twice. But I have told him I won't see him again—although that was before I knew...'

'What will you do, Lydia? What are you going to do?'

'In truth, Emily, I really don't know.'

Emily was all sympathy. 'Don't be downhearted. You made the same mistake thousands of other women have.'

'And now I will have to live with my mistake just as they did. What is done cannot be undone.'

Silence fell between them. Lydia stared down at the counter, resting her hands on the box of handkerchiefs. A lump clogged her throat in the way it did when she was going to cry. She did not, but when she looked up suddenly her eyes were dark with pain.

'It's so unfair, Emily. Everything was going so well.'

'Will you tell Mr Golding?'

'I don't know. When I told him everything was over between us he—he asked me to marry him.' If Emily was surprised, she didn't show it.

'And? What did you say?'

'No. I said no. How could I possibly accept? Look at me—what I am. And look at him. He's way above me in social class. He inhabits a world that is so very different to mine, with friends and colleagues I could never feel equal to. I have never dared to reach above myself and never aspired to be a lady. No, Emily, marriage to me would be hard on him. It would do him no good at all.'

'That's silly. You could adapt. I imagine you would be good at that. But you have to think of yourself—and the baby now.'

'But how can I continue working with a baby to care for? The business is bound to suffer. No one will want to purchase clothes or anything else from a fallen woman. Cruel censure is always directed at a woman alone with an illegitimate child. The shame and the stigma would be hard to bear. Society can be pitiless and it is always the woman who is to blame for being in the condition they will say she brought on herself.'

'You'll manage—we'll manage. We can take on another pair of hands if necessary, which may not be a bad thing anyway the way the orders are coming in. But whatever you decide to do I will help in any way I can—you know that. But one thing I will say is that Mr Golding has a right to know about his child. You have to tell him.'

'I know,' Lydia said miserably. 'And my father. He will be so disappointed in me when he knows about my condition.'

'From what I have seen of your father and what you have told me about his years in Australia, I think he will understand. And don't cry,' she said when she saw Lydia trying hard to stem the tide of tears. 'It will do you no good and will only make you feel ill. You must be brave if you are to overcome this ordeal.'

Emily was right about Lydia's father. He called that same day and, over tea in her office, she told him about her relationship first with Henry Seymour and then with Alex Golding.

It was a different matter entirely from telling Emily, for she found it difficult discussing such intimate matters with her father.

For a moment she hesitated, but her father's fading eyes regarded her with such a spontaneous sympathy that, lowering her gaze, in quick, broken sentences, she told him her story. She grew calmer as she talked, telling him how Henry had almost duped her into a bigamous marriage, of how Alex arrived in time to stop the ceremony. Finally, she told him of her relationship with Alex and that she was to bear his child. She held nothing back.

Seated on the sofa, he listened quietly, attentively, stirring restlessly more than once, and when she had finished he thought over what she had said.

Waiting for him to speak, anxious about what his reaction would be to what she had told him, with her chair drawn up close to him, Lydia watched him. Of late, he appeared to be more relaxed, but he was still frail and the haunted look had not left his eyes. Tears sprang to her own when she realised how disappointed he must be in her.

'You—you do not judge me too harshly, I hope,' she said quietly, having expected anger, instead of which there was a sigh and a faint, sardonic smile. Leaning forwards, he patted her hand as it lay on her lap and sighed deeply.

'I have not the right to judge you, Lydia. I forfeited that when I left you.'

'You are not shocked?'

'Indeed I am. I would be lying if I said I wasn't.'

'I'm sorry. I know how disappointed you must be,' she said forlornly, looking down at her hands. 'I've brought disgrace on myself.'

Her father smiled at her gently. 'Nonsense, my dear. Sometimes a person cannot help the things that happen to them. They are just the victim of circumstance.'

'Or Alex Golding,' Lydia murmured.

'Or Alex Golding. I am glad you did not try to keep this from me. I do not blame you, Lydia. You merely followed your heart. I should have stayed to watch over you, to take care of you, instead of leaving you like I did.' Lydia knew his sorrow and regret over what he had done was genuinely felt. 'I will not speak one word of blame—not to you or Alex Golding.'

'Thank you. I am in this predicament because of my own foolishness. I—I compromised myself when I agreed to—to...'

He touched her arm in an affectionate, comforting gesture. 'Enough. What is done is done.

What we have to do now is consider the future. He does not know of your condition?'

'No.'

'And yet he proposed marriage to you. He must want to marry you very much. What I do not understand is why you refused his proposal.'

Lydia sighed, looking down at her hands folded in her lap. 'Believe me, I was tempted. I found it difficult saying no. But his world—Oh!' she cried, standing up and pacing the floor in frustration. 'It is so very different from mine. He is wealthy, with friends in high places, a grand house in Belgrave Square and a country house in Berkshire. I could never live up to what would be expected of me. Besides, it is certain that his sister would discover my association with her husband. It would be awkward for all concerned. Alex and Miranda are very close. Something like this would be sure to drive a wedge between them. I could not bear to do that to them.'

'And this Miss…Hilton, I believe you said her name was. She warned you off Mr Golding. Does that trouble you?'

'No, not really—although she made it brutally plain that she wants him for herself. When I went to see Alex, she overheard our conversation—everything. If I continue to see him she will tell all to Miranda—who is also with child. Knowing this awful thing about her husband and her brother would distress her immensely. Unfortunately for Irene Hilton, Alex does not reciprocate her feelings. As for me—well, I have my business to think of. I have struggled so hard to get to where I am now. I cannot give it up for...' She fell silent and sighed, shaking her head with dejection.

'For a child,' her father finished calmly.

'Yes—something like that. But I know I can't possibly continue with my work with a child to care for.'

'Why not? Your mother managed it.'

She stopped pacing and smiled down at him. 'Yes—yes, she did—despite all the hardships.'

'There you are then. And you are not alone. You have a good friend in Emily and you can rely on me to help you all I can. You can take on someone to help in the shop when necessary. I am sure that when Mr Golding learns of your condition he will want to marry you all the more.' Seeing doubt cloud his daughter's eyes before she turned away, he felt a moment of alarm. 'You are going to tell him, Lydia?'

She nodded and turned back to him. 'Yes— yes, I will,' she said softly. 'It wouldn't be right not to.'

'Good. Would you like me to be there when you do?'

'No—that will not be necessary. I will write to him at his house in Belgrave Square. I can't imagine how he will react. We did not part the best of friends. I will not marry him, though. I—I cannot. That, I am sure of.'

Three weeks had passed and Alex was still feeling dejected after his bitter parting from Lydia. He sought David's company at his club and often David would call at the house with his sister almost always accompanying him. He had an aversion to Irene and he only put up with her for David's sake. There was a time when he had enjoyed her company, her low, throaty laugh and her enjoyment of life. But she lacked the things he had come to appreciate. Her eyes weren't that wonderful shade of green, her hair was not shining black and she didn't stir the emotions and desires only one woman could stir in him.

She wasn't Lydia.

He busied himself with his business affairs, he even drank more than he normally would to dull the ache, the void, Lydia's absence had left inside him. He remembered how warm and loving she had been and how she had kissed him and caressed him with such tender passion. He couldn't believe that the time had come when his resolve not to become entrapped by a woman had given way to such a battle against his own desire.

Impatient to get out of London where he was constantly reminded of Lydia, he was about to leave for Aspen Grange when David arrived. His baggage was being carried out to the carriage. David found him in his study, sorting through some papers and packing them into a leather case.

The two men were as close as friends could be and as different as night and day. David, with his ash-blond hair and deep blue eyes, was well liked, good-natured and easy going, but he lacked the aura of authority and power that always surrounded Alex.

'I heard you were deserting us for the country, Alex.'

'I have things to take care of. I've neglected things at Aspen of late. I can take care of my business interests from there.'

'How long do you expect to be away?'

'I'm not sure.'

'And the delightful Miranda? Is your sister no longer with you?'

Alex shook his head. 'She's gone home to Surrey—and Henry. She thought he'd been punished enough. I can only hope that with a child on the way he'll mend his ways.' He looked at his friend. 'If you have any plans to go to Berkshire, come and see me at Aspen. We can do a spot of fishing.'

'I might take you up on that.' David turned to look back into the hall. His sister had followed him in and had stopped to speak to the housekeeper. 'Irene is put out that you are leaving town. You know how much she likes your company. She attaches herself to you like a shadow. You'll not shake her off until you find someone else.'

David sensed that Alex was definitely not himself and he suspected the cause was something to do with the young woman Miranda had told him about. 'Speaking of which,' he said with a wicked gleam in his eyes, 'when I last saw Miranda she hinted that there just might be a young lady in the offing.'

'Miranda always did let her tongue run away with her.'

'At the risk of intruding into your thoughts, Alex, might I ask why you are wearing such a formidable frown? Could it be that not everything is going well in that particular department and the young lady is preying too much on your mind?'

'I seldom think of her—if it can be avoided.' Which was true—but impossible. It seemed that whenever Alex thought of Lydia his thoughts became angrily chaotic. She was like some dancing, irrepressible shadow embedded in his mind.

David gave him a laughing, sidelong look. 'So you would have me believe. But I imagine you think of her more than you care to admit. Didn't you help her start up her enterprise or something of the sort?'

'I loaned her some money—which she returned shortly after. Apparently, her estranged father came forward to invest in her enterprise. I suppose I could have dealt with the matter in a more gentlemanly manner. I must admit that I've been unfair to her.'

David quirked a brow, his blue eyes twinkling with light mockery. 'What's this? Are you becoming sentimental in your old age?'

'I am never sentimental,' Alex replied shortly. 'But for the life of me I can't understand why she turned my money down in favour of her father's.'

David regarded his friend with mild cynicism. 'Can't you? Think about it, Alex. For the first time in your life it would appear you have met a woman who is no scheming fortune hunter. From what Miranda has told me she is not a

brainless simpering miss but a proud, respect-
able working girl who has just achieved her
heart's desire—to own her own business.' He
grinned. 'It puts me in mind of you, Alex, when
you were starting out. Remember? Perhaps Miss
Brook doesn't want to drink the finest cham-
pagne and wear expensive jewels.'

'You're right, David. She left me in no doubt
that she wasn't interested in any of that.'

'You mean you discussed it with her? Good
Lord, Alex! Did you ask Miss Brook to marry
you by any chance?' Alex threw him a black look
and said nothing as he opened a drawer in his
desk and took out more important-looking papers. David's amusement could not be restrained
and he laughed out loud. 'You did, didn't you,
you old rascal? And she rejected you? I must say,
I would like to meet your Miss Brook.'

'She is not *my* Miss Brook.'

'She soon could be. Will you see her again so
you can introduce me?'

'I very much doubt it. We didn't exactly part
the best of friends.'

'Methinks Miss Brook gave as good as she
got. Am I right?' Alex merely threw him another thunderous look and continued packing
papers into a case. Becoming more intrigued
about Miss Brook, David said, 'Perhaps you

should write to her and apologise for your behaviour. If you were hard on her—if you tried
to be more understanding—you might find her
more amenable. Try a softer approach. Smooth
her feathers and you'll soon have her purring
like a kitten.'

Alex stopped what he was doing and looked
at his friend as though he'd taken leave of his
senses. 'God in heaven, David! There is nothing
docile about her. Lydia Brook is twenty years
old and has proved to be the biggest distraction I
have ever known in my life. Try a soft approach,
you suggest! Impossible! We are at an impasse.'

'Why?'

'Because we see things differently. We come
from completely different directions. It makes
everything complicated—difficult. We are ill
matched.'

'Difficulties can be surmounted.'

'Not this time. She rejected my offer of marriage. I will not give her a second chance.'

Stupefied, David stared at him, still thoroughly amused. It was unbelievable that Alex,
who always had absolute control over his emotions, who treated women with a combination of
indifference, relaxed tolerance and indulgence,
could have been driven to such an uncharacteris-
tic outburst of feelings by a twenty-year-old girl.

Fastening the straps on his leather case, Alex picked it up and strode into the hall where Harris, his secretary, was waiting. David followed.

'Have any correspondence sent on to Aspen, will you, Albert,' he said to his butler. He looked at David. 'If you take me up on my offer for a spot of fishing, David, perhaps you would be good enough to call here first. There might be correspondence you can bring with you.'

'Of course. I'd be glad to.'

'Does the invite to Aspen Grange extend to me, too, Alex?' Irene asked, sidling forward.

'Of course it does. Although I feel I must warn you that you may end up feeling neglected and become bored with us—unless you like fishing.'

'Not really, but I suppose I could learn—with the right teacher.'

Alex merely smiled. Irene might be charming and pleasing to the eye, but she was greedy and ambitious, and too much like his deceased wife for him to take their relationship further than friendship.

Feeling a little better now that she had shared her secret and some of her anguish with her father and Emily, Lydia managed to get a decent night's sleep. She awoke the following morning, feeling refreshed.

Although she was quaking inside, she sat down to write to Alex. It was the most difficult letter she had ever had to write. Once it was sent, all she had to do was wait for his reply. She knew she somehow had to get through this unpleasant time—and the thousands of other times over the days and weeks and years when, because of her moral transgression and the unfortunate predicament she found herself in as a result of that transgression, she would have to suffer severe censure and ridicule if he did not marry her.

Then began the wait for Alex's reply to her letter.

She would have been outraged if she knew how it had fallen into the wrong hands. Calling at Alex's house in Belgrave Square before going on to Berkshire, David had collected what correspondence there was. Setting it aside while he dealt with other matters, he did not see Irene thumb through it and see how her eyes narrowed when she saw a letter addressed to Alex in a familiar hand. It was the same neat, sloping writing she had seen in Lydia Brook's ledger. A *frisson* of anger shot through her. When her brother's eyes were averted, she slipped it inside her reticule, closed it and let out a long breath. She would take it out and read its contents when she was alone.

Lydia immersed herself in her work, grateful to have something to keep her busy. She was certain Alex would contact her in some way. Would he write back or would he come to see her? He didn't come the next day, nor the next, and after a week had gone by and then another, a terrible fear gripped her and it was all she could do to conceal it from everyone, but Emily watched her closely and tried to take some of the workload from her. Her father called on her every day when the shop was closed. Unable to hide his concern, he offered to call on Alex, to speak to him on her behalf, but Lydia didn't want to involve him.

As more time went by, she was determined not to give in to her fear, telling herself that she must be patient, that she must have faith in Alex, that he would come soon. And so she continued to immerse herself in her work with a cool demeanour that belied the anguish roiling inside her, unable to understand why he had not come. She was glad she had a heavy work schedule because she wanted to keep busy. But she wasn't sleeping well and she grew pale. She knew men took advantage of foolish, inexperienced young women, that when they had got what they wanted they walked away without any remorse. But Alex wasn't like that. He had asked her to marry him. This fact alone kept her hope alive.

Five weeks passed and Alex had made no attempt to see her or contact her. Every time the shop door opened, her heart would leap with anticipation. He could not have known how deeply he had insinuated himself into her heart, how much he had come to mean to her, to be someone she held dear and whose absence had become a source of grief.

She could see Emily and the girls she employed watching her, and it seemed to her that she read some pity in their eyes. But at that moment in her life, pity was one thing she could not endure. And so she lifted her chin, took herself in hand and forced herself to smile and to laugh, no matter what, as long as it hid her feelings. Alex wasn't coming, so she resolved to get on with her life without him. She told herself that she didn't need him.

A note was delivered to the shop by hand from Lady Seymour, informing Lydia that she was back in town and staying at her brother's house in Belgrave Square and she would be grateful if Lydia would call and measure her up for some new gowns. She explained in her letter that she was putting on weight at a tremendous rate with her pregnancy and she needed some new gowns to see her through. She added that she should have thought about it sooner, but she had been at home in Surrey for the past weeks. Henry had to come to London so she had decided to accompany him.

The unexpected request threw Lydia into a quandary.

'What should I do, Emily?' she asked in desperation. 'When I left Alex's house I honestly thought my association with that family was over—and yet here I am in a predicament I would not have chosen. Being asked to make some gowns for his sister is the last thing I want.'

'She probably thinks she's doing you a favour,' Emily said without breaking off doing some fine stitching to a rather delicate chemise. 'It would be good for business and probably bring in more clients of her class. I thought she seemed nice when we met her in the park with her brother. I saw how he looked at you that day—and so did she. Whatever the truth about the letter you sent to Mr Golding, she might be trying to do a bit of matchmaking on her own. I don't see why you shouldn't go to the house and measure her up.'

'I can't, Emily,' Lydia said firmly. 'If Alex wants to contact me he must do it directly and not through his sister. I wrote informing him that he was the father of my baby and for reasons I may never know he has decided not to reply. I have no wish to go to his house again. Besides, what if Henry is there? I really don't want to have anything to do with him. It would place me in a situation that would be unbearably awkward and far too embarrassing to contemplate. It could cause no end of trouble—trouble I would rather avoid.'

'I don't blame you—but what happened was not your fault. What he did to you was disgraceful, but you cannot let it affect your business. If his wife wants you to fit her for some gowns, then I see nothing wrong with that. But if you feel you would rather not then I understand.'

And so Lydia sent a second letter to Belgrave Square. She thanked Lady Seymour for choosing her above more experienced and well-known seamstresses in London to make her some new gowns, but it was with regret that she must decline her order. She stated overwork and that she was afraid Lady Seymour's child would be born before she could complete the order. She hoped she would understand.

* * *

It was Lydia's birthday. As a special gift and to cheer her up, her father called with tickets for the theatre. Lydia was pleasantly surprised.

'Why—yes, I'd love to go. I've never been to the theatre. But—are you sure you are up to it?' she asked, unable to conceal her concern.

He chuckled. 'Absolutely. Don't look so worried. It will do you good to get away from the shop. It's time you had a bit of fun—you, too, Emily. I'm as much of a stranger to the theatre as you are, so it should be an interesting—and entertaining, I hope—evening. It will be my honour to escort two beautiful young ladies to the theatre.'

Emily immediately began planning what she would wear.

When all the stitching and fitting was done and the evening arrived, Lydia was wearing a pale lavender satin dress with slashed inlets of deep purple and a matching satin sash at her waist. Her pregnancy did not yet show and she was relieved the dress fitted her to perfection. Emily looked lovely in a sumptuous sky-blue satin gown with a low bodice and blue lace ruffles. Both girls wore fashionable cashmere shawls to guard against the cool autumn evening. Samuel, despite his frail appearance, looked dapper in his black dress coat and white shirt and waistcoat.

A hired carriage took them to the Royal Lyceum Theatre on Wellington Street, just off the Strand.

'Oh, Lydia, I'm so excited,' Emily whispered, gripping Lydia's hand as they stood their ground among the crush of people. 'I can't believe we're here,' she breathed, smiling broadly, her eyes dancing with delight as she watched titled, wealthy and influential theatre-goers alight from their carriages and enter the theatre. 'I keep having to pinch myself to make sure I'm not dreaming.'

Lydia laughed, amused by her friend's wide-eyed awe and unconcealed excitement. 'Take it from me, Emily, you are not dreaming.'

That they were both looking their most alluring was confirmed by the smiles and appreciative glances of those around them.

With seats in the Royal Circle, they had an excellent, uninterrupted view of the stage. Never having been to the theatre before, both girls were dazzled as they watched a James Planché's fairy extravaganza, featuring spectacular stage effects that held them spellbound.

* * *

It wasn't until the interval that Lydia allowed her eyes to idly scan the audience in the auditorium. It was filled with noise and laughter and people moving about to pay courtesy calls on their friends. Her gaze was drawn across the circle to a lady who was returning to her seat between two gentlemen. Lydia was about to look away when one of the gentlemen rose to let her in. Her eyes became riveted on the group and a sick paralysis gripped her when she recognised Alex as one of the gentlemen.

Feeling her heart slam into her ribs, she froze for an instant, her thoughts scattered. He was seated beside Irene Hilton, beautiful and vivacious in a sumptuous gown of sapphire and silver lace, her hair gleaming and her red lips parted in a wide smile of sensuality. When she saw Irene's hand rest on Alex's arm with a possessive familiarity, leaning close to speak to him, a pain like she had never experienced before bit savagely into her heart.

Not wishing to attract attention to herself, Lydia sat as far back in her seat as she could, hoping her father seated next to her would shield her from view. It was not to be. When the curtain rose, she was unable to resist another glance in Alex's direction and it was at that moment that he seemed to sense himself being watched. He glanced across the distance and saw her. Their eyes locked, but then Lydia looked away and leaned back in her seat again, and Alex's view of her was mercifully blocked by her father. She had not foreseen this—how could she?

Never in the whole of her life had Lydia felt so agonisingly, unbearably jealous of anyone as she did of Irene Hilton at that moment. She swallowed down the tears that almost choked her, wishing she could leave the theatre and not have to sit through the words and music she was deaf to while blind to those about her. Her only conscious thought was that Alex was close by, dancing attendance on another woman.

She could feel his presence with every fibre of her being, and, despite the shock of seeing him again after so long, an increasing comforting warmth suffused her. A strange sensation of knowing he was close at hand pleased her. But the memory of their parting, of the pain and the hurt he had caused by not acknowledging her letter, still pained her.

Emily, noticing her friend's strained profile beside her and sensing that she was not paying attention to what was being acted out on the stage, leaned towards her. 'Are you all right, Lydia? You're not ill, are you?'

'No, no,' Lydia was quick to reassure her, preferring to keep what she had seen to herself. 'I am quite well.'

When the curtain came down and everyone began making their way out of the theatre, Lydia hoped she could avoid seeing Alex. Managing to get outside without a hitch, she began to breathe more easily, her eyes scanning the throng. She caught a brief sight of him standing with another gentleman, even more powerfully masculine and attractive than she remembered, and looking striking in his black-and-white evening attire. For a second their eyes met again, then he looked away, seemingly without interest.

Her father left them to find the carriage, having arranged with the driver who had brought them to the theatre to drive them home. Jostled from every direction by people standing around discussing the performance as they awaited their carriages, Emily was positively bubbling over with her enjoyment of the performance. She had never seen the like.

Waiting patiently for her father to return, Lydia visibly jumped when a female voice said her name.

'Why, Lydia! How lovely to see you here.'

Lydia turned to see Miranda coming towards

her, pushing her way through the throng congregated outside the theatre. Resplendent in a green-satin dress, her face and figure positively blooming with her pregnancy, she was genuinely pleased to see Lydia. It would seem she wasn't too put out by Lydia's polite refusal to take her on as a client.

'Lady Seymour, you take me by surprise. You remember Emily,' she said, drawing her friend forward.

'Yes, of course I do. Have you enjoyed the performance? It was quite a spectacle, don't you agree?'

'We enjoyed it enormously,' Lydia replied. 'We're here with my father. He's gone to see what has happened to the carriage but I'm sure he will be here in a moment,' she said, hoping he would be since she had no wish to see Alex up close. 'I—apologise for not being able to take on your order. I was afraid we would be unable to complete it in time.'

'I understood perfectly. Alex told me some of what transpired between the two of you when you came to see him. I hope you don't mind. Of course it would be difficult for you to take me on after that.'

'Yes—yes, it was something like that.'

'But now you are here you can't leave without saying hello. Like your father, Alex has gone to find the carriage. He shouldn't be too long.'

Before Lydia could make an excuse, Miranda was beckoning to a group of people. Her heart fell when she saw Henry. All she wanted at that moment was for the ground to open and swallow her up. Unable to escape his wife's prompting, Henry, followed by Irene Hilton and another gentleman, came towards them. On seeing Lydia he paled visibly and hung back. She had been so overwhelmed at seeing Alex again that she had failed to look properly at his companions.

Chapter Nine

Miranda drew the stranger forward. 'David, I would like to introduce you to Miss Lydia Brook. You will recall I told you all about her dressmaking enterprise.'

'You did indeed, Miranda,' he said, glad to be introduced to the tantalising young woman who had turned his friend's world upside down. 'May I say I am truly delighted to meet you at last—having heard all about you from Miranda—and Alex, of course.'

'Thank you.' Lydia liked David Hilton at once and for the life of her she could not understand how such a charming and amiable man could possibly be the brother of a woman like Irene. Looking past him to his sister, she smiled. Without opening her mouth to make any polite greeting, Irene merely smiled tightly and turned away.

Miranda looked at her husband standing uneasily behind her, shifting uncomfortably on his feet. 'Henry, come and say hello to Miss Brook.'

'Yes, Henry,' Irene drawled, turning to face them, a smug, knowing glow in her eyes. 'Do say hello to Miss Brook.'

Glancing from Irene to Lydia, Henry turned a queer shade of purple and reached for his handkerchief, clearly wishing he were somewhere else. He murmured a few incoherent words, looking anxiously to Lydia for support. Rising instantly to the occasion, Lydia drew herself up and, desperate not to say or do anything to give Miranda reason to think anything was wrong, she smiled calmly and inclined her head politely, before turning away to look for her father.

Alex was not as immune to Lydia's presence as she might think. He was surprised to see her at the theatre. Having located his carriage, he turned to his companions. Seeing Lydia speaking to his sister with Henry hovering somewhat awkwardly behind her and wishing to avoid any unpleasantness, he hurried towards them.

Nothing had prepared him for his first sight of

Lydia after five weeks apart. His heart wrenched when he looked on her unforgettable face—so poised, so provocatively lovely that he ached to hold her. She was collecting the attention of some of the gentlemen—and to his chagrin he had to concede that dressed in a lavender gown, which set off her stunning figure to perfection, she warranted such admiring regard.

Lydia watched him approach, her mouth dry. After weeks of not seeing him, it was like coming face to face with a stranger. That well-remembered gaze slid around those gathered around her before coming to rest on her. She had not forgotten how brilliant and clear his eyes were—or how hard they could be. As she waited for him to speak to her, her eyes searching his granite features, she saw no sign of the passionate, sensual side to his nature, of the man who had held and kissed her with such tenderness.

'Hello, Alex,' she said quietly, unable to wait any longer to hear his voice. She was painfully aware that all eyes were focused on her. 'I am surprised to see you here.'

'And I you. I did not know you frequented the theatre.'

'I don't,' she replied, trying to remain calm, relieved to see out of the corner of her eye David Hilton take his sister's elbow and escort her to their carriage. She looked again at Alex, gazing at him intently because she wanted to read him and what she wanted to understand was why he had not tried to contact her when he had read her letter. 'I have been so busy of late that my father thought it was time for some recreation.'

'It's also her birthday,' Emily enthused with a happy smile. 'Mr Brook arranged for us to come to the theatre as a special treat.' Never had she been in such illustrious company and she was determined to make the most of it.

'Your birthday?' Miranda repeated.

'Happy birthday,' Alex murmured.

Lydia drew her shawl tighter about her shoulders. She wanted something more from him than happy birthday, but with all eyes upon them she couldn't bring herself to speak to him. Their eyes were locked together. He was good at reading her, at understanding, and he knew this was neither the time nor the place for a discussion between them.

Lydia wasn't aware that her father had returned until he said, 'Aren't you going to introduce me, my dear?'

'Oh—yes, of course.' Lydia made the introductions.

It was an awkward moment for her and she was more than a little anxious when she introduced him first to a sheepish-looking Henry, who was still doing his best to hang back and having very little to say, and then to Alex, wondering how her father would react to the two men who had hurt her. But she need not have worried. Her father could be charming when it suited him and he was now playing the role of a proud father. She was amazed how he had adapted to the refinements of London life— smart clothes, polite manners. No one who did not know him would imagine for one moment that he had spent seven years as a convicted criminal halfway across the world in a penal colony.

'Mr Brook. What a pleasure it is to meet you,' Miranda said. 'Have you only recently arrived in London?'

'A few weeks now—in time to invest in my daughter's enterprise.'

'How fortunate,' she said. 'Where were you before?'

'Travelling,' he said, looking directly at Alex. Lydia had told him that Alex Golding knew about his past and he was hoping he could rely on his discretion. Alex merely nodded.

'I've been out of town myself for the past five weeks—in Berkshire. I only returned yesterday.'

That was the moment Lydia realised he didn't

know about the baby, that he had not received her letter.

Samuel looked at his daughter, aware of her hidden strain. 'The carriage is waiting for us, Lydia. We don't want keep it waiting.'

The look she gave him was of relief. 'Of course.'

Hasty farewells were said and everyone went to their respective carriages.

Alex was quiet on the journey back to Belgravia. Seeing Lydia tonight had been unexpected and a shock. He was torn between torment and tenderness. After spending some time in Berkshire, he felt his anger and pain had finally diminished enough and he could think more rationally about Lydia. Recalling her agonised face when she had left him in his study at Belgrave Square, how vulnerable and hurt she had looked, he ached with remorse. That was when he had decided to return to London.

How could he have thought for one moment that he could purge her from his heart and mind? In his anger that day he would have said he could, but not now. Seeing her once more, in a calmer mood, he knew it was impossible. It mattered to him what happened to this beautiful, intelligent young woman. For the first time in his life he had found a woman who was rare and unspoiled, a woman who had succeeded in touching his heart, which was something all the other women in his life had failed to do.

Alex was on the point of leaving the house the morning after the theatre when he had a visitor. Indeed, it was Samuel Brook, come to speak to him on his daughter's behalf.

'I thank you for receiving me,' Samuel said, handing his top hat to a hovering servant. 'I have come to have a word with you about Lydia. I will not keep you long.'

'You are welcome, Mr Brook. Please, come into the study. We can talk there.'

Inside the study, Alex seated himself by the fire, offering Samuel the seat opposite.

Samuel took the chair and looked straight at the man who had seduced his daughter—although Lydia refused to call it seduction since she had been a willing participant. He couldn't help but admire Alex Golding's calm manner.

'You want to speak about Lydia,' Alex said. 'Does she know you are here?'

'No, she doesn't. But she has given me a full account of her actions since meeting you. As you know I have not been present while she was growing up, which I deeply regret. I know she has told you the reason why, so I will not go into that. I have no right to play the heavy-handed father—I lost the right to interfere in her life a long time ago—but I want you to do right by her. I believe you to be an honourable man.'

'I try to be.'

'Then I expect you to do the honourable thing by Lydia. After your last encounter, she wrote you a letter. I have come to ask you why you did not have the courtesy to reply to her.'

Alex weighed his words carefully before he spoke. 'Had I received any such letter which warranted a reply, I assure you, Mr Brook, I would have done so.'

'So what are you saying? That you did not receive her letter or that in your opinion it did not warrant a reply?'

'The former. I had all my mail sent on to my home in Berkshire, but there was no letter from Lydia. I have a feeling you know its contents.'

'Yes, I do. I also know that you asked her to marry you.'

'I did. She refused.'

'I know that, too. Do you still want to marry Lydia?'

'Why?'

'Because she is carrying your child.'

Alex was struck dumb. His heart pounding

with disbelief, he experienced a wrenching pain of unbearable guilt and a profound feeling of self-loathing. Getting to his feet, he walked to the window while he gave himself over to his thoughts. What had he done? Yes, she had given herself to him willingly, but he should have practised more restraint. How could he have done this to her, when all he wanted was to love her, to be her husband and her friend, to share her hopes and dreams, her laughter and her tears?

When he turned to face Samuel Brook once more, he was thoughtful, impassive—the expression he normally used to shield his thoughts when troubled or angry. A muscle began to twitch in his cheek.

'And this was in the letter?'

'Yes. She wanted you to know—said it was your right. But that does not mean she will marry you—even though she loves you.' He smiled when Alex started at this information. 'Yes, she does. She doesn't know it herself yet, but my instinct tells me this is so. You will have your work cut out persuading her to be your wife. I do not have the power to compel you to do what is right. All I can tell you is what I learned while I was doing brutal, back-breaking penance in Australia. It opened my eyes to the truth of my real crime—that which I did not want to see—the betrayal of the two people that I loved most in the world. They suffered a wound I can never heal. I was a failure and a fool, and I have to live with that for ever. What I want now is for my daughter to be happy. After all she has been through she deserves to be.'

'The possibility that she might refuse to marry me is beyond the bounds of feasibility in my estimation. I would as soon end my life than see her come to harm.'

'Think about that when you go and see her. She values what she has—what she has achieved. She will fight tooth and nail to keep that. But whatever argument she puts to you, don't lose her—or you will end up being the kind of fool I was.'

Lydia was in the shop when Alex came in. Her father had told her that he had paid Alex a visit. She would rather he had left well enough alone and let her deal with it in her own way, but it was done now. One lady being attended to by Emily was in the process of choosing fabric for a new gown and another was browsing through some designs. Lydia stopped what she was doing and gave Alex her full attention.

Conscious of those searing blue eyes on her, she watched him come towards her. Everything was obliterated but that invisible physical force exploding through her body, so that she felt her every nerve spring to a trembling awareness of him—and instinctively she knew it was the same for him.

An unbidden flare of excitement rose up in the pit of her stomach, followed quickly by dread when she thought of the reason that had brought him here. Warily, she watched him, wishing she could cool the waves of heat that mounted her cheeks—wishing she could run away.

Everything about him spoke of control and command. He was aloof, his eyes icy, metallic. His gaze swept over her, narrow, assessing, as if expecting to see her waistline already thickening with child. She stood quite still, her hands folded quietly in front of her, and with her large eyes, which were as wide and solemn as a baby owl's, she had an ethereal quality. Her head was poised at a questioning angle, the darkness of her hair framing her face. But there was a shadowed hollowness to her cheekbones and she was pale, which told Alex that the first weeks of her pregnancy were not going well.

But apart from this he thought she was different, somehow, and his heart took a savage and painful leap at the sight of her. She seemed younger, like a child, making it hard for him to believe he had made love to her—and yet it was a woman who looked at him, with a woman's eyes.

'Can we talk—in your office, perhaps?'

Lydia couldn't help recalling what had happened the last time they went into her office. If she had not succumbed to temptation that day, then she would not be in this predicament now.

'Of course. Please come this way.' When the door had closed behind them she looked at him directly. 'You have spoken to my father.'

'Yes. He came to see me. He told you?'

She nodded. 'I wish he hadn't taken matters into his own hands. I would rather deal with this in my own way.'

'He was concerned about you.'

'I sent you a letter. I even paid someone to deliver it. Do you know what happened to it?'

'No, I don't. I am looking into it. This is a damned unfortunate business, Lydia, and I bear the entire weight of this on my conscience.'

'I agree. It is an unfortunate business, but I was as much at fault as you.'

'The responsibility is all mine,' Alex replied curtly, dismissing Lydia's well-meaning attempt to absolve him. 'Your father and I have discussed the matter and it is our intention to see that things are done right.'

'Indeed?' She tilted her head to one side as she considered him coolly. 'And will you? Do the right thing by me, I mean?'

'I want to—if you will let me.'

'I did not ask for this, Alex. I certainly did not want it. I made a mistake—a grievous mistake. But it has happened—the damage is done—and I must face the consequences.'

'That is something we will both have to do. My lust for you has led me into a trap of my own making—now I, too, must pay the price of my passion.'

'A trap?' she retorted heatedly, hurt by his unfortunate choice of word. 'Is that how you see it? Well, you need not. I know you proposed marriage to me on our last encounter—which was said in the heat of the moment and which I am sure you have had cause to regret. I am certainly not asking you to marry me now—nor would I wish you to under such circumstances. There are still too many issues between us.'

'Those can be easily resolved.'

'You are a gentleman. I am a seamstress. Men of your class make mistresses of women like me, but they don't marry them. You would be ostracised and I would never be accepted.'

'Do you seriously believe any of that matters to me?'

'Maybe not—at least not now. But it might, in the future.'

Alex looked at her with that straight, disconcerting gaze of his. The line of his lips was grim and hard and some new darkness seemed to move at the back of his eyes. 'What of you? Think about it, Lydia. You must be aware of the stigma attached to an illegitimate child, that it will be an object of censure and ridicule throughout its life. And a woman alone with an illegitimate child is prey to the pitilessness of society.'

'I know that. I think of nothing else. At present my consideration is only for the child.'

Alex turned away from her and in earnest meditation he wondered how best to deal with a situation such as she had presented him with, whilst saving her from public humiliation. But one thing stood out above all else, something that was more important to him just then than his feelings for Lydia. After his common sense had done battle with his conscience, his feelings had become possessive, and he knew he could not, would not, disown a child of his blood.

His mouth sat in a bitter line, his black brows drawn in a straight bar across his eyes as he turned back to her. 'You may rest assured that I shall make suitable provision to provide for its future, but I would despise myself if I did not try to do better than that. My obligation is towards you *and* the child.'

'I've told you I want nothing from you.'

Alex's jaw tightened, his eyes burning furiously down into hers. 'Be that as it may, Lydia, you must see that marrying me is the only possible solution to your problems. These are not the most romantic circumstances in which to propose marriage and I am more than likely wounding you by discussing the arrangements in such a blunt way, but we have no choice.'

'Yes, we do. I don't *have* to marry you and it is arrogant of you to assume that I would accept you. You speak as if I have no control over any of this. Well, I have. I recall you telling me on our first encounter that you were not looking for a wife—you gave me the impression that your marriage was something of a disaster, which is why I am surprised that you are willing to repeat the experience.'

'My wife certainly burned almost every emotion out of me.'

'I would have imagined you would have too much common sense to attribute to all women what you have experienced in one,' she said cuttingly.

'I don't. When we met in Scotland—what we

did—you showed me so much vulnerability, so much generous passion. A woman who in her loving was so unlike my wife that I was put on the defensive.'

'Hence your harsh words when I mentioned the word love.'

'I had told myself that I no longer knew what the word meant. That aside, can you deprive a child of its father?'

A lump of nameless emotion constricted Lydia's throat. Abruptly, she turned her back on him. She was struggling against the insidious feeling of surrender which was steadily crushing her, her immediate sensation being one of drowning. How could she endure living the kind of life that would be thrust on her if she married Alex? Then came the realisation that she might have no option. What did it matter whom she married as long as her child was spared the stigma of illegitimacy?

Suddenly nothing seemed important any more. Everything paled beside this. He was right, she thought, with all the bitterness that came with defeat. But when she considered what her feelings were for Alex, she could not deny that he drew her like a magnet. In fact, where he was concerned her mind was all confusion, for she wanted to be his wife, to belong to him, as much as she wanted to be free of him.

As if all the strength had drained out of her, she turned to face him. 'Give me a little time. You may be right—I don't know. But with so many differences between us there will be difficulties and I need to be sure.'

Reading panic overlying her inner tension, Alex softened his expression a little. For the first time in his life he was finding it difficult to tell a woman—this woman—that she was the most alluring and desirable he had ever known. Even now, when the consequences of his actions were so grave, he wanted her. She had become a passion to him, a beautiful, vibrant woman, and he had hurt her very badly.

'Few couples know each other really well before they marry. You will have to take me on trust,' he teased gently.

'If I decide to marry you, then it seems I shall have to—as you will have to take me on trust.'

'We neither of us know what the future holds, but if we are to have any kind of life together we must strive for an amicable partnership. For the sake of the child. In one way or another our parents were never there when Miranda and I were children. Despite the care and kindness of our grandfather, who became responsible for us, it is a dreadful lack for a child when one's parents are absent.'

'Yes, I know—at least what it's like to be without a father.'

'Of course you do. I won't press you now. We both have much to think about. I am leaving for Aspen Grange for the weekend. I invite you and your father to come with me. Perhaps when you see where I live—where I hope we will live together—it will help you to make up your mind.'

'And my work? I cannot abandon what I have started. I have come so far. It means a great deal to me.'

'I know. As my wife you will find there is no need for you to work.'

'I do not do it out of need, Alex. It means more to me than that.'

'I do realise how important it is to you. We will discuss it at some length if you decide to marry me.'

One week later, when Lydia had arranged for a suitable woman to assist Emily during her absence, Lydia travelled to Aspen Grange in Alex's large coach. Her father was unwell—he had come down with a chill which had forced him to decline the invitation. Lydia didn't like leaving him, but he had assured her that he had Mrs

Danby, his landlady, to take care of him and she mustn't worry. Alex had invited Miranda to accompany them, thinking that Lydia would be more relaxed with another woman present. Henry had been invited, too, and, to avoid any awkwardness, Alex was relieved when he declined.

For most of the journey, Lydia stared out of the window of the luxurious conveyance. It was a long time since she had ventured out of London and, despite her underlying anxieties about what might await her at Aspen Grange, she delighted in the scenery fanning out around them. Between pastures and woodland, oaks, beeches, chestnut and alders were draped in red, gold and yellow of autumn. There were villages and farms with chimneys from which grey smoke curled.

Alex sat across from her next to a sleeping Miranda. She was glad when the carriage turned in through tall wrought-iron gates that marked the driveway to Aspen Grange. Nothing had prepared Lydia for the house's exquisite splendour. It was timeless and brooding, its elegant beauty expressing power and pride. The portico at the front of the house overlooked well-manicured lawns surrounded by a flagstone path which disappeared into flowering shrubs and woods beyond.

'Oh, my goodness,' Lydia breathed, with a growing sense of unreality. She had read about the grand houses the English gentry lived in, but never had she envisaged anything as lovely as this. Alex must be very rich to be able to afford to live in such a house.

'Do you like it?' he asked, hoping she wasn't going to be so overwhelmed by Aspen Grange that it would send her haring straight back to London.

'Why—it's beautiful. Is it very old?'

Alex smiled at the dazed expression of disbelief on her face, well satisfied with her reaction. 'I'm afraid it is,' he replied, folding his arms across his chest, preferring to watch a myriad of expressions on her face rather than the approaching house. 'Built over a hundred and fifty years ago, the structure survives relatively unaltered.'

'And all those windows,' Lydia murmured, watching as the late afternoon sun caught the three storeys of huge windows, lighting them up like a wall of flame, contrasting beautifully with the green and yellow tints of fiery shades of the finest autumn foliage. 'I wonder you can bear to leave it for London.'

'Frankly, I wish I had more time to be here more often. With all my business commitments and travelling to consider new investments with new industries starting up all over the country and abroad, I'm actually fortunate to get here once a month.'

The four bay mounts pulling the coach danced to a stop in front of the house. Alex got out, extending his hand to help his sister and Lydia. Servants appeared out of the house and descended on the coach to strip it of its baggage as its occupants entered the house.

At a glance Lydia became aware of the rich trappings of the interior, the sumptuous carpets and wainscoted walls. A fire burned in a huge fireplace, with two sofas facing each other in front of it. An ornately carved oak staircase cantilevered up to the floors above. The butler, a tall, dignified man with rather austere features, stood aside as they entered, keeping a keen eye on the servants to remind them of their duties as their eyes kept straying with curiosity and frank approval to the young woman who stood beside Mr Golding.

Alex turned to a middle-aged woman who had appeared with a rustle of stiff black skirts. 'I'm sure you would like to settle in, Lydia. Mrs Senior, my housekeeper, will show you to your room. Settle in and refresh yourselves before dinner. I thought we'd have a quiet dinner this evening.'

* * *

Later, having freshened up and changed her clothes, Lydia went to join Alex and Miranda in a small candlelit dining room off the main hall. Presenting a pleasing appearance, having donned a deep rose silk gown which complimented her figure, she managed to maintain an outward show of calm, despite the tumult raging inside her.

The opulence and elegance of her bedchamber, offering a splendid view of the gardens, had taken her breath away, and as she had made her way through the rooms of Aspen Grange, filled with treasures representing decades of possession by the Golding family, it was the kind of lineage that Lydia could never claim for herself. The walls were hung with a varied selection of artwork—not family portraits, which was what she had expected to see, but beautiful landscapes and paintings of an equestrian nature, indicating the owner's love of horses and field sports.

Alex was standing by the sideboard, pouring red wine into three glasses. Lydia was struck by his stern profile outlined against the golden glow of the gas lighting—newly installed, the housekeeper had proudly informed her. He seemed preoccupied somehow, which was hardly surprising, considering everything that had happened in the past week. He turned when she entered and moved towards her, his narrow gaze sweeping over her with approval.

'I hope I haven't kept you waiting.'

'Not at all. Miranda isn't down yet.' Alex handed her a glass of wine.

Leaning against the mantelpiece, Alex watched as she sank onto a green-and-gold striped sofa and carefully arranged her skirts. 'Have you thought any more about my proposal, Lydia?'

'Yes,' she replied, wishing he hadn't asked her that question straight away. 'Nothing has changed since last we spoke, but I expect I shall have to concede in the end. Although I must stress that I value my freedom and independence too highly to give it up lightly.'

Alex's jaw hardened. 'So, unlike others of your sex, you harbour no ambition to snare a wealthy husband.'

Her eyes flared. 'That was uncalled for, Alex. Material wealth does not interest me. I would marry the meanest pauper if I loved him and he returned that love.'

'And me?'

She looked at him directly. 'Why, Alex, do you love me?' Her question seemed to take him by surprise. When he failed to answer, her lips curved in a disappointed, bitter smile. 'I'm sorry. I should not have asked you that. When I marry

I want a man who will be a true husband to me, with whom I can share a love everlasting—not a man who will marry me for no other reason than that I am to bear his child. I am in charge of my own destiny, Alex, not you.'

'Not when you are carrying my child,' he stated coldly.

'You cannot force me to marry you.'

His eyes glittered like shards of ice. 'No? We'll see about that. I always get what I want in the end. It would serve you well to remember that.'

'Always is a long time.'

'Don't be difficult, Lydia. There will be no choice,' he stated bluntly.

Lydia was unable to argue further for at that moment Miranda swept into the room. Rejuvenated after her nap on the journey, she was her usual chattering self. If she noticed the tension that existed between her brother and Lydia, she gave no sign of it. As yet she did not know that Lydia was to bear Alex's child, but Alex had made no secret of the fact that he wanted to marry her, and Miranda was openly delighted.

Throughout dinner Alex presided over the meal with his usual calm composure. He was politely courteous and attentive to both Lydia and

Miranda, giving no hint of his feelings, but sensing his perusal, as if he were feeling compelled and at liberty to look his fill, Lydia met his intent gaze and, hot, embarrassed colour stained her cheeks. He responded with a querying, uplifted brow.

As the meal progressed and the more Lydia's mood softened, there was something in Alex's eyes which made her feel it was impossible to look at him. There was also something in his voice that brought so many new and conflicting themes in her heart and mind that it made her wonder why she was making everything so difficult for them both. Why did she not just tell him she would marry him and that would be that?

In danger of becoming hypnotised by that silken voice and those mesmerising eyes—the fact that he knew it, that he was deliberately using his charm to dismantle her determination to stand against him, confused her. As soon as she had finished her dessert she pleaded tiredness and asked to be excused.

'Oh, but would you like some coffee before you leave?' Miranda asked, hoping she would say yes. 'Or perhaps you would like to stay a while longer and play a game of cards—or chess, perhaps?'

'No…thank you, Miranda. I…have a head-ache. Perhaps tomorrow night.'

Alex accompanied her to the door, opening it for her. 'I am sorry you are leaving us so soon.'

Meeting his gaze, Lydia felt her flesh grow warm. His nearness and the look in his eyes, which had grown darker and far too bold to allow her even a small measure of comfort, washed away any feeling of confidence. The impact of his closeness and potent masculine virility was making her feel altogether too vul-nerable—it was just the sort of situation that had got her into this predicament in the first place.

'It's been a long day. I'm sure I'll feel better after a good night's sleep.'

'Of course. I hope you sleep well. I must warn you that the old timbers creak and groan, so don't be alarmed if you hear anything untoward in the night. Tomorrow I will show you around. I have something I want you to see.'

Lydia felt a sudden quiver run through her as she slipped away from him, a sudden quicken-ing within, a quickening she was all too famil-iar with every time she was with him. She went up the stairs quickly, feeling his eyes burning holes into her back as she went.

'Where are you taking me?' Lydia asked, when she sat next to Alex in the open carriage the following morning. 'And why is Miranda not with us?'

'Because I want to spend some time with you alone—which is also why I've left the driver behind and taken the reins myself.'

The day was fine although the night had seen considerable rain. But now the air was crisp and clean and the sky displayed a wealth of cumulus clouds. They drove through a stunning rolling parkland defined by magnificent trees of oaks and beeches and copses of birch and poplars and firs. Deer lifted their heads, as if to evaluate these intruders into their territory, before scampering off into the trees.

Lydia was transfixed by all she saw. 'Do you own all this?' she asked, completely entranced.

'No. Just Aspen Grange. All this belongs to David. We are neighbours—in fact, if you look into the distance, above the trees you can just see the rooftops of his house, Sunninghill Hall.'

This was news to Lydia. She could make out the house Alex pointed out to her, but she didn't ask him about his friendship with Sir David Hilton since it would remind her of his hostile sister. Any conversation they had about that particular woman would ruin her day.

Alex halted the carriage on the brow of a hill overlooking a small hamlet. The sun was high, but it had rained earlier. Two rows of gardenless cottages ran down the hill. Some dwellings were inhabited, some derelict. A narrow road ran like a ribbon of mud between them. More cottages stood away from the hamlet, some standing alone in their own gardens, giving the feeling that the families who lived in them were superior to the those who lived in the rows.

Alex climbed down from the carriage and urged her to do the same, holding out his hand to assist her. The silence was broken by birdsong. Three ragged children emerged from one of the cottages and stood looking at them.

Puzzled as to why he had brought her to this place, which seemed like the end of nowhere to Lydia, where poverty seeped out of the dwellings and looked out of the empty eyes of the children like a visitation of the angel of death, she looked at him. 'What is this place? It is difficult to imagine that anyone can live in this place. Those children are barefoot.'

'It's called Low Field Row.'

'Does it have any particular significance?' she asked, uneasily conscious that he had brought her to this place for a purpose.

He nodded. 'I wanted you to see this. I could not bear to tell you about this before. You have a vision of me in your head, a picture of a man you believe to be me. I am about to spoil that image.'

Something in his voice, in his manner, broke through Lydia's defences. 'Tell me.'

'There is still too much between us, too many misunderstandings. I want to recover the closeness we shared before I went to France. I cannot let you go, Lydia. I thought if you knew more about me, you'd understand why it doesn't matter to me what you do, where you come from or the fact that your father was a convicted criminal. Do you see the dwelling at the bottom of the row on the right-hand side?'

'Yes,' she murmured, seeing a crumbling house with holes in its roof and heavily overgrown with ivy, brambles and weeds.

'That was where I lived for the first ten years of my life. It was my home.'

There was something about the hardness beneath his tone that made Lydia feel he was about to disclose something important. 'What are you saying?'

'I was born in that house—Miranda, also.'

Lydia's unease grew. 'But...you live at Aspen Grange. I—I believed it to be your ancestral home.'

'You were wrong. There is no ancestral home. When I was a boy I would often find my way to Aspen Grange. I had an insatiable drive to learn, to succeed in everything I set my mind to. I was determined. I would tell myself that I would own that house one day—or one like it. I was fortunate. Eight years ago it was up for sale. I bought it.'

Lydia stared at him. His disclosure certainly explained the absence of family portraits hanging on the walls of Aspen Grange. As far as she knew, Alex was a wealthy English gentleman who spent a great deal of his time working on his many business enterprises, a man who succeeded in everything he did.

Reading her thoughts, he gave her a bitter smile. 'I'm sorry to have to shatter any illusions you may have about me, but the truth is that I grew up in squalor—like those children down there—without shoes on my feet. I was not born with a title like Henry—or with a silver spoon in my mouth. My childhood was not in the least like you imagine it to be. My parents were drunkards. My father was a violent man—drink made him that way. Most of the time he wasn't fit for work. What we had came from my maternal grandfather. It was hell for Miranda. My grandfather lived in Newbury. He did what he could, spending every penny he had on my education. He managed to send me to Marlborough. When my parents died, both Miranda and I went to live with him.'

'But...your parents... What happened to them?' The pain in his eyes made her heart ache.

'They died within months of each other when I was ten years old. I don't come here any more because I never want to remember.' The memories nearly choked him.

'I am appalled by what happened to you. How could your parents do that to you? I am so sorry for what you suffered, Alex.'

He looked at her. 'Don't feel sorry for me.'

'But you were just a boy.'

'Maybe, but I was not the one to feel sorry for, Lydia. It was harder for Miranda. I once told you that we had more in common than you realised—that we weren't so very different. Well, now see for yourself. This is it. This is where I lived with Miranda.'

Lydia could hardly bring herself to believe the beautiful Miranda and her brother had lived in this squalid district. 'Your friend—Sir David Hilton—he must know you lived here as a boy.'

'No. This place and Sunninghill Hall were close but might as well have been a thousand miles apart. We neither of us knew each other until we met at school.'

'And you didn't tell him?'

'No. He knew Miranda and I lived with our grandfather in Newbury—but not here.'

'Were you ashamed, Alex?'

He looked at her, the pain undiminished in his eyes. 'Yes, I admit it, I was ashamed. Who wouldn't be—living down there?'

'Who do the houses belong to?'

'The owner of Sunninghill Hall.'

'David Hilton?'

He nodded. 'The people who inhabit them are estate workers and their families.'

'And was that your father's occupation?'

He nodded again. 'When he was sober enough to turn up. David's father died recently and now David is in charge he is to demolish the houses—thank God—and not before time.'

'What will happen to the people who live here?'

'They will be found new accommodation—better than this.'

When he fell silent Lydia looked at him, really looked at him. His mouth was compressed. She could still see the pain in his light blue eyes, a great deal of pain that shocked her out of all feeling for herself. She looked at his proud, lean face with its firm jaw and stern mouth, but all she saw was a dark-haired little boy—alone, frightened, trying to do the best for his sister and determined to succeed.

How could she have been so wrong about this man? He had been hurt almost beyond bearing, so badly that he'd kept his pain hidden, allowing no one to come close enough to uncover it. That he was doing so now, to her, told her he very much wanted her in his life. She knew how much it was costing him to open up his past to her, because he possessed as proud a spirit as she.

'I can't imagine how you survived that,' she whispered achingly, feeling a lump of poignant tenderness swell in her throat. Unthinkingly, she took his hand and raised it to her lips. 'I'm so sorry, Alex.'

'What for?'

'For being so difficult.' There was so much more she wanted to say to him, but she felt unfamiliarly nervous and ashamed. She stared at the strong-boned face, the face she loved so much. 'I convinced myself that there was a social gulf between us.'

'And just how antiquated do you think that sounds? Good Lord, Lydia, we are not living in the dark ages.'

'No, I know that. What we experience as children, along with our backgrounds, moulds us from the very beginning to be who we are as adults—without the culture and tradition that guides one through life.'

'It's in the past—a past that for a long time refused to leave me. It followed me around like a starving dog, making me more and more determined to succeed in whatever I set out to do.'

'Why didn't you tell me all this before? Is it because you are ashamed, because if you are then you shouldn't be. You are one of the bravest people I know and you should be proud of the way you turned your life around, of all you have achieved.'

'I had to. Miranda looked to me—depended on me. I had to take care of her, to try to give her a better life. When she met Henry and fell in love with him, even though I had my doubts about him, I could not deny her.'

'Little wonder she adores you.'

Alex's expression softened. 'What of you, Lydia? Will you adore me?'

'I think I already do. I don't care where you came from—who your parents were. It's who you are now that counts.'

'That's what I tried telling you, but you wouldn't listen.'

'I will now. Whatever our pasts, Alex, we cannot allow it to affect how we feel about each other. Do you still want to marry me?'

'Of course I do,' he said, taking hold of her and drawing her into his arms, 'and not for the sake of duty or because I feel obligated.'

'Then tell me why. I need to know,' she whispered. Her body became still in his arms, her cheek resting against his chest as she waited, not breathing, anticipating his next words.

Tightening his arms around her, Alex placed his lips on the top of her head. 'It's because I love you,' he said fiercely. 'When Blanche died I persuaded myself that I would never fall in love again, that I would have the strength of character to withstand such a debilitating emotion, but then I had not met you. I cannot remember when I came to love you, but I can't deny that I have been unable to get you out of my mind since the moment I set eyes on you in Scotland. I love you very much indeed,' he whispered. 'I knew straight away that you were different to any other woman I have known. I didn't recognise what I was feeling. But suddenly you became the light of my life and my body and my soul craves for you.'

Lydia turned her face up to his, her eyes shining with all the love that was in her heart. 'I can't bear to think I could have lost you.'

His mouth quirked up in one corner. 'Does this mean that you are finally warming to me?'

She nodded, looking up at him with tear-bright eyes. With sudden heartbreaking clarity the fact that she might have lost him when he had come to mean everything to her was overwhelming. 'I think I must be. I can think of no other reason why I am crying.'

'Even though you refused my proposal of marriage—when I would have made you my wife, child or no child.'

'I know. It was foolish of me. I'm a very complicated woman.'

His lips curved in a leisurely smile. 'I'm beginning to realise that.'

The smile she returned was tremulous. 'Do you mind?'

'Not in the least. I'm beginning to warm to you, too.'

'I'm glad. You see, I love you, too, Alex. Very much indeed.'

An unbearable sense of joy leaped in Alex's heart. The yielding softness in her eyes, the rosy flush that bespoke her youth, brought faint stirrings of an emotion he'd thought long since dead. Reaching out, he cupped her chin in his fingers, tilting her face to his and gently placing his lips on hers.

'Thank you,' he murmured. 'I'm relieved we have finally reconciled our differences.'

Lydia tilted her head sideways. 'So you would like to think. There is still one important matter that concerns me.'

'Which is?'

'My work.'

'You will have a child to focus your energies on. Why would you want to work?'

'Because I do. I will not give it up, Alex.'

He looked at her hard, love glowing in his eyes as he considered her words. Taking her face in his hands, he gave her a light, lingering kiss full of promise for the days and years to come. 'I will not expect you to do that. We will work something out.'

'Thank you.'

She was glad she had heard what he had to say. It was strange to think she had held herself from him, from his proposal of marriage, because of who she was, because of what she was. Now she wondered if it even mattered.

Chapter Ten

Surfacing from a deeply passionate kiss, seated beside Alex in the carriage before they set off back to the house and knowing their newfound happiness could not be concealed, Lydia sighed, relieved that all the deliberations and heart searching were over. For better or for worse she was going to be Alex's wife.

Holding her in his arms, Alex was content to let his eyes dwell on her beloved face, to gaze into the depths of her eyes, to glory in the gentle sweep of her long dark lashes which dusted her cheeks. Unable to resist her and overcome by a strong desire to draw her mouth to his and taste the sweetness of her quivering lips once again, he placed his mouth on hers and she parted her lips to receive his kiss, her heart soaring with happiness. He kissed her slowly and deliberately, and Lydia felt a melting sweetness flow through her bones and her heart pour into his.

With a deep sigh Alex drew back and gave her a searching look, his gaze and his crooked smile drenching her in its sexuality.

'There are times, Lydia Brook, when you confound me,' he murmured, placing his warm lips on her forehead before he took up the reins. 'Now enough of this—you are in danger of being made love to here and now if we do not get a move on. We should get back. There's going to be rain soon.'

Lydia sighed and settled against him. 'I can't believe I am to marry you.'

'Believe it, my love. I intend to marry you as soon as it can be arranged.'

'You know I am not cut out to be a lady of leisure, Alex, with so many servants to do my bidding.' She smiled. 'Still, when I'm not designing my dresses, I can always look after you—iron your shirts…whatever it is that wives do.'

'I have a housekeeper for that.'

'Then I can help you with your work—take notes. Write letters.'

He turned his head and grinned at her. 'I have Harris to do that.'

She stared at him and then she laughed, which

was a joyous sound to Alex's ears. 'There you are then. Heaven forbid that I should tread on Mr Harris's toes. Since you are so well taken care of there will be nothing at all for me to do except die of boredom if I don't work.'

'You are forgetting that you will soon have a baby to take care of.'

'I haven't—but no doubt we will have a nanny and a nursemaid to help me with that as well.'

Falling silent, she settled down to enjoy being with him. She could hardly believe how deep her feelings were running and the joy coursing through her body melted the very core of her heart. She loved Alex. She knew that now and that perfect certainty filled her heart and stilled any anxiety she might otherwise have had.

Except one, and she was somewhat deflated by the thoughts that suddenly assailed her.

Attuned to her every mood, Alex glanced across at her. 'What is it? You look troubled.'

'How long do you think it will be before Miranda gets to know what happened in Scotland—how Henry betrayed her with me?'

'Do you want her to know?'

'Perhaps it would be best all round if we were honest with her and told her the truth. Then we could move on. Although I don't want the subterfuge to cause a rift between the two of you.

There is something I haven't told you. Irene Hilton knows about us.'

His jaw hardened. 'Irene? How?'

'She overheard our conversation that day I called to see you—when you asked me to marry you. The fact that she is holding this information that will devastate Miranda if she lets it be known does concern me.'

Alex nodded, thoughtful. 'I agree. Better if it comes from me. Miranda already knows Henry was involved with a woman so that part is taken care of. How she will feel and react when she realises that woman was you is another matter entirely.'

When they arrived at Aspen Grange they were surprised to see a carriage in front of the house. Lydia's stomach sank when she saw David and Irene Hilton climb out.

'Oh, dear,' she breathed.

'What the hell are they doing here?' Alex growled. 'I certainly didn't invite them.'

Lydia found it difficult being in the presence of Irene. When Alex stepped forward to greet them, automatically she held back, but sensing her reluctance, Alex drew her forward.

'I knew you were coming to Aspen for the weekend so I thought I'd call,' Sir David said with a smile that embraced both of them. 'Hope you don't mind, but I couldn't resist meeting the charming Miss Brook once more.'

'Of course I don't mind,' Alex replied. 'And I'm sure Miss Brook would want you to call her Lydia.'

'Yes,' Lydia said, responding quickly. 'Please do.'

Eager to meet once more the tantalising young woman who had bewitched his friend, David moved towards her. As he reached for her hand, his handsome face broke into a brilliant, reassuring smile and his eyes twinkled with delight. 'Your servant, Miss Brook,' he said, bending over and pressing a gallant kiss on the back of her hand. 'And may I say I am truly delighted to meet you again—and looking just as lovely,' he said meaningfully, casting his friend a mocking, lopsided grin.

On seeing Lydia's cheeks flush a delicate pink, Alex laughed. 'Don't be embarrassed by David's flattery. He's harmless enough. Irene, his sister, you have already met.'

'Yes, we've met,' Lydia replied coolly, noting how Irene held back. She liked David Hilton—he had made a pleasing impression on her when she had met him at the theatre and for the life of her she could not possibly understand how such a charming and amiable man could have such an obnoxious sister.

'You must stay for lunch,' Alex said. 'Miranda's here as well—somewhere.'

'And Henry?' Irene asked, sliding her eyes to Lydia with subtle meaning. There was something in their depths, something malevolent, which no one else saw but Lydia.

'Not Henry. He has things to do in Surrey.'

Irene smiled, showing her perfect teeth. 'Really? How convenient,' she replied blandly, turning from them and sweeping into the house in search of Miranda.

Aware of Irene's hostility towards her—she clearly resented sitting down to lunch with a woman who had to work for a living, for in the world in which she lived, class and distinction were to be observed—Lydia was mostly quiet throughout the meal, content to listen to the conversation with a polite interest, conscious that Irene tried to exclude her from any discussion.

Her appetite having deserted her, she toyed with her food, mostly cutting the meat and moving it around her plate. Alex watched her. His eyes were warm and his lips curved in a secret smile. It was meant to encourage her, to tell her all would be well soon enough. Talk was of matters in general and the time David and Irene had spent in France. They also discussed horses, the main topic being the winter's hunting.

'We often come during the winter months for the hunting—fox hunting, you understand,' Irene said condescendingly to Lydia. 'Is that not so, Alex?' Without waiting for him to reply, she went on, 'There is always a good turnout. Do you hunt, Miss Brook?' she asked, watching Lydia like a hostile cat while knowing full well that she didn't.

'No—I don't ride, let alone hunt. I don't think I would care for it.'

'Goodness! Don't tell me you are one of those people who are against hunting, Miss Brook,' Irene said imperiously.

'It is not my idea of a pleasurable pastime, if that is what you mean,' Lydia replied, becoming increasingly irritated by Irene's manner.

'Alex always enjoys country pleasures—is that not so, Alex?'

'Very much, as it happens, but that does not mean Lydia has to share our enthusiasm for field sports, Irene.'

Irene's eyes narrowed. 'I don't suppose she has to. However, it is hardly a pastime but a way of life—as it has been for generations past.'

Determined to keep calm, Lydia looked her in the eye. 'That does not mean to say it is right.'

'But everyone enjoys it—you only have to ask them, riders and hounds alike.'

Lydia had to admit that she wouldn't mind learning to ride over the open countryside, but she couldn't help saying, with a delicate lift to her eyebrows, 'Then it's a pity no one thought to ask the fox.'

Two angry spots appeared on Irene's cheeks and she pursed her lips. Knowing that she was silently fuming, trying desperately to control her temper for fear she'd made a fool of herself, Lydia exchanged looks with Alex, and he grinned lazily, frankly amused by the short interchange between them. However, sensing a skirmish, Miranda put her napkin on the table and rose.

'I think I'll take a walk on the terrace. It is rather warm in here. Would anyone care to join me?'

Lydia stood up, glad of the reprieve Miranda was offering. 'I will join you in a few minutes, Miranda. I'll just go to my room for a shawl.'

In her room she lingered a while, reluctant to face Irene again and wishing she would leave. Eventually, draping a shawl about her shoulders to guard against the chill, she found her way to the terrace, where Miranda and Irene had been joined by Alex and David.

Irene watched her walk towards them, 'Miss Brook! I am bemused as to why you are here. I would have expected you to be far too busy in that shop of yours to spare the time for a visit to the country.'

Alex overheard what she said and moved to stand beside Lydia, taking both her hands in his. He smiled down at her, his lips lifting at the corners in his joy. She allowed her hands to remain in his. What he was showing her in his warm light blue eyes told her of his feelings. Raising her hands before the three spectators, he kissed them, a declaration that none of them could ignore and caused Irene's eyes to narrow with anger.

'I invited Lydia to spend the weekend here.'

'Why on earth would you do that?' Irene asked.

'Because, Irene,' Alex said, glancing down at Lydia, 'and I hope Lydia won't mind if I make an announcement—but she has done me the honour of consenting to be my wife.'

There was a long moment of absolute silence in which everyone seemed to hold their breath, then Miranda rushed forward, her expression one of genuine delight as she hugged both her brother and future sister-in-law, happy for them both.

'I knew it,' she said. 'I knew you would eventually agree to his proposal, Lydia. I am so happy for you both.'

'Me, too,' David said, slapping Alex good-naturedly on the back and kissing Lydia warmly on the cheek.

Irene's body was rigid with hatred as she watched Miranda and David pour their good wishes on the happy couple. It was evident she would never forgive this woman for stealing the man she had earmarked for herself.

The sudden change in the weather put an end to the congratulations. It began to rain so they went back inside into the drawing room. Miranda made herself comfortable on a sofa at right angles to the fireplace. Irene sat next to her. Alex and David moved to the library next door to drink a celebratory brandy. Reluctant to be too near Irene, Lydia went to look at the pictures that adorned the walls.

She had nothing to talk about with Irene. Irene had no interest in hearing what she had to say and Lydia had no interest in her, which rather limited the conversation between them. But it seemed that now Alex and David were no longer within earshot, Irene had plenty to say.

'Naturally I was surprised when David told me Alex had invited you to Aspen Grange for the weekend—and now we know the reason why. And you are here, too, Miranda, and without Henry. I did think that rather odd—but, thinking about it, I don't suppose it is. Is it, Miss Brook?'

Lydia felt her nerves tighten. A searing white light seemed to dance in front of her eyes. She felt hot, blazingly hot, and physically sick as she waited for Irene to do her worst. Irene got to her feet, facing her so that her focus was on her and not Miranda. It was a tense moment in which Lydia waited for more. She felt her heart pounding in her chest and the blood started singing in her ears. Outside, a gust of wind and the rain that had begun to fall hit the lead-paned windows of the room. Lydia was the one to flinch.

Irene smiled. 'Worried, are you, Miss Brook?' She laughed, a thin strident sound, clearly enjoying sticking in the knife. 'You should be. You are a sly one. How well you have engineered all this.'

Lydia paled. 'I don't know what you mean.'

'Then let me explain. When you found you couldn't have Henry—you turned your sights on Alex. You're a quiet one,' Irene sneered. 'The quiet waters of your outward appearance run deep enough for us all to swim in.'

Miranda gave her a puzzled look, for Irene's eyes and her voice were full of something she did not care for. And what did Henry have to do with this? 'What on earth are you talking about, Irene?'

Irene felt it was time to inject her poison, knowing full well the effect it would have on Miranda when she saw the awful truth about her precious husband and brother—and the up-start who thought she was good enough to marry Alex. 'I am talking about Alex—and Henry. Clearly, you don't know.'

Miranda's brain was numb, for all her senses told her that something was badly wrong, that what Irene was about to tell her was not going to be pleasant. 'Tell me. I don't understand.'

'You will,' Irene said, her eyes narrowing and glittering viciously as she prepared to de-liver her trump card, 'when I tell you that Miss Brook was the woman who ran off to Scotland with Henry to be married. When you know for yourself who she really is, then I doubt you will want to welcome her into the family.'

It became so quiet in the room that the steady tick of the clock on the mantelpiece sounded like a gun being repeatedly cocked.

Finally, Miranda said, 'What did you say?'

Irene's face expressed a look of malicious triumph, but before she could repeat the words that damned three of the people in the room, David, along with Alex, who had just arrived in the open doorway in time to witness the scene unfold, said, 'Stop it, Irene. This isn't necessary.'

'I'm afraid it is at this point.'

Miranda digested the knowledge slowly, unable to believe what Irene had disclosed. There was an appalled silence as she stared wordlessly from Alex to Lydia, giving them both a look of condemnation. Irene watched and rejoiced with gloating eyes. In alarm, Alex went to his sister, for in that instant he could see Irene had dealt her a crippling blow.

Miranda looked at Lydia in a way that made Lydia feel that the thousand truths she had hidden from Miranda were there, openly displayed, and she was reading them all. The blood had drained from Miranda's face and her eyes had a haunted, almost desperate expression.

'You and Henry?' she asked, looking at Lydia, who nodded dumbly. 'I didn't know.'

'How could you?' Irene said, excitement over the disastrous effect her revelation had caused bringing a bright glitter to her eyes and showing in every line of her body. 'It would appear that the three of them have deceived you in the most cruel manner. And you were taken in by Miss Brook just as well as I—which goes to prove she's a better actress than either of us realised. She has an artful tongue and it is clear that her powers of persuasion are so remarkable that she managed to capture both your husband and your brother.'

Alex straightened from Miranda's side. There was no softness in his expression, no emotion either, and the ice-cold slivers in his eyes and the marble severity of his face left Irene in no doubt of his anger. 'Shut up, Irene. I think you've said quite enough.'

Irene's vicious outpouring had left Lydia speechless. Still, perhaps it was better that what had transpired in Scotland was out in the open, but it did not justify the cruel brutality of Irene's words and the devastating impact they had on Alex's sister.

'I am so dreadfully sorry about this, Miranda,' she whispered. 'We—Alex and I—intended to tell you when we returned from our drive this morning, but when we saw Sir David and Miss Hilton...'

'Please don't say anything,' Miranda said hoarsely, pushing her brother's hands away as he tried to draw her close again. 'Not now. I—can't take it in.' With her head lowered she turned away. 'I'm going to my room. Excuse me.'

'I suppose you'll be leaving now,' Irene said calmly to Lydia as Miranda went out of the room, her eyes aglow with smug satisfaction and a triumph that ever since she had seen Lydia in Alex's carriage she'd obviously been waiting to savour.

Lydia looked at her, her face cool and exquisitely set. Yet inside her the anger that she managed to keep under ruthless control swirled around her in waves. 'I am not. And did you have to tell Miranda in such a brutal manner with such malicious joy? It doesn't matter to me—or to Alex, for that matter—but Miranda is with child. What you have said today might have done her untold damage.'

A brief flash of contrition came and went in Irene's eyes. 'It's as well that she knows what her husband gets up to when he's not with her.'

'Miranda already knew and she dealt with it in her own way. I congratulate you. You have most certainly done your worst.'

'There is one thing before you leave, Irene,' Alex said, finding it virtually impossible to restrain his anger. 'I have a feeling you can clear up a matter that has been giving me one hell of a headache. It concerns a letter Lydia wrote to me—a letter which mysteriously disappeared around the time I left for Aspen on my return from France. I suspect you know all about that letter, don't you, Irene?'

Her face chalk white, Irene stared across the room at his relentless features. In an attempt to lie her way out of a predicament she had not foreseen, she said, 'Letter? What letter? I know nothing about a letter and that is the truth.'

'Truth?' David said sharply. 'You wouldn't know how to tell the truth if it leapt up and hit you in the face.'

Irene cringed at her brother's tone. 'Really, David! This is quite preposterous. I have no idea what you are talking about.'

'Do not insult my intelligence with your denials. Tell the truth, Irene. You removed the letter from the pile I picked up in Alex's London house, didn't you?'

'Don't be ridiculous. How on earth would I know if it was from her?'

'Because you recognised my handwriting,' Lydia said quietly. 'You saw me writing in my ledger when you called to see me at the salon. You would have recognised it on the envelope.'

David was astounded. 'Why did you call on Lydia, Irene? And for God's sake do not tell me it was to order a new gown. You went to warn her off Alex, didn't you, because you wanted him for yourself?'

Alex saw the truth mirrored in her eyes. 'If that was what you wanted, Irene, then you deceived yourself. Not once have I given you reason to believe you are anything more than the sister of my closest friend. Yes, I always knew you were available, too ready to grasp everything I could give you, but you were too much like my first wife to even consider making you my second. You did take the letter, didn't you?'

Irene's hands were clenched by her sides and her face so contorted with rage that it was almost ugly. 'Yes, all right, I did. I admit it.'

'And you also read the contents so you must know that Lydia is carrying my child.'

'Yes,' she hissed, 'I do know that—that you have fathered a brat on a common shop girl—for no matter what she tries to aspire to, she will always remain what she is. A plain nobody.'

The callous bluntness of her reply jarred every one of Alex's nerves. He moved close, looming over her, and never had Irene seen such an expression of fury in any man's eyes. 'And you have a warped definition of how a well-bred young woman should behave. Lydia could give *you* lessons in the art of being a lady.'

Irene stiffened. 'How dare you say that to me?

She may put on a hoity-toity manner and boast a superiority of mind that is positively sickening, but what do you think will happen if it gets out what sort of woman she really is? It will do her no good—her shop even less.'

No human emotion could be traced on Alex's face. In a silky, menacing voice, he said, 'If it is your intention to disclose any of this, or cause Lydia and Miranda any unnecessary suffering, then I advise you to reconsider.' He looked at David who, like himself, was finding it difficult keeping his rage under control. 'Take her home, David. Make sure that if she is nothing else she is discreet on this matter.'

'Don't worry, Alex. There will be no scandal. If she so much as breathes one word that will bring disgrace on either Lydia or your sister and your good name, I swear I will personally wring her neck.' These words were spoken in a cold, lethal voice, leaving Irene in no doubt that he meant it.

She drew herself up with nervous hauteur. 'You can't threaten me, David.'

'No?' Alex inquired. 'But I can. David meant every word. There is one thing you should know about me, Irene, and that is that I am a very determined man and if any harm comes to any of mine through your hand, I will destroy you. Believe me when I tell you that you don't want me for an enemy. Now leave us. You have said quite enough,' Alex said sharply.

There was a moment of impasse during which no one moved. Finally, David took his sister's arm and escorted her to the door. 'Go to the carriage and wait for me there,' he ordered his sister. He turned and looked at Alex and Lydia. 'I am so sorry about this. She has caused immense and unnecessary distress to all concerned—especially to Miranda. I had no idea...'

'Don't worry about it, David,' Alex said. 'What is done cannot be undone. None of this is your fault.'

'I have the full measure of my sister and you may be assured that you will not see her for a very long time. I intend to send her back to Paris. Fortunately she has a liking for all things French so with any luck at all she will find herself a rich French aristocrat and settle down. I will call on you just as soon as she has gone back to London—oh, and one thing more,' he said, a smile curving his lips, 'congratulations. You seem to have put the cart before the horse when it comes to matrimony—but I am happy for you both.'

When David had gone, Lydia stared at the closed door. Standing in the wreckage of her dream of marrying Alex, she realised it was over. There was no coming back from this, for how could Miranda possibly forgive her? For the rest of her life she would remember this moment when the bottom had dropped out of her world. She could not forestall the inevitable conclusion for which she was entirely to blame. Irene's declaration meant the end of everything between her and Alex, and deep within herself Lydia was furious, furious at the injustice done her and furious at the pain she had caused Miranda. Her voice when she spoke was intense.

'This is all my fault,' she said. 'It's down to me—all of it. I've ruined everything between you and Miranda. Tell me how I'm supposed to live with that?'

Alex looked at her. She stood near the window where he could see her face. It was one of torment, strained with the pain inside her, and for a moment he felt himself responsible for this although she and not he had been the one to allow Henry into her life. But he couldn't help himself. He needed her so desperately that from the moment he had met her he had questioned nothing about her as long as he could be assured that her need for him was as great as his was for her. Subconsciously, they had both been looking for a place of permanence where they could abide. He would not allow Irene Hilton's malice to take that, or their love for one another, which had grown from a moment of wonder, away from them.

Her pain and anguish tore at Alex. He went to her and tenderly took her in his arms. 'None of this is your fault, Lydia. Henry has a lot to answer for—but I must tread with care for Miranda's sake. This is a difficult time for her, but we will get through it. We have to.'

She turned her face up to his. 'I know that. But what can I do? Miranda will never forgive me.' The pull of his gaze was too strong for her to resist. It was as though he were looking into the very depths of her heart. She felt the touch of his empathy like healing fingers soothing away her pain like a balm.

'She will. We must give her time.'

'This must be breaking her heart.'

'I know. Let me talk to her.'

Before he could do that Miranda walked in.

Lydia stood beside Alex. She closed her fingers over his hand for support. She felt him look at her, but he said nothing. Instead, his hand turned and he wove his fingers with hers.

'Miranda... What can I say?' Lydia said hesitantly. 'I want to explain.'

'I don't want an explanation.'

'No, but you're unhappy. I am part of that. I didn't intend—'

'Oh, people never do, do they?'

Lydia heard the bitterness in her words. Its presence didn't surprise her.

'We hadn't been married very long before I found out what Henry was like. When I first became aware of the rumours, read the signs—whatever you wish to call them—I chose to ignore them rather than face the truth. But then I realised it's better to know the truth than to live a lie. I thought I knew him. And then I realised I didn't know him at all. But I can't believe—with you...'

'Please believe me when I tell you that nothing happened between us, Miranda—nothing like that. I had no idea he was married, I swear it to you.'

Miranda looked at her, her eyes wide and brimming with tears and hurt and betrayal and all the other things a woman feels when the man she loves, a man she'd hoped loved her back, lets her down in a way she cannot forgive.

'Then why?'

'Because I was desperate—desperate to get away from London, from everything,' Lydia explained.

'Why? What were you running away from?'

Miranda demanded. Her throat was aching so badly that she found speaking difficult.

'My father,' Lydia replied quietly. 'I was running away from my father.'

Miranda stared at her, trying hard to understand. 'But...why would you want to do that? According to Alex, your father is a gentle, lovely man.'

'I didn't know that then. You see, my father left me and my mother to fend for ourselves when I was a small child. I had to watch the love my mother bore him turn to bitterness and then hate. Inevitably that hate rubbed off onto me.' She told Miranda of her meeting with her father. She spoke of his theft and being sent to Australia, and how the letter he wrote to her sent her into a panic. 'That was when I met Henry. I can't pretend I wasn't flattered by his attention, and when he told me he was to go to America, where he lived, and he would marry me, I saw it as a way out of my predicament.'

'So you returned to London when it fell through. And your father? Have you forgiven him for deserting you and your mother?'

'Yes, yes, I have. I have no intention of punishing him any further. He has paid in his own way for what he did.'

'Tell me truthfully—honestly. Would you

have agreed to go America—to marry Henry—
if your circumstances had been different?'

'Honestly? No, Miranda, I would not. I didn't
love him—not that I knew anything about that
kind of love until I met Alex in Scotland, when
he arrived to stop the wedding. Henry wasn't
honest with me. I swear I would not have given
him the time of day had I known he had a wife.'

Miranda looked at her intently, trying to see
behind the words for a lie, but unable to find
one. She sighed. 'I believe you.'

'I am sorry to speak ill of Henry to you of
all people, but he wanted me for no other reason than to win a wager he had made with
his friends. I rejected any amorous moves he
made. In the end the only way he could win the
wager—to save face—was to come up with the
ridiculous tale he spun me about his family in
America and that he wanted me to go with him
as his wife. Like a stupid fool I believed him,
when all the time his intention was to whisk me
off the Scotland, to enter into a bogus marriage,
and afterwards…he intended to desert me.'

'How did you feel when you found out—
when Alex arrived and stopped the wedding?'
Miranda asked.

'I was devastated and deeply hurt, then furious at the way I had been duped and used to fulfil a wager. Henry almost ruined me.'

'I think I understand why you refused to make my dresses now,' Miranda said with a sigh.

'Yes. I'm sorry about that,' Lydia said. Unable to look any longer at Miranda's anguished face, she went to her. Taking her hand, she drew her down onto the sofa where they sat facing each other. 'You have no idea how I agonised over my decision. You see, Alex had asked me to marry him and I had refused. I simply could not enter into any kind of permanent relationship, knowing what I did and unable to tell you without hurting you. I felt dreadful deceiving you and I assure you I am not that sly, manipulative woman Irene painted me as being.'

'I do realise that. Alex has told you—about our childhood—our parents, hasn't he? He told me he intended to do so when you went out in the carriage with him earlier.'

'Yes, he showed me where you as lived a child. I'm sorry, Miranda. I realise how difficult things must have been for both of you.'

'It was. I couldn't have got through it without Alex—and our grandfather. I haven't told Henry about that part of our lives.'

'Will you?'

'Perhaps—one day. With everything that has

happened recently, I don't think that's important. I asked Henry to come with me to Aspen. He said he had things to do on the estate—things he had neglected of late. He made no comment when I told him Alex had invited you. I realise now that it was because he was afraid of the truth coming out.'

'I can see that. What will you do?'

'I don't know. I shall have to have time to think about it—to consider all the ramifications of what you have told me. I don't know when I'll be able to sort through my feelings on the matter. I can't see you as a bad person—after all, you were deceived as well as me. Besides, Alex loves you and he is a good judge of character. Henry has promised me things will be different from now on. He's looking forward to the birth of our child.' She swallowed, a look of desperation on her face. 'I have to believe him. What else can I do?'

Lydia looked at her. She wanted so desperately to believe Henry could be the husband Miranda wanted and needed. Lydia wasn't so sure—and one look at Alex's face told her he wasn't convinced either. Henry had lied to Miranda from the start because he was used to lying, because that was what he did. Lydia doubted very much that he would change.

'There is one more thing we should tell you, Miranda, something you don't know and will probably shock you when you do.'

Fully expecting to be told something further that would upset her, Miranda looked at her warily. 'What is it?'

Lydia looked at Alex, holding out her hand for him to take, which he did.

'I am pregnant, Miranda. Alex and I are to have a child.'

Miranda gasped and looked from one to the other. 'Oh—I wasn't expecting that.' Clearly shocked, but delightedly so, she stood up and embraced her brother and then Lydia. 'I don't know what to say. I am amazed… I am happy for you both… Oh,' she exclaimed, clasping her face in her hands, 'what a day this has turned out to be. I suppose now there will *have* to be a wedding.'

Later that day, when the rain had stopped and dusk cast a shadowy darkness over the gardens, Lydia strolled beside Alex, trying to forget the day's happenings and to appreciate the simple pleasure of walking by Alex's side. Reaching a rose-twined arbour, they stopped and breathed in the scents of the rain-washed garden. Lydia looked at Alex, at this man she had known for such a short time and whom she knew with absolute certainty, she would follow to the ends of the earth if he asked her to, and everything else—her work, her father, those aspects of herself that she had not even been aware of—suddenly fell into place.

'Are you warm enough?' Alex asked, drawing her shawl close around her shoulders. 'The rain has left a chill in the air.'

'The cool air doesn't bother me. I spend so much time indoors with my work that I like to get out in the open when I get the chance—especially when I have such lovely gardens to stroll through—on the arm of the man I love.'

She fell silent, feeling awkward suddenly. Her eyes, which she'd cast down when she declared her love for him again, fluttered upwards and clung to his. They never left his face. In the beginning she had told herself that she had been drawn to him because of his compelling good looks and his powerful magnetism. She had almost convinced herself that it was so, that this strange hold he had over her was merely his ability to awaken an intense sexual hunger within her. But that was just the tip of the iceberg, because what she felt for Alex Golding went way beyond the physical. It was something far deeper, something dangerously enduring, which had been weaving its spell to bind them inexorably together.

The light from the windows of the house fell on his face. She was enchanted, it seemed, by the line of his strong jaw and the curve of his throat.

It was as though the gardens had cast a spell on them and they had not the strength, nor perhaps the desire, to escape it. Alex smiled, and then the smile slipped away and his eyes darkened to the deepest blue as they travelled slowly over every inch of her face. He was fascinated by the wisps of hair that clung to her cheeks. He felt heat pulsate through his veins and he could not look away.

'Have you any idea how precious you are to me, Lydia? I want to make you my wife just as soon as it can be arranged.' The husky whisper was as potent as a caress. He felt inside his coat and pulled out a narrow box. 'I have a gift for you. It's something I meant to give you when I returned from Paris, but somehow the moment never arose.'

Lydia gasped when he raised the lid to reveal the diamond and emerald necklace and earrings nestling on a bed of black velvet. Tentatively she touched the precious stones with her finger, never having seen the like.

'Alex…they are beautiful.' She raised her eyes to his. 'Did you buy them in Paris?'

He nodded, lifting out the necklace and holding it next to her face. 'There. I was right. They do match your eyes.'

'I…don't know what to say. No one's ever given me anything like this.'

'Think of them as a wedding gift from me. You might like to wear them on our wedding day.'

Just one month later, Alex and Lydia were married at the small Norman church in the village close to Aspen Grange with no more than twenty guests. It was an emotional moment for Lydia when her father gave her to Alex for safekeeping, before stepping back and looking proudly on as they exchanged their vows.

A beaming Emily was her only bridesmaid. Emily had made Lydia's wedding dress, a simple gown of ivory silk, skilfully designed to conceal Lydia's expanding waist. Alex's diamond and emerald jewels sparkled about her throat and dripped from her ears. Miranda, several months into her own pregnancy and blooming with health, attended with a very quiet and sheepish-looking Henry, who never left his wife's side during the entire celebrations.

It was Miranda's idea that Henry should speak to Lydia. 'The sooner the better,' she said adamantly. 'We belong to the same family now. We have to get over all that unpleasantness and put it behind us.'

Lydia was afraid that talking to Henry would bring back all the bitterness she had felt at the time. But it had to be done and this was as good a time as any. For Miranda's sake she would strive to be civil to him.

'I want to say I am sorry,' Henry said. 'I never did apologise to you.'

'No, you didn't and I have not forgiven you for what you did to me. You would have ruined me. I only hope that where Miranda is concerned you treat her better than that. She deserves to be happy, Henry.'

'I know that. I couldn't bear to lose her. At least one good thing came out of all that—you and Alex. I never would have thought it when I left Gretna that the two of you would… Well, you know what I mean. When I came back from Scotland I promised Miranda that I would make a fresh start with her and our child.'

'Then keep your promise and behave yourself.'

As she turned to rejoin to her husband of two hours, she didn't think for a minute that Henry would keep his word. Oh, he meant it now. He was truly sorry for trying to seduce her, probably for hurting Miranda as well. But how long would he abide by his promise? Now Lydia could see Henry for what he was—a handsome, dangerous individual who lived by his impulses and would never know how to control his feelings.

Alex had observed her short exchange with Henry with concern and was relieved that it went without mishap. He smiled warmly when she made her way to his side. He took her hand and pressed his mouth against her open palm.

'I shall love you until my dying day, Alex Golding. Promise me that nothing will come between us.' She raised her hand and tenderly brushed his cheek.

'Nothing will, I promise you,' he said fervently. 'I look forward to this night when I can love you as my wife.'

When he bent his head and placed his lips on hers, Lydia realised how lucky she was. Ever since she had been old enough to know what she wanted—her own establishment, her salon, her customers and most of all to design gowns— she had never stopped to think until she had met Alex of the lonely life she had mapped out for herself. Here, now, was her love, her beloved

Alex. Her life was complete—or it would be when she had given birth to their son or daughter.

With extra help in the shop Alex and Lydia spent their weekends at Aspen Grange, often accompanied by her father, who had become a much-valued part of her life. As Lydia's confinement drew near they spent less time in London. There was a new confidence in her, an elation. Alex was relieved and impressed by the way she had settled down to married life, and amazed how quickly she had learned to manage Aspen and its huge contingent of staff while designing gowns for her rapidly expanding enterprise.

Her enterprise wasn't the only thing that was expanding and as the weeks passed she was impatient for the baby to be born. Miranda gave birth to a son and with the coming of spring, the Golding baby—a boy who was named Charles William—was born.

Lydia had never felt such softness, such tenderness, such sweetness, when she looked at this little human being she had given birth to who was sleeping in the cot beside her bed. Alex came and sat beside her on the bed, one arm about his wife and his eyes on the child. With his closed eyes, the feathery eyebrows, the tiny rosebud mouth, he was perfect.

'Thank you, my love. You are a beautiful mother. Just remember one thing and brand it into your heart—I love you dearly and I promise you that nothing will come between us.'

Gathering her up into his arms, he kissed her then, with all the old passion and fierce possessiveness she knew so well. She felt the strength of his muscles as he held her and was aware again of the vitality in him and of the nearness of his beloved, strong face. She felt comfort in the closeness, weakened by the birth of their child. But tomorrow she would be strong again, and they would grow closer together. She felt her heart and mind almost burst with a joy too much to contain. These two people were hers, her family. They were all she had. All she wanted.

The world had taken on a wonderful glow.

* * * * *

MILLS & BOON®

 HISTORICAL

AWAKEN THE ROMANCE OF THE PAST

A sneak peek at next month's titles...

In stores from 25th January 2018:

Just can't wait?
Buy our books online before they hit the shops!
www.millsandboon.co.uk

Also available as eBooks.

MILLS & BOON®

Coming next month

THE MARQUESS TAMES HIS BRIDE
Annie Burrows

'Don't be ridiculous. I am not your fiancée. And I don't need your permission to do anything or go anywhere!' Clare said.

'That's better,' Rawcliffe said, leaning back in his chair, an infuriatingly satisfied smile playing about the lips that had so recently kissed her. 'You were beginning to droop. Now you are on fighting form again, we can have a proper discussion.'

'I don't want to have a discussion with you,' Clare said, barely managing to prevent herself from stamping her foot. 'Besides, oh, listen, can't you hear it?' It was the sound of a guard blowing on his horn to announce the arrival of the stage. The stage she needed to get on. 'I have a seat booked on that coach.'

'Nevertheless,' he said, striding over to the door and blocking her exit once again, 'you will not be getting on it.'

'Don't be absurd. Of course I am going to get on it.'

'You are mistaken. And if you don't acquiesce to your fate, quietly, then I am going to have to take desperate measures.'

'Oh, yes? And just what sort of measures,' she said, marching up to him and planting her hands on her hips, 'do you intend to take?'

He smiled. That wicked, knowing smile of his. Took her face in both hands. And kissed her.

And just as she was starting to forget exactly why she ought to be fighting him at all, he gentled the kiss. Gentled his hold. Changed the nature of his kiss from hard and masterful, to coaxing and...oh, his clever mouth. It knew just how to translate her fury into a sort of wild, pulsing ache. She ached all over. She began to tremble with what he was making her feel. Grew weaker by the second.

As if he knew her legs were on the verge of giving way, he scooped her up into his arms and carried her over to one of the upholstered chairs by the fire. Sat down without breaking his hold, so that she landed on his lap.

Continue reading
The Marquess Tames His Bride
Annie Burrows

Available next month
www.millsandboon.co.uk

LET'S TALK

Romance

For exclusive extracts, competitions
and special offers, find us online:

Or get in touch on 0844 844 1351*

For all the latest titles coming soon, visit
millsandboon.co.uk/nextmonth